A VERITABLE HOUSEHOLD PET

Viggy Parr Hampton

First edition, January 2026

ISBN Paperback: 979-8-9898755-8-0

ISBN Hardcover: 979-8-9898755-9-7

ISBN Ebook: 979-8-9898755-7-3

Illustration by Jaime Stearns

Book Design by Nuno Moreira, NMDESIGN

A VERITABLE HOUSEHOLD PET

Viggy Parr Hampton

For my husband Ryan,
who is thoughtful, supportive, kind, and brilliant…
and therefore nothing like any man in this book.

A Cold Night for Alligators
A determined CDC epidemiologist goes rogue to tackle a
mysterious outbreak in Savannah, only to find himself entangled
with a pair of urban explorers and a dangerous, tortured soul in
an abandoned theme park where dark forces stir.

Much Too Vulgar
Disturbed pre-med student Keely Rexroth is unable to take
'no' for an answer when she is denied entry into a prestigious
research program. As her ambition curdles into dark mania, she
embarks on her own curriculum of twisted experimentation,
fighting to keep her secrets from a campus priest who is too
perceptive for his own good. If she can't get what she deserves
on her own merit, she'll eliminate her competition.

The Rotting Room
When a young nun with a troubled past joins a new religious
order, she quickly comes to realize that this abbey has its own
share of sinister secrets, along with a disturbing burial ritual. She
must race to uncover if the abbey is full of divine miracles—or
unspeakable evil.

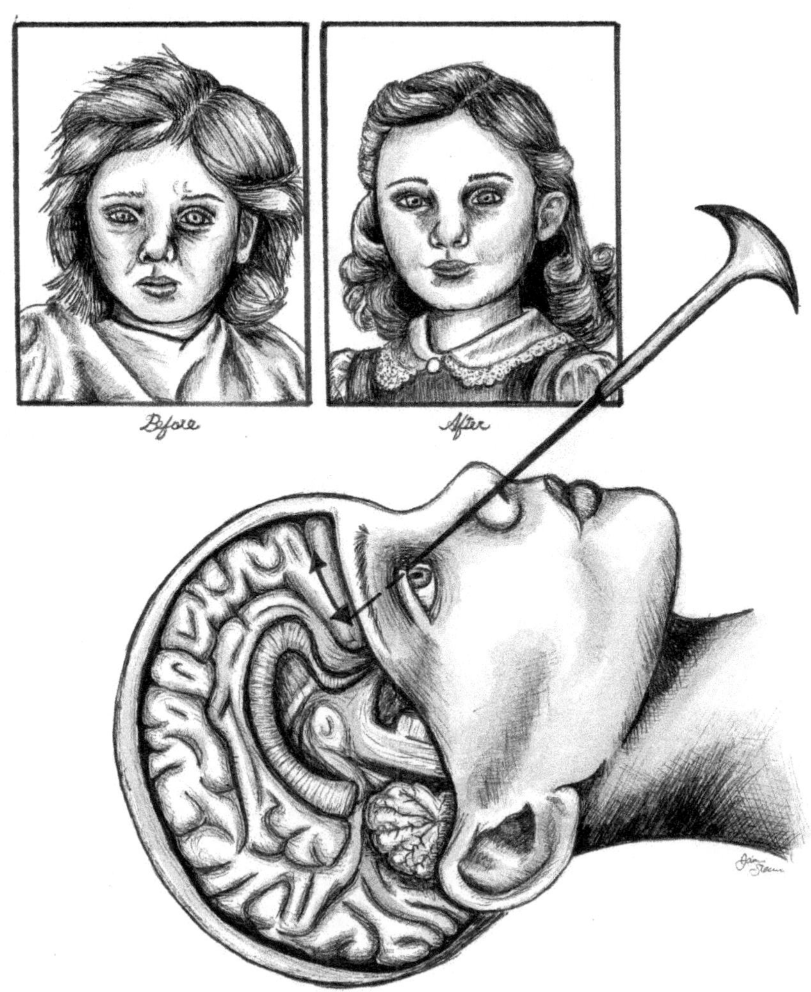

Before
After

SCRIBE'S NOTE, 2025

[Scribe's note: This is my sister Darla's story, as dictated to me. I have tried to remain as faithful to her diction and voice as I can, while also making it intelligible and coherent. I have added notes, interpolations, and supporting documentation where necessary to clarify or explain, or to add my own experience if relevant.

If you're curious as to why it took so long for you to read this, I'd encourage you to keep your bratty thoughts to yourself. You're lucky I'm telling you the truth at all. This is the last thing I have to do for her, and I hope you're finally mature enough to handle it.]

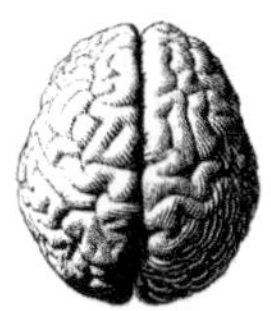

1 9 6 0 - 1 9 7 1

You might be wondering why you're reading this, but just trust me—it's important. I'm going to tell my story the best way I can, because you need to hear it. I have no doubt that you'll be better than I ever was or could ever be, but given what I've been through, it's amazing I can do much of anything at all. [Scribe's note: Darla has progressed considerably since the surgery, but as of this writing, she is still unable to live independently or write by herself.]

I don't remember any one thing that made me the way I am—or, I guess I should say, the way I was. Ma and Pa weren't mean, at least in the beginning. They never raised their hands to me, I never almost died as a baby. Nothing like that. I had a good relationship with my older sister, Ellie. [Scribe's note: 'Good' may be too strong and simplistic a word. I always viewed our relationship differently. Darla is my blood, yes—I can't and won't deny that, and our bond comes with certain obligations, even extending to this document you're holding in your hands. At the same time, ever since the day she was born, Darla seemed to suck up all the air in the room, so there was none left for me.]

I had this real strong fear, for as long as I can remember. My memory isn't too good, but that is one thing I do know. This fear was a part of me, as close to my soul as Jesus used to be. The fear of sickness, of germs, and, most of all, of vomiting, ruled everything I did, everything I was, everything I knew, everything I thought. There was nothing physically wrong with me. I was a healthy child, and I played with the neighborhood kids, and I loved following my sister around. [Scribe's note: Darla followed me around like a lost puppy until the phobia became so severe that she refused to leave the house. At that time, she was around eight years old. I was ten.]

It started off slow, but got bad real fast. I caught a stomach bug, just the simple sort of thing all kids deal with and forget about as soon as it's over. Mine wasn't even that bad, I don't think. But even after it was over, I still felt that there was something I'd done that had gotten me sick, that if only I had just changed my behavior or done one thing different, I would have been okay. The physical pain of the vomiting went away after a few days, but the mental pain never did.

I remember watching "I Dream of Jeannie" with Ellie and seeing Jeannie and Major Anthony Nelson kissing. All I could think about was how sick he could make her, with that quick touch of the lips. She didn't know what germs he was carrying around. How could she risk it for that brief contact, even though Major Anthony was handsome? I wanted to scream at the TV, "It isn't worth it, Jeannie!" [Scribe's note: In actuality, Darla often did scream at the TV. Any time characters would perform actions she felt, in the depths of her despair, were unsafe or insalubrious, she would yell, cajole, whimper, and cry at them, begging them to do something different. Being unable to hear her, the characters, of course, carried on with their fictional lives, oblivious to the self-imposed pain of the little girl watching them.]

Sure, I saw Ma and Pa kiss—not often, that sort of behavior wasn't always appropriate around children, I learned—and every time I saw it, this pit of anxiety opened up in my belly, and I thought I would fall into it and drown. I felt the same thing when I saw them share a cigarette, which they did often. I knew married people did those sorts of things, which, at my darkest times, even as a little girl, made me consider the likely possibility that I would live out the rest of my life alone. I didn't think I was made for companionship.

I don't know if I can fully tell you just how dark and hopeless things became. Shortly after I got that stomach bug, I stopped going to school. I absolutely refused, because I was certain that if I wanted to not get sick again, I had to never again be a part of the things I'd done around the time I'd come down with the bug. That meant no more school. No more playing with the neighborhood kids, even if Ellie was right outside with them. I just stood at the window, staring out, wishing I could play with them, while at the same time wishing more than just a window separated us, because they were too close, and getting too close meant sickness. It meant pain.

No more peanut butter sandwiches, which had been my favorite food, because that was the last meal I had before I began vomiting. No more milk, either, and no more chocolate cake, which pained me even more than not being able to play outside. Ma's chocolate cake was the best in the whole town, everyone knew it, and until then, it was the one thing I always asked for on my birthday. The day I got sick, she'd made the cake for her friend Mary Hortman's daughter, Lisa, and she'd let me have a little piece. I sure wish she hadn't.

Ma and Pa thought I was going through a phase, at first. They knew I'd always been a nervous kid, but they plum didn't know what to do with me when I started refusing to go to school. Pa wanted to force me to go, but Ma said I would get over it on my own, if they just gave me a little time and space. **[Scribe's note: Darla probably doesn't remember, but Father did try to force her to go back to school. He had to physically carry her, kicking and screaming, to his car. She tried to escape several times and dash back into the house, but each time, he caught her and hauled her back into his Impala. She was raising such a racket, our neighbors were coming outside to see what could possibly be the matter. When she broke out of the car the** last time, shrieking and bawling, Father just let her go back inside. He didn't want the neighbors—especially that odious busybody Mrs. Knowles—to see him manhandling his hysterical daughter into the car. I believe that was the moment Father's affection for his baby girl started to wane. How sad.]

How would things have been different if Pa had gotten me back to school? Would he have broken my fear like a cowboy breaks a wild horse? Or would I only have made a scene and embarrassed our family, and everything would have turned out the same? Sitting here, alone, I ask myself that question a lot. I never get any answers.

Some time must have passed. I can't remember it too well, but I know I was in my room, shut up like an invalid, for awhile. I wouldn't even go into the living room anymore to stare out at the kids playing. Ma would come in and sit on my bed, try to talk me into leaving my room, but it didn't work. The only thing I looked forward to was Ellie coming in. She'd bring my second-favorite food, strawberry Jell-O, and we'd sit together on my bed and eat it. She wanted to play games with me, like Yahtzee or Candy Land, but I was afraid to touch the same pieces as her. Ellie wasn't too disappointed, and she didn't judge me, she just talked about what she'd done at school that day, or what game her friends were playing outside. [Scribe's note: Darla completely missed the point of my visits. If I couldn't draw her out with the games she used to love, then I wanted to make school and the larger world feel so vital, so fun and unmissable, that she'd throw off her covers and come outside with me. It never worked. That was back when I thought I could fix her, could make her normal enough that mother and father wouldn't spend every waking moment talking about her, worrying about her.]

Ma and Pa started arguing. I could hear them in their room next door to mine, and I could smell the smoke from their cigarettes floating through the air. The walls in our house were thin, and if I pressed my ear to the plaster, I could make out exactly what they were saying. Usually, Pa was angry-whispering that they needed to do something about me, that

I couldn't stay in my room forever, that nobody could live like that. Ma would whisper something back, about how it was a phase, and Pa would say it's not just a phase if it never ends, and how something was wrong with me. Hearing that hurt pretty bad, but I guess I already knew that, deep down. But at the same time, the pastor at our church had always said God made us just the way we were, so I thought maybe there wasn't anything wrong with me after all, because God doesn't make mistakes. [Scribe's note: God makes mistakes all the time. After nearly forty years of being a surgeon, this is something I can tell you definitively. Darla and I didn't talk about God, so I didn't have a chance to tell her that directly. As you've already gathered, Darla was very much in her own world and only heard what she wanted to hear, which was anything that was consistent with her delusions.]

Since my surgery, it's hard to really remember what I felt back then, but I'll try as best I can.

I started losing weight, that I remember very well. I wasn't exercising or playing with the other kids outside, but I was slowly limiting what I would eat. Once, during one of Ellie's visits, she told me that Cynthia Marlow had thrown up all over her desk during homeroom. I started breathing real fast and heavy, and all I wanted was for Ellie to leave right then, because if she'd seen it, then she was contaminated, but I also had to know—what had Cynthia done before it happened? What had she eaten? Ellie told me Cynthia always ate the same thing for lunch, a tuna sandwich, and from then on, I refused to eat tuna. It had never been my favorite food, but it was something I would eat, and Ma brought it to me once or twice a week for lunch. She was exasperated—that was the word she used—when I told her I couldn't eat tuna anymore. I actually cried when she brought me a tuna sandwich. [Scribe's note: I made up the story about Cynthia Marlow. I only told it to Darla because I thought it might be a good sort of exposure therapy for her. At the time, I didn't realize how deep her fear ran, how much it had already poisoned the well of her mind. After she panicked, I didn't tell her the story was false because, quite frankly, I didn't want Mother or Father to spank me. They were always quite liberal with the belt, when it came to me. With Darla, she never felt the sting of the leather on her backside. Father would have done it, but Mother always insisted Darla was 'too delicate.' I don't know what it was about me that screamed 'indelicate.']

It was around that time I stopped keeping up with my classes. Until then, Ma had asked Ellie to bring home my schoolwork, and that's what I worked on all day. Ma still hoped I would grow out of the phase I was stuck in and go back to school one day, and she didn't want me to get too far behind. After Ellie told me about Cynthia, I stopped trusting anything that had come in contact with the school or with the other kids. I was too afraid to touch the papers or the notebooks, even the textbooks. And when Ellie came in to visit me, I asked her to sit on the floor across the room instead of on my bed. That was the hardest part of all. [Scribe's note: I didn't mind Darla pushing me away. I was tired of this self-imposed imprisonment. She was completely resistant to change, and she was making ridiculous choices. She stopped eating almost every food except for Jell-O, which stained her teeth red. She was confining herself completely to her room, even going so far as to install a bucket in the corner for her waste. Visiting her in her room became a chore I loathed. The room stank of excrement, and Darla herself was so bedraggled and filthy, I wouldn't have hugged her even if she'd begged.]

Pa finally convinced Ma to do something when he found out about the bucket. I didn't want to share the bathroom anymore—there were too many germs, too many people touching things. Too much risk. So I used the bucket when I had to go. I got used to the smell, after a while. Ma was horrified at first, but she usually just dropped a tray with my food on it at the foot of my bed and left. [Scribe's note: Every time Mother left Darla's room, she would run into her own, slam the door, and sob until Father either went in to comfort her or yell at her for enabling Darla's behavior. I spent a lot of time on my own. Mother and Father were too busy either catering to Darla or arguing about Darla to worry about me. She was the squeaky wheel, even though she was useless. Therefore, I had to run smoothly. If I brought home grades that were anything less than perfect, Mother would nosedive into yet another a crying jag so intense I thought she would make herself sick. Father would yell at me that he couldn't handle this from me, because my sister was already so enfeebled.]

The first thing they tried was yanking me out of my room by the back of my nightgown and forcing me to take a bath. Boy, that did not go well. It seems so silly now, how I scrabbled around like a cat with its tail on fire, clawing, screaming, yowling. I think I actually scratched Ma's arm so deep she bled. I'm not proud of that. [Scribe's note: It was worse than that. After the ill-fated bath, Mother tried to clean her wound as best she could. In the ensuing days, infection set in, causing Mother's temperature to spike to 105. A trip to the emergency room, heavy antibiotics, and much chiding later, and she was back home, weak but alive. Mother didn't tell the doctors the full story of how she came to receive that wound, but privately, I believe there was excrement caked under Darla's nails, and when she scratched Mother, the bacteria burrowed into Mother's arm, setting her off on the road to infection. Not unlike how the Viet Cong coated their tapered punji sticks with feces to incapacitate American soldiers.]

After it was all over, I ran back into my room, shivering and wet, and burrowed into my bed. Coming back into my room after weeks of not leaving it made me realize just how horrible the smell had become. It's easy to ignore the filth if you never experience anything different.

I wish I had snapped out of it after that, but I didn't. I couldn't. Ma had some sort of bout of illness, and after she recovered, Pa insisted I see someone. That's all he would say—that I 'see someone.' I didn't know what that meant. He didn't say the word doctor. I asked Ellie about it, and she said they wanted me to see a head shrinker. That scared me real good, let me tell you. I didn't want my head shrunk! I had enough problems as it was! But then, I thought about it some more, and I figured my head, with all my thoughts, was what was causing all my problems, and maybe shrinking it would shrink my problems, too.

After what happened with the bath, Ma and Pa didn't try to take me out of my room again. They brought the head shrinker to me. He stood outside of my open doorway, pinching his nose, and talked to me in this nasally voice. I don't remember much, but I do remember how he kept asking me how something made me feel. Everything made me feel the same way: scared. [Scribe's note: The idiot psychiatrist wouldn't even walk into Darla's room, even though Mother and Father were paying him a pretty penny they couldn't quite afford (although, given the smell, I can understand his reticence). Darla got a fruitless appointment with a useless quack, and I got socks for Christmas because there wasn't enough money for a real gift that year.]

When the head shrinker left, my head didn't feel any smaller. It actually felt bigger, like I was about to get a headache, and I cried for what seemed like a very long time. I cried so hard my stomach started to hurt, which terrified me, which made me cry harder. I only stopped when Ellie came in, pinching her nose like the head shrinker had, and stood in the corner. She helped calm me down. She was always so good at that. [Scribe's note: I told her what I'd done in school that day. Every time I visited her, I tried to think up ways to lure her out of her room. Who could resist a pool in the hot summer, or a cold ice cream cone? Who could say no to a street carnival with clowns, or a rousing game of double dutch jump rope? Darla could, apparently. After awhile, I began to realize that my anecdotes weren't helping her. Quite the opposite, in fact—she was living vicariously through me, and my stories only served to provide the social outlet she craved.]

The head shrinker told my parents to give me some medicine that would make me better. [Scribe's note: The quack prescribed Darla Thorazine. I'm sure you've heard plenty about the side effects of Thorazine and why it is no longer widely used. If you haven't, avail yourself of the

Internet and fill this shameful gap in your education.] Ma and Pa told me the medicine was meant to take away nausea, and that people used it so they wouldn't throw up. That's all I needed to hear to swallow it. If the medicine could keep me safe, then I had to have it.

At first, the medicine just made me feel detached from everybody, like I was floating. It wasn't unpleasant… until it was. I couldn't think. I couldn't eat. I couldn't close my mouth, and I kept drooling on myself. Ma would come in and help me change my shirt over and over, until she finally put a bib around my neck to cut down on the amount of laundry she was doing. Even though I was drooling so much, my mouth was so dry, drier than I'd ever felt before. No amount of water made it feel better.

Even though I had no appetite, I started gaining weight. I'd been an active kid, up until I stopped leaving my room, and I had never been heavy. The medicine made my belly soft, my thighs squishy, my face puffy. The few times I caught a glimpse of myself in the mirror hanging on my wall, I almost screamed, because I didn't recognize the person staring back at me. I think Ellie came to visit me every now and then, but everything is kind of hazy. [Scribe's note: I did make occasional visits to see Darla, but they were, like her, utterly hopeless. I would try to talk to her, but she would just stare at her bedcovers, eyes downcast, slobbering all over herself. She'd been useless before the medicine, but this was worthlessness at an entirely new level. The medicine incapacitated her. She was experiencing tremors, and she could barely walk to the bathroom (which she had, mercifully, begun using again), often resulting in accidents in the hallway when she couldn't make it in time. If she still felt the effects of her emetophobia, she didn't discuss it. I heard Mother and Father talking about Darla, saying they'd traded one intolerable condition for another—and this one was far worse.]

I remember hearing Ma and Pa arguing one night. My medicine must have been wearing off, because I can recall it quite clearly. Pa was yelling, saying they couldn't take care of me here anymore, that I was ruining their lives, and that it was about time they put me somewhere. Ma was crying, begging him to stop yelling, saying she would never let him put me in one of those places. [Scribe's note: I was sitting on the couch during this argument. The 'place' they were referring to was an asylum, which, by that time, were in short supply thanks to the deinstitutionalization movement that led to the closure of many such facilities around the country in favor of medicines like the Thorazine that had so hollowed out Darla. Asylums were, no doubt, barbaric, and I agreed with Mother, but I can understand Father's side. Darla wasn't getting better, and our lives were getting worse. At this point, Darla had been confined to our home for over two years.]

Not long after that, Ma stopped giving me the medicine, but I don't know if Pa knew that. As the medicine wore off, all of my old thoughts came rushing back. I refused to leave my room, and the bucket had to be brought back for my toilet. I couldn't force any food besides crackers and bananas into my body, because no other foods seemed safe. This restrictive diet combined with coming off of the medicine made me lose weight again, and when I looked in the mirror, I still didn't recognize myself. I was so skinny, my cheekbones were like blades sharp enough to cut. My eyes were sunk into hollow pits. For the first time, I really scared myself.

For the first time, I thought I might die.

Not long after that came the really dark time.

I was in my room, burrowed into the nest my blankets had become, reading a book I'd read too many times to count. I'd stopped letting Ellie bring me books from the library—too many people had handled them. I'd just eaten a sleeve of crackers when I felt a flutter in my stomach, and my throat got thick.

I felt nauseated, and with the nausea came a fear so heavy I felt crushed by the weight of it. I couldn't take it. I knew with perfect certainty that I'd rather be dead than vomit. So I threw my water glass on the floor as hard as I could, over and over until it broke.

I picked up the biggest, sharpest piece I could find, and I started digging into my wrist, watching the blood seep out.

Ma burst into my room. She'd heard the sound of the glass, and when she saw what I was doing, she screamed bloody murder. She rushed over to me, grabbed the piece of glass, and flung it away from me. That's the last thing I remember.

[Scribe's note: We were lucky Darla lost consciousness. She never would have let us clean and bandage her if she were awake. When Mother finally pulled herself together, she called me in, and together we disinfected Darla's wound, which wasn't deep enough to cause any real harm. We swept up the broken glass, emptied Darla's bucket, and even changed her sheets, which smelled almost as horrendous as the bucket. We opened the windows and let in fresh air. By the time Darla awoke, we had put everything back the way it was, but from then on, Darla was only allowed paper cups and plates and dull, plastic utensils.]

It was some time after that when I first heard the word that would change my life forever. I don't know who said it first, or how my parents ever heard of it, but one day it appeared in our house like an unexpected guest.

Lobotomy.

I first heard the word from Ellie. She told me, from her perch across the room, that Ma and Pa were talking about getting me this special surgery, a surgery that could help me. She told me she was more in favor of electroshock therapy, but Ma thought it was horrendous and wouldn't let it happen. Ellie told me this surgery, this 'lobotomy,' was quick and easy, and I wouldn't feel a thing. [Scribe's note: I tried never to lie to Darla unless I thought it would benefit her in some way (such as my unsuccessful experiment with the lie about Cynthia Marlow vomiting at school); she told herself enough lies as it was—but I did lie about the lobotomy. It would be quick, but I knew it wouldn't be easy. After her suicide attempt, Mother and Father were at the end of their ropes, and they wanted the most radical solution possible. I would have preferred electroshock for her, but Mother wouldn't listen to me, and Father was so fed up by then, he barely cared what happened to Darla. Looking back, I should have seen what happened to him coming, but I was wrapped up in the normal struggles and foibles of a girl in the throes of puberty, and the possibility that my parents were not invincible had failed to occur to me.]

We weren't rich like Savannah Munro's family, I'll say. Savannah always had the newest toys, the best clothes, the biggest house, which I visited a few times before I couldn't make myself go out anymore. The Munros even had a maid who came twice a week to clean. I know Ma would have loved to have that kind of money.

I'm telling you all this so that you can understand how big of a decision this surgery really was for Ma and Pa. The lobotomy did not come cheap, but Ma would do anything to make me normal again. For myself, I knew I didn't want to live like I was anymore, and I didn't want to be so scared I tried to hurt myself again. I knew I wasn't really living, not like the other kids did. I knew my family didn't think much of me anymore, and that hurt me—but the anxiety, the fear, hurt me more, made it impossible for me to change. That fear feels so far away now, but at the time, it was more real than anything else in my small life.

Like I said, we weren't wealthy, but we were okay. We owned our house, and even though I wore mostly hand-me-downs, me and Ellie always had plenty of presents under the Christmas tree. [Scribe's note: We weren't as financially healthy as Darla thought. Late at night, I could usually hear Mother and Father arguing about money, if they weren't arguing about Darla. Father's job as a machinist at Richmond Tool and Die paid a decent wage, but Mother always had a taste for nice things, especially when it came to her daughters. Darla may remember the presents under the tree; I remember the stiff department-store dresses Mother made us wear to church, which cost a fortune we didn't have.]

Now, I don't know the exact cost, but I know that the surgery was expensive. [Scribe's note: Mother and Father consulted with several doctors before finding the right one to perform the procedure. Mother's criterion was a long list of successful patient outcomes; Father's criterion was how much he would have to pay. Although the transorbital lobotomy had fallen out of favor in the late 1960s, there were still enough morally bankrupt doctors who were willing to take a whack at it for $250, which is about how much Mother and Father happened to have in the entirety of their savings account. Well, I suppose I should say his savings account—Mother's name wasn't on anything of note, not the deed to the house, not the car registration, nor on the bank account. I know she squirreled away money whenever she could, just to have some semblance of financial security and control—or maybe that was the source of the funds for the horrible Christmas dresses I wanted to burn more than I wanted to wear. The year I got socks instead of a dress, while pitiable, was still preferable.]

The doctor insisted on meeting me before agreeing to do the lobotomy. He was short and thin, with dark brown hair that puffed around his head. Ellie stood in the corner of my room, and the doctor was in the doorway, wearing one of those surgical masks, which I appreciated. Dealing with sick people all day, there's no way he wasn't contaminated. He asked me questions about my life, about why I didn't leave my room, about what scared me so much and why I felt that way. Every now and then I'd look at Ellie, and she looked so angry. I couldn't figure out why. [Scribe's note: Even as a child, I knew what was happening wasn't right. The man looked more like an actor playing a doctor on a television show—and not a very good one—than an actual practitioner of medicine. The mask he wore made it difficult to understand what he was saying, so he kept shouting. He looked like he needed a shower, and his shoes were scuffed and dirty. I was surprised Mother let him in the house with those shoes still on. All he did was talk to Darla—he never approached her, he never physically examined her. He was almost indistinguishable from the psychiatrist quack in his lack of thoroughness. I couldn't believe it—this was the man Mother and Father were going to pay a small fortune to stick needles in their daughter's brain? So, yes. I was very angry.]

When the doctor left my room, I could hear him talking to Ma, and then he left. Ellie was still in my room, shaking her head. When I asked her what was wrong, she wouldn't tell me. [Scribe's note: How do you explain to an eleven-year-old something like that? How do you explain how much our parents were sacrificing, how much risk they were taking, all because they couldn't stand Darla anymore? I… I couldn't accept that. Worse still, I heard Mother ask the doctor if Darla would require a hospital stay. The doctor answered her far too quickly, saying an office procedure was more than sufficient, and a hospital stay would double or triple the cost of the procedure. At that point Father grunted, his universal way of saying 'no,' and that was that. Even as a child, I couldn't fathom it—my sister was going to have brain surgery, and she wouldn't even be in a hospital? It was madness.]

A date was set for the surgery, and Ma explained to me what would happen as best she could. Ellie did a better job, even though I didn't really want to hear her version. It sounded scary, but if there was a chance I could be permanently fixed, I was willing to take it. [Scribe's note: Mother and Father used all of their savings in this last-ditch effort for a permanent solution to the problem of Darla. At the time, we didn't know about Dr. Walter Freeman, or how he had been banned in 1967 from performing the surgery he pioneered after his final patient died of a brain hemorrhage. All Father knew was that there was a procedure that had the potential to make Darla normal, to fix what was broken inside of her for good. Father didn't say this to Darla, but I heard him tell Mother that if the lobotomy didn't work, they had to send her away, to somewhere that could take better care of her. He tried to phrase it as if he cared about Darla, but I could see right through it. I knew he was fed up with her, disgusted by her, enraged by her. I couldn't help feeling protective of my younger sister, even though I, too, was consistently frustrated by her. I'd lay awake at night, wondering why she couldn't just shake herself out of it and be normal again, like she used to be. In my darker moments, when the night was blackest and it seemed as though morning would never come, I cursed the psychiatrist quack who forced us to this point because he couldn't do a damn thing but take our money and turn Darla into a drug-addled zombie.]

When the day of the procedure came, Ma told me to take some of the medicine she'd saved from before, the medicine that made me feel numb and slow. She said it would help calm my nerves before the surgery. Even though I didn't want that medicine anymore, I took it.

I don't remember too much after that.

1 9 7 1

Excerpt from Medical Notes of Brian Tanner, M.D., Psychiatrist

Patient appears timid and anxious. Face pale, eyes gray. Her hair is dirty, clumped around her face. Patient cannot remember the last time she had a bath. Patient urinates and defecates in a bucket in the corner of her room, which she refuses to leave. Patient seems not to notice the stench. Patient speaks in a very soft voice and expresses intense fear of vomiting. The emetophobia has become so severe that she has become a recluse and has limited her diet. Signs of malnourishment are present, but mother and father show no indications of abusive behavior.

Besides the emetophobia, patient shows social withdrawal, detachment, and self-isolation, classic signs of schizoid personality disorder.

I have prescribed Thorazine to dull the patient's fear and allow her to return to a normal life, or, at the very least, allow her parents to more easily care for her.

*   *   *

Excerpt from Notes of Michael Hupman, M.D.

Darla Gregory, age eleven, complains of severe phobia of vomiting. Due to her fear, she prefers I remain just outside the entrance to her room, in which she has been confined for the past two years, with a brief respite during which she was medicated with Thorazine. Mrs. Gregory withdrew Thorazine several weeks ago, stating she could not accept the medication's side effects.

Darla is small in stature for her age, but her restrictive diet and recent use of antipsychotic medications has aged her beyond her years. She is anxious and groggy, with a lack of muscle tone and pale, almost sallow, skin.

Mr. and Mrs. Gregory are unhappy with Darla's experience with Thorazine and wish for a more permanent intervention. They inquired about a lobotomy, and we discussed my training with the acclaimed Dr. Walter Freeman. I explained how a transorbital lobotomy could successfully rid Darla of her phobia and help her function more normally in society. If she continues as she is without treatment, it is my professional opinion that she will not survive beyond puberty.

We also discussed the risks of the surgery, which are minimal. Mrs. Gregory expressed hesitation, but Mr. Gregory insisted we go forward with the procedure. He said he no longer had the patience to deal with Darla's 'craziness,' and that he couldn't let her ruin their family. The Gregorys have an older daughter who has also been negatively affected by Darla's illness. Mrs. Gregory relented and agreed with her husband. I believe Darla is an excellent candidate for a lobotomy. Receiving this surgery early in life is highly beneficial, as evidenced by Dr. Freeman's work with other mentally defective children.

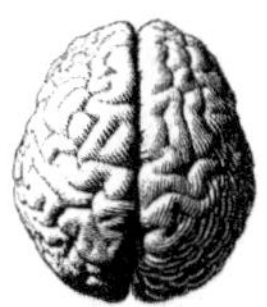

1 9 7 1

There was a sharp pain, and then a bright light. I didn't wake up for what felt like a very long time after that.

[Scribe's note: If Mother had known the lobotomy required electroshock sedation, she probably would have resisted more fiercely, but as it was, they had already paid their money by the time Darla entered Dr. Hupman's office. Father stayed at home, so Mother brought me along in case she needed help with Darla after the surgery. Mother had given Darla several times the normal dose of Thorazine so she would be pliable enough to leave the house. On the way to the doctor's office, Darla's head and neck kept twitching, like she was a marionette with her strings being randomly pulled. Even when I spoke to her, she was unable—or unwilling—to respond. Darla had not left the house in several years at this point, but in her drugged state, she did not seem to notice the change in environment. She even gripped my hand at one point, but whether that was some sort of muscle spasm or a genuine search for connection, I've no idea. I hadn't felt my sister's touch in years, due to her phobia that other people were contaminated and had the potential to infect her.

When we arrived, Mother and I helped Darla into the building. The receptionist led us into the doctor's office, which looked more like a gentleman's study than a surgical suite, with the exception of the hospital bed at the edge of the room. Dr. Hupman smiled at Darla, and without his surgical mask, I could see it was a greasy grin. From then on, I didn't believe a word he said (not that he'd engendered much credibility before, but at least at this juncture, he looked less disheveled). He positioned Darla against the wall, then snapped her photograph, before helping her onto the bed. He placed the electrodes on her temples, turned on the power, and the room filled with the stench of burned hair. Mother gagged into her handkerchief, then kept it pressed to her face for the duration of the procedure. Her gaze was fixed on the ground, tears leaking from her eyes, soaking her handkerchief. I, on the other hand, was riveted. I couldn't look away from Dr. Hupman. After sedating Darla with the electric current, he pulled a long, pointed instrument, very similar to an icepick—in fact, it could easily have *been* an icepick—from a small table set up next to the bed. He inserted the tip into the corner of Darla's right eye, grabbed a small hammer from the table, and hit the end of the icepick once, twice, three times, until there was a crack. Mother sobbed when she heard that sound, earning a sharp look from Dr. Hupman. The icepick sank into Darla's head, whereupon Dr. Hupman swiveled the handle around in a circular motion. With the pick still embedded in Darla's skull, he again lifted his camera and took a photograph. He then removed the pick and repeated the actions on Darla's left eye. When he finished, he set the icepick—which was only slightly bloodied—on the table along with the hammer and looked up at me and Mother. "Well, that'll do it," he said. The surgery took barely eleven minutes, a minute for each year of Darla's life, I remember thinking. Mother finally looked up, choking back sobs. "Thank you, Doctor," she said, and wiped her face with the wet handkerchief.

Darla lay on the table, unmoving. For a moment, I thought she might be dead. After all, a man had just shoved an icepick into both of her eye sockets and twirled it around. How could anyone survive that?

"She'll likely be groggy for awhile, and she'll have two shiners," he said. His lack of professionalism galled me. I wanted to take my sister and leave immediately, but Mother was the type who was easily cowed by fancy credentials, so she stayed, listening to Dr. Hupman describe how Darla would feel after, what we should do to care for her, and the cost for any follow-up visits. He also made Mother sign some sort of document, which I have reason to believe released him from all culpability in the event Darla's condition worsened as a result of the surgery. His nurse came in with a wheelchair, and Dr. Hupman hefted Darla's unconscious body into it as though she were a sack of potatoes, and just as meaningless. He took a final photograph of her, grinned at us again, then ushered us out of his office, with Mother pushing Darla's wheelchair.

There was a brief follow-up visit, and then the last time I saw him was in the newspaper.]

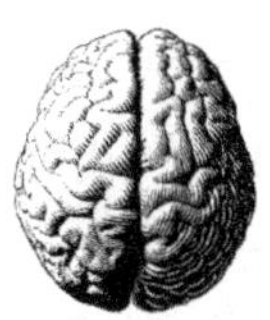

1 9 7 1 - 1 9 7 2

Everything is very hazy after that. The next thing I remember is being back at home, in my bed. Memories come in bits and pieces, like a jigsaw puzzle I can't quite put together. When I try to think back on that time, it feels like drifting. But at least there was no fear. [Scribe's note: Darla can speak for herself. She might have felt no fear, but that's only because she didn't feel much of anything. When Darla regained consciousness at home, she promptly wet herself, vomited, moaned, and fell back asleep. Mother insisted we change the sheets, which involved quite a bit of heavy lifting to move Darla, all while Mother furiously chain-smoked to quell her anxiety. It's too bad Darla didn't have a coping mechanism like that for her emetophobia. For our part, we certainly felt fear.]

My head hurt, I do remember that. And I was hot—so hot, sweating like a pig. [Scribe's note: Shortly after the surgery, Darla developed a fever of 104. Mother panicked and insisted we take her to the hospital. When we arrived, they admitted Darla and gave her fluids. Her bloodwork showed an infection, and they pumped her full of antibiotics and pain medication. Mother had to explain the precipitating circumstances—the lobotomy, of course. The doctor and nurses had the decency and good sense to be horrified. By then, the transorbital lobotomy, especially for a child, was seen as utterly barbaric. Looking back, I believe it was one of the nurses that notified the state licensing board. From there, the press ran with it. Thank goodness they kept our names out of it.]

I think I went to a hospital—there was bright light, which made my head hurt worse, and I was so thirsty. [Scribe's note: Darla was admitted to the hospital for five days, until her fever broke decisively enough for us to take her back home. Mother was afraid the doctor was going to call social services. If he did, nothing ever came of it.]

I remember Ma and Ellie helping me back into my bed. I was so weak, I could barely stand on my own. [Scribe's note: Darla couldn't stand at all. Mother and I had to carry her between us. Father refused to help. He was incensed about the hospital bill, yelling about how the lobotomy was supposed to keep Darla out of the hospital, and instead we'd now saddled him with an enormous debt he'd have to work for years to pay off. I'm not sure what he thought the alternative was—should we have let Darla die at home, sweating through her mattress?]

My head still hurt every now and then, and Ma or Ellie would spoon-feed me chicken soup and little sips of water. [Scribe's note: Darla was little more than a vegetable for three months. She would go in and out of consciousness, never communicating anything clearly. Mother and I took turns changing her diapers. When she was awake, Mother and I would try to feed her, but she wouldn't chew, so we had to blend everything or rely on mostly clear soups. She lost more weight, and she had accidents daily, completing soaking through her diaper, until Mother finally decided to do away with the sheets and use waterproof pads instead that could be more easily changed out. We were terrified Darla would be that way forever—completely unable to take care of herself, worse off than she was before the surgery.]

My first truly clear memory after the surgery is of Ellie. She came into my room and sat on the edge of my bed, which had been stripped of sheets. I must have been mighty out of it before, because Ellie looked so surprised when I opened my eyes and looked at her. The only thing she said to me was, "I hate you." [Scribe's note: Yes, this happened. I'm not proud of it, but I'm not going to apologize for it, either. Darla had been incontinent and incoherent for three months. Mother and Father fought constantly, filling the entire house with secondhand smoke from the cigarettes they sucked down by the pack. Father yelled that Darla seemed drunk, and Mother would respond that this was his fault, and he would scream back something along the lines of, "Damn it, Kelly, Darla is worse off now than she was before! She's wearing diapers, for God's sake!" Mother would say he's the one who pushed for the surgery, and Father would get very quiet, which was when I knew she had gone too far. Sometimes the quiet hung there for awhile; other times, it ended with a resounding slap and Mother's pathetic sobs. Either way, the disintegration of our family was obvious. Darla was even more useless than before, Father was angry, Mother was a mess, and I was left to hold everything together as best I could.]

Slowly, very slowly, I returned to myself. But what came back wasn't the same version of me. I was still Darla Gregory, but in some ways, I was a completely different person. [Scribe's note: It took five months for Darla to be able to speak coherently again. By then, Mother and Father fought daily, screaming matches that could be heard out in the street. Father berated Mother for the choice of doctor, telling her Dr. Hupman was a disgrace, a joke. He wasn't wrong, but Mother, when she was feeling feisty, would say that Hupman had a good reputation, and besides, they'd tried everything, even a psychiatrist before, and that had been worse. Of course, Father would then say what could be worse than what we've got now, because the thing in that room is no daughter of mine.

By the time Darla resembled more of an animal than a vegetable again, Father was so consumed by his anger that there was no turning back.]

I remember feeling serene, like a pond in the middle of a field no one ever visits, its surface never rippling. Sometimes my face would ache from smiling. I smiled more than I had my entire life. [Scribe's note: Father found ways to be angry about this new development, too. He said the crazy doctor had turned Darla into a moron, and they'd have to take care of her for the rest of her life. For my part, even though I hated what Darla had done to our family, how she had splintered us into a thousand sharp pieces, all pointed at each other, there was something about caring for her that I appreciated. Darla never moved, she never escaped; she was like a hamster I could keep in a cage and caress when I saw fit. She was no more than a veritable household pet.]

I couldn't remember how to do basic things, the sorts of things even very young children can do—eating solid foods without leaving my mouth hanging open, using the bathroom on my own, even speaking became difficult. I would try to form the words I wanted to say, but they either got lost on the way to my mouth, or my tongue got so twisted up that nothing sensible would come out. Ma would try to work with me, to get me to say little words, but it took a very long time for even the most basic 'Hi.' Pa would get so angry with me, and I should have been upset, but nothing much ruffled the serene pond I had become. Even the fear that used to plague me had gone away. I could remember feeling afraid, but what used to terrify me felt so distant—funny, even. If I thought about the fear for too long, it began to seem so silly that I started to laugh. Once I laughed, I couldn't stop, which would set Pa off again if he was home, which wasn't too often. I don't think Pa was around much then. [Scribe's note: Darla remembers correctly. Father started staying away for longer and longer stretches, saying he had to work late. Towards the end, he stopped even making excuses or manufacturing reasons for his absences. He just didn't come home, except for the occasional shower or to change clothes. I could hear Mother in her room at night, crying softly. I want to say it broke my heart—perhaps it should have—but I felt numb by then. I knew there was no saving our family.]

I saw Dr. Hupman one more time that I can remember. He came by the house to ask how I was doing. He looked different. Smaller, more shriveled, like an old apple, and he smelled sharp and sour, like dirty sheets. He tugged at his collar from the doorway to my room, where he stood, shifting on his feet. Ellie was in the room with me, sitting on my bed, and she just about snarled at the doctor. He asked me what I remembered, how my head felt, if my fear was still there. [Scribe's note: I wanted to do far more than snarl. I wanted to roar and bare my teeth; I wanted to charge and leap upon that horrid, dirty man, who had obviously been drinking, to boot. I wanted to claw his face to shreds, then rip out his teeth one by one. He was no doctor. He was the worst, most repulsive creature of all: a man whose massive ego prevented him from realizing just how stupid and incapable he really was.]

Ma came up behind Dr. Hupman and asked him if he'd like to speak in the living room. When he left, Ellie jumped off the bed and followed. Pa wasn't home, and I think Ellie just wanted to watch after Ma with another man in the house. [Scribe's note: Not exactly. I wanted to do what all children love most—eavesdrop. I wanted to know the real reason for the man's visit. Darla wasn't wrong—he did look paler, more disheveled, as though he'd suffered some great crisis and was barely hanging on. Truth be told, I relished in his anguish. How could I not? He'd destroyed my family.

I hid around the corner, just out of sight of Mother and the man in the living room. Mother was stammering something, about how Darla did seem to be doing better—the woman had always been intimidated by men with advanced degrees, no matter how spurious or repugnant they truly were—and the man was interjecting every now and then with an "Excellent!" or "How wonderful!" Something was off, and it didn't take me long to understand exactly what that was.

Their conversation was wrapping up when the man pulled something crinkly out of his pocket, the sound obscenely loud in the otherwise silent house. He spoke quietly, but I could still make out what he said: "Mrs. Gregory, I want to thank your husband and you sincerely for your discretion in this delicate matter." I heard the crinkly paper slide across the coffee table, then the sound of Mother's fingers grasping it. I couldn't see her, but I could imagine that she brought the paper closer to her face, squinting at it, as though narrowing her eyes would help her better understand.

"But I don't understand," she said, futilely.

I could hear the man shifting uncomfortably on the scratchy orange couch. "Consider this an expression of my gratitude." When Mother didn't respond, he added, "For keeping this experience to yourselves."

I could almost hear the wheels click in Mother's mind. "Is this hush money?"

The man gulped. "No, no, of course not. Like I said, just an expression of my gratitude."

"This is more than we paid for the procedure," Mother said flatly.

"I... I am very grateful," the man stammered.

Mother, to her credit, managed to find some mettle deep within her bones. "I'd like you to leave my home now, Doctor." The action would have carried more gravitas if she'd thrown what I now know was a check back at him, but even at such a young age, I was under no illusions about the state of our family finances. Mother needed that money, so I'm sure she tucked the check into her pocket.

"Yes, yes, of course," the man said, and I heard the couch creak as he stood up, then the shuffle of footsteps toward the front door. "I believe—"

"I believe you've done quite enough," Mother said, then opened the door and ushered the man out.

For one rare, fleeting moment, I felt somewhat close to proud of my Mother.]

When Ellie came back in, her face was bright red. I asked her what had happened, and she told me not to worry about it. That was good enough for me—nothing much worried me in those days. [Scribe's note: Darla didn't need to know. Even if I'd told her the truth, I doubt she would have understood or grasped the full implications of what had just taken place. I sat back on her bed and resumed clipping her toenails, a task I hated the least out of my various caretaking chores.]

After Ellie left the room that afternoon, Ma came in with my dinner. I still had trouble getting the food from the tray to my mouth, so she helped me. Sometimes she had to hold my mouth closed so I could chew without spilling food all over myself. Ma tried to make me my old favorites, even her chocolate cake, but I didn't much care, even though I was hungry. I don't remember tasting the food; everything around me had become black and white, even flavors. I floated for a long time.

Pa almost never came to my room anymore. The only way I'd know if he was home or not was from the shouting that I could hear through my bedroom wall. I know what he said about me, and it should have hurt, but it didn't. I couldn't feel anything in full color. Everything was just shades of what it had been before, and I simply didn't care.

[Scribe's note: The next time Father was home, two days after Hupman's visit, he screamed at Mother so loudly I thought the neighbors might call the police. I don't know if she told him the full story or showed him Hupman's wrinkled hush money check, but he knew enough to be furious. In my opinion, Mother had more of a right to be angry—it was Father, after all, who had insisted on the lobotomy—but she had lost her spine and turned back into a mouse upon Father's return.

The next day was the worst fight yet. That was the day we saw the newspaper article.]

1972

THE RICHMOND-TIMES DISPATCH

April 24, 1972

Doctor's Medical License Revoked Following Death of Lobotomized Patient

In a recent press release, Richmond Marshall Hospital announced that it has severed ties with Dr. Michael Hupman. Dr. Hupman, a staff physician at the hospital for the past twenty-two years, has had his medical license revoked after a patient's tragic death, which has in turn spurred nearly two dozen patients and their families to file complaints of medical malpractice, alleging unauthorized and unsafe surgeries.

A World War II veteran and father of three, Dr. Hupman specialized in neurology, and trained with Dr. Walter Freeman at The George Washington University. It was under Dr. Freeman that Dr. Hupman learned how to perform the transorbital lobotomy, a procedure that has since fallen out of favor among clinicians, with many calling the surgery barbaric with little to no efficacy.

The transorbital lobotomy, invented by Dr. Freeman and modeled after the prefrontal leucotomy of Dr. Egas Moniz, involves inserting a sharp instrument, similar to an icepick, into the eye sockets to sever a portion of the brains' internal connections. Dr. Freeman pioneered this procedure, which does not require anesthesia and can be performed in an office instead of a surgical suite, with the goal of curing mental illness and helping patients confined to asylums return to their homes.

Despite its purported beneficial outcomes, the transorbital lobotomy has been shown to be far less effective than Dr. Freeman promised. After Dr. Freeman's final patient died as a result of the procedure in 1967, he was no longer allowed to perform surgery.

Dr. Hupman has been an avid proponent of lobotomy as a curative surgery for those suffering from extreme mental illness. When Richmond Marshall Hospital banned the procedure in 1967, coinciding with Dr. Freeman's final surgery, Dr. Hupman allegedly continued to operate in his own offices.

Following the death of Ava Christine Lionetti, 56, in February after an alleged lobotomy, her family has brought a wrongful death lawsuit against Dr. Hupman. Many additional patients and their families have followed suit. It is unclear whether criminal charges will also be filed.

"We are shocked and saddened to hear of the death of Mrs. Lionetti," a representative from Richmond Marshall stated. "We do not condone Dr. Hupman's actions in any way, shape, or form. Our thoughts and prayers are with the families affected by this tragedy."

Dr. Hupman did not respond to our requests for comment.

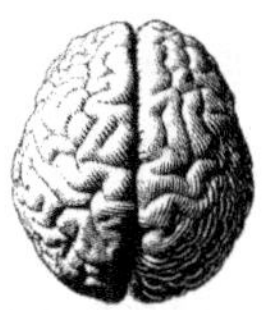

1 9 7 2

There was some commotion one day in the spring after my surgery. I was used to hearing Ma and Pa fight, but this was something different, something worse. Usually, they argued in their room, and I could hear them pretty easily if I pressed my ear to the wall. This time, they were out in the living room, and even though I couldn't make sense of everything they were saying, I could tell it was bad. Pa was furious, and Ma could barely talk, she was crying so hard. I should have cared more—they were my parents, after all, and they were hurting bad—but everything slipped over me like Ma's silk dressing gown. I'd been going on like I was, sitting in my bed, staring at the wall, occasionally talking to Ellie when I could make the words come out right, for so long, and I figured I would spend the rest of my life doing the same. It should have bothered me then. It should bother me now, I can tell you that. But my ability to care deeply was gone, and all I could do was sit there, listening, but not comprehending or reacting. I felt like a painting in a museum, but far less pretty.

[Scribe's note: Father and Mother had sent me to my room before the real screaming started, but I crept out and listened anyway, crouched around the corner. They weren't trying to be quiet, so I didn't feel ashamed of eavesdropping. The evening began as usual, with Mother flitting to and fro trying to think of something to cook for supper, the sort of supper we used to all have together but now mostly ate in our own corners of the house, tucked away. I was in my room, doing my homework. Darla was in her bed, as always, staring off into the distance and drooling. We'd had to bring back the bib; at least it was less drool than we'd dealt with while Darla was on Thorazine. Father came home, the door slamming behind him, and I knew something bad was coming. I rushed into the living room in time to see the front page of the newspaper Father had thrown onto the coffee table. The headline read, "Doctor's Medical License Revoked Following Death of Lobotomized Patient," and even though I didn't see Hupman's name, I knew exactly who that article was referencing.

"Kelly!" Father yelled. "Kelly! Get in here!"

Mother scurried into the living room, her face pinched even more than usual. "What is it?"

"Have you seen the goddamn paper today?"

"No," Mother said, shrinking back into herself.

It was at this moment they both noticed me, and Father snarled, "Get out of here. This is between your mother and me."

I thought about lingering, just to see what he would do to me—how far he would go—but I didn't want to disrupt the conversation. I pretended to go back to my room, then took up my place around the corner.

Father picked up the paper and threw it down again, the *slap* echoing throughout the house. "Read it," he growled at Mother.

There was a rustling of pages and the sigh of a cushion as Mother sat down to read.

The silence was broken only by Father's heavy breathing. After what felt like a very long time, there was another crinkle of paper as Mother set the newspaper down. Then she began to weep.

"Jesus Christ," Father said. "What a fucking mess."

Back when things were good, Mother would have scolded him for swearing, but she did no such thing. She only continued weeping as Father stomped around the room, his footsteps heavy, almost violent.

"That man destroyed Darla," Father finally huffed. "Just look at her, Kelly! She can't talk, she can barely eat, she can't even use the goddamned toilet on her own. At least before, she could go in that fucking bucket by herself!"

Mother managed to choke out, "I didn't want her to have that procedure. I never wanted that."

This was the wrong thing to say, and Mother must have known it immediately, because there was a fleshy *thwap* as Father's hand connected with Mother's cheek.

"Are you saying this is my fault?" Father said, his voice icy.

At least this time, Mother had the good sense not to respond.

"It's your side of the family that has all the crazy," Father said. "The Gregorys are far sturdier. I should have listened to my mother, goddamnit. She tried to tell me any children we had would be fruit of the poison tree."

These words were absolutely venomous, even for Father, whose tongue had always been on the sharper side. It was true that Mother had several cousins, aunts, and uncles who had suffered from melancholy or delusions, but I'd never thought too deeply about it until then. If Mother had the 'crazy' in her, too, maybe it was her fault. I couldn't help but wonder if the crazy was in me, too.

Mother pulled herself together enough to ask, "Should we call a lawyer?"

I thought Father would slap her again, but instead he sank into a cushion of his own. I couldn't see him, but I imagined he was hunched over, head in his hands, defeated. "Hell, no. If we call a lawyer, people will find out what happened to Darla. They'll ask questions."

"But maybe we could get some money, you know—"

Father cut her off. "I don't want money from that man."

On this point, we could agree.

"But it could help pay for her care—"

"I said no, Kelly!" Father yelled, but the venom had dissipated. I could tell he was bone-deep exhausted. "It's nobody's business but ours. We can take care of Darla here."

What he didn't say to Mother was clear: *You* can take care of Darla. *Ellie* can take care of Darla.

The room was quiet again, except for the gentle rasp of Father's labored breathing. I wanted to get my hands on that newspaper, read the article for myself, but I'd have to wait. When I heard the creak of the couch as one or both of them stood up, I ran back to my room and quietly closed the door.]

When all the yelling stopped, Ma came and stood in my doorway. She looked so sad. She looked at me as though I were already dead. Like most things during that time, it should have hurt.

But it didn't.

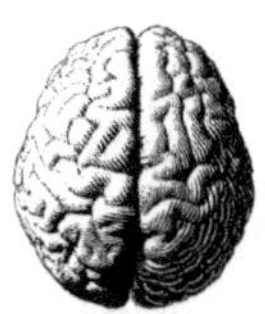

1 9 7 2

The fog lifted slowly. It felt as though one minute, I was in a cloud of heavy gray, and then, as if the sun were rising, the murk burned off, and I could see. Things weren't as bright or as clear as they were before what happened to me, but at least they weren't fuzzy. [Scribe's note: This started happening about seven months after the lobotomy. I noticed the light starting to creep back into Darla's eyes, how she would look at me when I spoke instead of through me. We had conversations that held some meaning, even if they were inane or unimportant. We spoke mostly of the weather, or I would tell Darla what was happening at school. More importantly, we didn't talk about what was happening at home, or about Hupman, who, after the civil lawsuits were filed, was charged with involuntary manslaughter and arrested. He posted bail, but without his medical license, he could do little harm in the outside world. Still, I hated him with a passion I hadn't felt before in my young life. Even at that young age, I knew manslaughter didn't carry as heavy a sentence as murder, but I wished it did. I wanted him to fry for what he'd done to our family. How dare that man call himself a doctor, when he'd done more harm than anyone else I could ever imagine.]

One morning, I had to go to the bathroom. I wanted to take myself to the toilet. When I got out of bed and walked to the doorway, I stumbled, and I couldn't catch myself in time. I went sprawling to the carpet. I must have yelled, because Ellie came running into my room. By the time she got me back on my feet, it was too late, and my bladder emptied all over the floor. [Scribe's note: It wasn't just the floor—Darla's urine soaked through her diaper and into my bellbottoms. I was beyond disgusted, but what could I do? Father was gone, as usual, Mother was at the grocery store, and I was the only one home on that Saturday morning. I helped Darla change out of her soaked nightgown and cleaned her off as best I could, then got her redressed in a fresh nightgown and diaper and back in bed. I figured the months—the years—of being confined mostly to her bed had atrophied her muscles, which hadn't been too much of a problem, because she still never left her room.

In fact, until that moment, she hadn't shown much of any initiative to go anywhere on her own, so even though I was angry, I felt hopeful, too. That was a good sign. Maybe there was some possibility, however slim, that Darla would be able to take care of herself one day. I could only wish that day would come sooner rather than later. Caring for Darla was already wearing on me. I was withdrawn at school. Sullen. What friends I had had begun to pull away, as if sensing the rot of our family on my skin. No one outside of our family knew about the lobotomy, but kids talk. Kids speculate. Kids can be cruel, and so many of them asked me questions that I eventually thought it would be easier to just tell them Darla went to live with our nonexistent Great Aunt Christine because she had a big house in the mountains, and doctors had told us the fresh air would help Darla heal from the mysterious illness I always alluded to but never named. Eventually, the kids stopped talking about Darla. Then they stopped talking to me. My world had narrowed to an ever-shrinking tunnel, and Darla was at the end, blocking the light.]

I knew Ellie was upset about my accident, and I should have been embarrassed, but I wasn't. I don't remember if I told her I was sorry. [Scribe's note: She did not.]

Ma still had to help me eat. My brain tried to tell my mouth to close when I took a bite, but my mouth wouldn't listen. I could bring a fork to my mouth, but I couldn't make my lips close. Ma had to push my mouth shut so I could chew, but I didn't have to chew too much. Ma mostly fed me soft things, like porridge, or tuna salad, or, every now and then, some of her chocolate cake. I heard her tell Ellie she wanted me to put some more weight on so I could get my strength back.

One day, Ma came into my room and announced that it was my birthday, and we were going to celebrate. She helped me out of bed, gave me a thorough scrubbing in the shower, and dressed me in a new dress. It was orange with little yellow flowers, and I liked it very much. Ma combed my hair back and put a barrette in it. I leaned on her as she brought me into the living room, which I hadn't been in for a very long time. She sat me on the couch and told me to wait for a minute while she got my birthday dinner ready.

Ellie came in and smiled at me. I remember her smile because she'd started wearing lipstick, and the bright red made her teeth look really white. She told me happy birthday and sat across from me. She told me about school that day, and I told her I didn't even know it was my birthday. [Scribe's note: Darla hadn't had much of a birthday party for several years, since she refused to leave her bedroom. Mother was committed to breaking the pattern, to making Darla appear more normal. I think she wanted to put on a show for Father, make him see that Darla was getting better because, Hey! Look! She's out in the living room, and she's dressed in something that's not dirty pajamas, and her hair is clean and brushed, and she's looking right at us when we speak!

Mother had gone to a lot of trouble to make Darla's birthday dinner. Roasted chicken, mashed potatoes (real, not instant), peas, and fresh rolls made from scratch. Then, of course, there was the obligatory chocolate cake, which she'd decorated with sprinkles and twelve pink candles. I didn't tell her, but I thought she was trying far too hard. I sat and talked to Darla, and even I could see Darla's improvement, while visible, was minimal. All she said to me was "I didn't know it was my birthday." There was no emotion in her voice, or on her face. She was like a ghost wearing a Darla suit, but at least she'd spoken a complete, coherent sentence.]

When Ma called for us to come to the kitchen because dinner was ready, Ellie helped me to my chair. I didn't remember the last time I'd sat at the kitchen table. I felt strange sitting in the chair, looking at the meal on the table. Ma had cooked so much, like she was feeding an army instead of just us. The food looked good, and I reached out my hand to grab a roll. Ma swatted my hand away and said, "Not yet, Darla dear. We're waiting for Papa." I couldn't understand why we had to wait. The food was getting cold, and my stomach was growling. [Scribe's note: I couldn't understand, either. I sat there, across from Darla, trying not to roll my eyes. Did Mother really believe Father would show up? He avoided us whenever he could. Why did she think tonight would be any different?]

I was about ready to try for the roll again when the door opened and slammed shut. Pa came into the kitchen. He didn't look happy. [Scribe's note: I was shocked. Mother must have begged him, that's the only explanation. He was scowling, even though I imagine most other men would be elated to come home to a delicious dinner and a happy family. Maybe that's my mistake—I wouldn't really call us happy. Father grunted, sat at his place at the head of the table, and picked up his fork without preamble. "John? It's your daughter's birthday today. Don't you have something you'd like to say to her?" Father grunted again, and, with his mouth full of potatoes, snarled, "That idiot isn't my daughter, Kelly, and you damn well know it." I wasn't altogether too shocked—I was used to Father's inappropriate and brutal outbursts by that point—but the way Mother's face crumpled, you would have thought Father had just told her the world was ending. I wanted to kick him under the table, but of course I didn't dare. Mother had gone to so much trouble; the very least he could have done was tell Darla happy birthday. Just two little words would have made the evening feel, if not normal, at least tolerable. Instead, Mother sniffled as she picked at her plate, scooting closer to Darla to help hold her jaw closed while she chewed. I wasn't very hungry (watching someone dribble half-masticated food from between their lips is hardly appetizing), so I focused on making a pyramid out of my peas.]

Pa was mean, but I don't remember exactly what he said. Something about how I wasn't his daughter anymore, which made no sense, because of course I was. I might be different than I was, but I was still his child. Ma got real sad, and her chin wobbled like she was going to cry. She still helped me eat my dinner though, which tasted good. My face started to hurt from all the chewing—I'd only been eating soft foods for a while, but it was worth it. I ate everything on my plate and then reached for another roll. This time, Ma didn't stop me. [Scribe's note: Father rushed through his food as quickly as possible. The few times he looked over at Darla, he scowled even more severely, which I didn't think was possible. He looked at her like she was a vile stranger, a creature unfit to live in his home. It made me wonder if he had ever loved Darla, and by extension, if he had ever loved me. How else could a father's affections switch off so completely?]

Pa ate real fast and then got up. Ma asked him if he wanted cake, and he said no. Then he went back into their bedroom, and I could hear him getting changed. [Scribe's note: What he actually said was, "I can't eat another damn thing if I have to look at her. She eats like a goddamn barn animal. Makes me sick."]

Ma and Ellie cleared our plates, and then Ma brought out my cake. She didn't light the candles, but I didn't care. I tried to count the candles, but my brain couldn't hold onto the numbers. They danced just out of my grasp. It wasn't until Ellie told me I was twelve that I understood. [Scribe's note: If Father had tried just a bit harder, I know Mother would have lit the candles. She would have brought the cake into the room with all the pomp and circumstance she used to expend for our birthdays—all smiles, cheers, and rounds of 'For She's a Jolly Good Fellow.' Instead, she plopped the cake onto the table and collapsed back into her chair. She didn't even bat an eye when Darla plunged her dirty fingers into the cake, tearing off chunks and shoving them in her mouth. Bits of cake and saliva dripped from her open jaws onto her new dress. There's no doubt—it was, indeed, a disgusting display. Mother didn't move to help Darla eat this time. Maybe she thought there was no longer any need to put on a show, since Father had, by that time, showered, changed, and left the house again, slamming the door on his way out. I can't say I blame her.]

The cake was yummy, and I almost ate half of it before Ma took it away. My stomach was full to bursting, but I still wanted more. [Scribe's note: In later years, during my medical training, I learned that the injury caused to the frontal lobe by lobotomy can damage the body's natural hunger and satiety cues.] If she'd left the cake in front of me, I would have eaten the whole thing, even though I was starting to feel funny and achy. It started like a wave, and then, before I knew it, I threw up right on the table.

There it was. The thing I knew I'd been so afraid of that I'd had to get surgery. I spat out the bits of chicken and potato that were still in my mouth. The whole room smelled like my sick, which made me throw up again. It wasn't so bad, but I think Ellie screamed, and then Ma was by my side, crying and dragging me into the bathroom. [Scribe's note: I was glad Father had left by then. If he'd been witness to that revolting scene, he surely would have throttled Darla right there, anything to rid her from his life. I did, in fact, scream, and I was also glad I had barely picked at my meal. The whole kitchen was enveloped in the bilious stench, and when Mother rushed to Darla's side, she was sobbing. I can't know if she was crying because of Father, or because of Darla, or because of the entire sorry state of our family, but I did know that her tears meant I had to stay strong. We couldn't both fall apart.]

Ma cleaned me up in the bathroom. She took off my dress and rinsed it off in the sink, then she changed my diaper, combed my hair again, and wiped off my face with a towel. She tucked me into my bed and closed my door.

I could hear her crying on the other side of the wall all night.

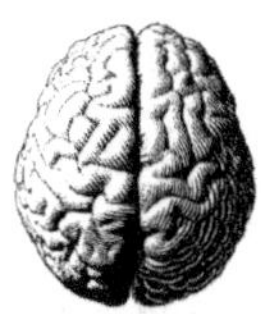

1 9 7 2

Before the surgery, I had really liked to read. I used to get new books from the library every week, but when things got really bad, I only read and reread the books I already had in the room, because the ones from the library weren't safe. Too many hands had already touched them. It's sad to think of a little kid being afraid of a book, right? [Scribe's note: Sad isn't the word I'd use. Mostly, Darla's crises during the height of her emetophobia led to infuriating exasperation. There were many times when I thought about simply slipping a library book onto her bed while she slept. Then, when she woke up, she'd find she hadn't succumbed to fatal illness despite the book's proximity overnight. I never went through with this, though. Yes, Darla exasperated me, but even though I couldn't understand her pain, I could feel it. It hurt me, too. Be thankful you do not have a sibling.]

Not long after my birthday, Ellie came into my room carrying books she was reading for school. I asked her if I could look at one, and she handed it to me. I wasn't really able to read the words, even still. My brain hadn't been able to make much sense of written letters since the surgery. I could see an 'A' or a 'D' and understand what they meant, how they sounded, even, but I couldn't read the words they formed. The letters would wriggle away like worms even as I reached for them. I would have been far more frustrated if I hadn't still felt numb.

I remember the name of the book Ellie gave me. It was *Anne of Green Gables*. I thought that sounded so fanciful, even though I didn't know what a gable was. Ellie asked me if I wanted to read it, and even though I wanted to, very badly, I couldn't make my mouth say the word 'Yes.' All I could manage was, "I don't know." [Scribe's note: This was Darla's common answer to most questions around that time, as if the act of thinking critically or making a decision was too overwhelming. Sometimes, in his crueler moments, Father would mock her, saying "I don't know," in a high-pitched voice whenever Darla was within earshot. It was very clear he wanted to wound her.]

I felt myself smile as Ellie opened up the book. She knew what I wanted, even if I wasn't really able to tell her. She started reading, and I was enchanted. I felt like I was being taken away to a happier place, where girls were smart and strong and powerful and could live their own lives. I knew that sort of place didn't really exist, but like all good fairy tales, it helped me escape for awhile. It helped me relearn how to feel, at least a little bit. [Scribe's note: Darla's eyes lit up when I started reading. I could tell she was enjoying herself, which was a very encouraging sign. Foolish girl that I was, I still held out hope that Darla would return to normal and our family would be saved. Clearly, Darla wasn't the only one who preferred living in a fairy tale world.]

Every day after school, Ellie would come into my room and read to me from *Anne of Green Gables*. Her visits to my room were the only thing I looked forward to—in fact, they were the only thing that made me feel much of anything at all. It was so simple, really, just reading to me out loud, but it affected me deeply. Ellie helped bring me back to something close to myself. I would never be the same Darla, the surgery had taken care of that, but Ellie's reading sessions made me think that maybe, one day, I could be someone worth knowing, someone worth existing.

Ellie was halfway through the book when it occurred to me that I could try to help myself. It's what Anne would do, after all. During the day, when Ellie was away at school and Ma was cleaning the house or cooking, I would take little trips around my room. Just little walks, getting my body used to moving again. My knees and hips were stiff and creaky, and sometimes my feet didn't move the way I wanted them to, and I would trip and fall to the carpeted floor. But I kept going, because it's what Anne would have done. And more than anything, I wanted to be like Anne.

Ma must have heard me fall one day, because she came rushing into my room, wiping her hands on her apron, and ran to my side. I was on the floor, attempting to push myself up all on my own. Ma grabbed me and got me back into bed. "You stay tucked up in here, Darla," she said to me, like I was an invalid. I guess, in her mind, I was. And maybe I had been ever since the surgery, but I didn't want to be like that anymore. The way Ma put me back in bed, without even trying to talk to me or give me a kind word or two about my efforts, made me think she wanted me to stay sick, to keep lying in bed for the rest of my life. [Scribe's note: Mother told me about this incident when I returned home from school. In her version of events, Darla had been crashing around in her room, and scared the devil out of mother, who then ran to Darla's room to see what the racket was all about. Mother said Darla had fallen out of bed, and she fretted about whether or not she'd need to get a bed rail to keep Darla from falling again, and then she collapsed at the kitchen table, her head in her hands, and wept until it was time to start cooking the dinners none of us wanted to eat anymore. All that is to say, I think Darla may have been somewhat correct about Mother's motivations. Mother could handle a sick child, a being with a constant, predictable need. She was not equipped to handle a child who wanted to claw her way back from the brink of nonexistence. Mother was not one to put in that sort of effort, the kind of hard work required of a real mother. I can empathize, because I became the same way.]

Even though Ma put me back in bed and told me to stay there, I didn't listen. To be honest, I didn't much care what Ma wanted. Like most things, her feelings toward me did not affect me. For that reason, at least, my numbness worked in my favor. If I had listened to Ma, I never would have walked again.

By the time Ellie got to the last chapter of *Anne of Green Gables*, I could walk back and forth across my room three times without falling. When Ellie read the last word in the book, I got out of bed and showed her what I could do. She clapped and cheered, which must have got Ma's attention, because she came into the room and got real mad at Ellie. I couldn't understand why, but Ma made Ellie go to her own room and told her not to bother me so much. [Scribe's note: Mother was upset because she came in and saw Darla out of bed, walking around. Instead of being delighted, she was furious—not at Darla, but at me. She was angry that I'd allowed Darla to get out of bed and move on her own, because, in Mother's words, "Darla isn't capable. She's going to hurt herself, and it's going to be your fault."

This was ridiculous to me. Didn't Mother want Darla to be able to move on her own again? I'd overheard a teacher at school talking about her husband's back pain, and how somebody called a physical therapist had helped him. I asked Mother, "Why don't you take Darla to a physical therapist? She clearly wants to walk again!"

Mother was unmoved. "Do you think we have the money for that? Who's going to pay for it? You?"

I was tempted to throw *Anne of Green Gables* right at Mother's head, but I refrained. I didn't want to upset Darla, even though she likely wouldn't have cared. Mother sent me to my room, then she went back to the kitchen for another crying jag. I was used to the routine by now—thirty minutes of pre-dinner crying, then a desultory meal we both only picked at, then Mother helped Darla eat in her own room, then Mother sat on the couch in the living room, staring at the front door, willing Father to walk through it. I can't blame Mother too much; after all, she'd been sold the lie all women of her time had gobbled up like candy: find a man to marry and he'll take care of you. Life will be easy. Life will be sweet. Life will be satisfying, as long as you have a family. In a way, Mother was living in her own fairy tale, too, but it was beginning to curdle.]

After *Anne of Green Gables*, Ellie read me *Treasure Island*, *The Lion, the Witch, and the Wardrobe*, and *The Secret Garden*, which was my second favorite after *Anne*. Every day, I kept willing myself to go a little further, a little longer, a little faster. I was regaining a little bit of the muscle I'd had before everything happened. My mind was starting to clear a bit faster. I still couldn't read on my own, but I found myself wanting to learn. I craved new things, which Ellie brought me in the form of her books. Things were okay, for awhile.

Until they weren't.

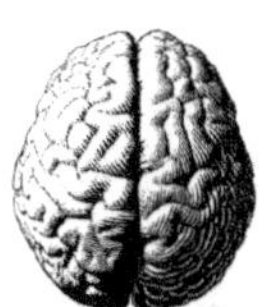

1 9 7 2

I don't remember seeing Pa again after my twelfth birthday dinner, where I ate too fast and got sick on the table. [Scribe's note: It was summertime, and I was home almost all the time. I saw Father sporadically—once when he stopped in to pack a bag of clothes, another time when he was pulling money from the cookie jar Mother used as her rainy day fund (and which I'm sure she thought he knew nothing about), and the last time when he stumbled in one night after dinner, drunk. Mother was in the shower, but I heard the door slam, so I crept out and found him on the couch. I wasn't done fighting for Darla, so I waited until he noticed me, and then I asked, "Do you think we could take Darla to a physical therapist? I heard my teacher talking about how her husband had back pain but then a physical therapist helped him feel better. I know Darla wants to get better, so maybe that would help her, too?" I was breathless when I finished. It was more than I'd spoken to my father in what felt like years.

He just stared at me, red eyes narrowed, then he scoffed. "And how will we explain to this 'physical therapist' what made Darla that way? I won't have people whispering about our family."

"But—"

"Did you hear me, young lady? Anyway, forget about her. Darla is a lost cause. She's not going to get better, Ellen."

Like Mother often did, he bent over and cradled his head in his hands. He looked so vulnerable, so small. I didn't think Darla was a lost cause, but I believe Father hoped that without any attention, Darla would wither and die, and therefore cease to be his problem. Looking for something to say, I asked him if he was okay.

"What do you think, Ellen?" he snarled at me. "Just what the fuck do you think?"

I'd heard him curse before, of course, but never at me. Disgusted with him, and, frankly, fearing he would escalate and bring the belt out again, I left him on the couch and fled back to my room. When I woke up in the morning, Father was gone.]

One night, Ellie ran into my room and grabbed my shoulders. She told me we had to get out of the house right away. I wanted to ask her why, but all I could manage was, "Yes." She helped me out of my bed and half-dragged me through the living room and out the front door. She sat me down on our porch and then went back inside. A couple minutes later, she opened the door again and pushed Ma out in front of her. Ma looked dazed, and she sat down hard on the steps. Ellie ran towards the garage, and Ma leaned over into the grass and vomited. I realized my head was hurting, so I laid down behind the bushes where it was dark and closed my eyes. The next thing I knew, the garage door was opening, and a cloud was escaping from the growing crack. I could hear the rumble of the car's engine, and then Ellie screamed. I expected Ma to get up and go help her, but she didn't. She just kept sitting there, hunched over the grass. I wanted to run to Ellie, but I couldn't. My body felt so heavy, like all the progress I'd made had disappeared while I was sleeping. I felt trapped, and Ellie just kept screaming and screaming. Eventually, our neighbor Mrs. Knowles came outside and asked what the devil was going on. It wasn't too long after that I could hear the sirens. Their flashing lights made me even dizzier, so I closed my eyes again and lay back down. I must have fallen asleep, because when I opened my eyes again, I was in a hospital bed. I started feeling really anxious, kind of like how my fear used to make me feel, and I didn't know what was going on, what had happened, where my family was. Just then, a nurse came in.

She asked me to settle down, told me the straps around my wrists were to keep me safe.

Then she told me my father was dead.

[Scribe's note: He was not a good father, I know that. I think he was incapable of the sort of deep, unconditional love a father should feel for his children. Like Mother, he'd been sold a lie: marry a nice girl, have a couple of kids, work for forty years, and then enjoy the fruits of your labor. No one had told him how cruel life could be, how wanton its vicissitudes. No one had trained him for a life where your child was not healthy, your wife not stable, your home not a sanctuary. I should have seen it coming—I knew he was unwell. Mother knew it, too, but she couldn't see past her own pain. She felt cheated and misled, and Father's suicide only added to her long list of grievances against life. In her darker moments, when she'd had an extra glass of wine, she'd confide to me that she wished I hadn't pulled her out of the house that day, that I'd let her die in there, too. In her darkest moments, her self-preservation instinct activated, and she instead whispered that she wished I'd left Darla in there. For my part, there are times I wish I'd left us all in there.]

I knew I should feel sad, and even though I could practically see the emotion, I couldn't make myself feel it. I was still the serene pond, and Pa's death was a pebble so tiny it didn't even cause a ripple. When Ma came into the room a bit later, she was crying. She hugged me, but it felt more like she was clinging to me than comforting me. Ellie came in, too, and sat at the end of my bed. She unbuckled the straps around my wrists and told me that because of my surgery, the doctors wanted to make extra sure that I was okay after what happened. [Scribe's note: Father had killed himself with carbon monoxide, which had leaked into the house through the open door leading into the garage. I still don't know if that was an oversight or intentional. Either way, when the paramedics arrived, they quickly realized there was nothing they could do for Father. The rest of us were hustled into the ambulance. Mother revived on the drive, but Darla still looked glassy-eyed. When we arrived at the hospital, Mother did not want to tell the doctors about Darla's lobotomy, which struck me as negligent to the extreme. When Mother left the room to get a cup of coffee, I called for the doctor and told him what had been done to Darla. He looked deeply unsettled, but he said I was right to tell him, and that they would do a thorough check to make sure Darla was in decent shape. I don't regret it, because, when Darla began thrashing violently, we were all prepared. The nurse told me they'd seen patients like this before, and they had trouble acclimating to new surroundings. The restraints were for everybody's safety until Darla had calmed down.]

I guess I was okay, because the doctors let me go home later that day. When we got back to the house, Ma went into her room and closed the door. I could hear her crying really loud through the walls. Ellie helped me inside and sat me on the couch. She didn't look sad. I'm sure I didn't, either. I don't think we were bad daughters, and I don't think Pa was a bad father. We were just bad when we were all together, like puzzle pieces that didn't fit. [Scribe's note: Darla was right; I wasn't sad, per se. I knew before Mother locked herself in her bedroom that she would absolutely fall apart. Even though Father had been pulling away for years by that point, Mother had always held onto a shred of hope that everything would turn around, and the rough time they were going through would be nothing more than a blip they could bury with better memories. Now that I think about it, that's probably why Father held so much animosity toward Mother. He accepted, very early on, that our lives would never be normal, and he resented Mother for clinging to the possibility of an idyllic future. I leaned more toward Father's viewpoint, but instead of hating our new reality, I embraced it. What else was there to do? I didn't want to kill myself like Father, and I didn't want to implode like Mother. I wanted to live as best I could, and if that meant I pulled Darla along with me, so be it. In the wake of my father's death, the most prominent emotion I felt was a low-grade buzzing anxiety. With Father gone and Mother left to bear the financial brunt of our lives alone, I knew things would drastically change, even if Mother hadn't yet accepted it. We weren't wealthy, and Mother would, no doubt, have to find work to keep us afloat. The woman hadn't earned a paycheck a day in her life, so I had no doubt the adjustment would be hard for her. And if it was hard for her, she would make it hard for us, too. She was not a woman to suffer in silence. Darla wouldn't be bothered, of course, but I knew my responsibilities would be doubled, if not tripled. With Mother working, I knew I'd likely have to become Darla's sole caregiver. I only hoped I would have time and energy left over for myself when I was done taking care of everybody else.]

Ma was different after Pa died. She didn't smile much, and if she did, her gray eyes still looked flat and hard, like little stones. Her skin got all wrinkly, as though she'd cried so much she'd sucked herself dry. For the first time I can remember, I thought she looked old. [Scribe's note: I noticed Mother's physical decline, too. Almost overnight, she shriveled into a raisin. Most disturbingly, she was only thirty-five years old. She was still young enough to have another baby, although none of us even remotely considered such an absurd possibility. We had all we could handle—more than we could handle, actually—already.]

Ma stayed in her room for a long time. Sometimes she cried, sometimes she screamed, and sometimes I heard her throwing things against the wall. She stopped coming in to help me do things, which I didn't mind, because it meant I could practice moving around without her putting a stop to it. I tried to stop peeing in my diapers, and soon, I could use the toilet again. I made a bit of a mess in the bathroom, but nobody ever mentioned it, and the next time I had to use the toilet, it had been cleaned up, like magic. [Scribe's note: It was not magic. It was me. I cleaned it up. I didn't enjoy that part, but it was far preferable to changing her diapers several times a day, especially since the summer ended shortly after

Father's death, and I went back to school.]

I got real hungry during the day. Ma stopped bringing me food. I don't think she ate much, either. I had to wait until Ellie came home. She'd gone back to school like everything was still normal. When she got home, she sat on the edge of my bed. I managed to tell her I was hungry, and when she asked what I'd like to eat, I could only say, "I don't know." She brought me a tuna fish sandwich. She didn't help me eat it, and I liked that. I made a little mess, but I was able to wipe myself with my napkin, and Ellie didn't make a big deal out of it. She even read to me while I ate. [Scribe's note: I was furious with Mother for neglecting Darla. Who did she think she was? Did she completely forget that the world didn't stop just because her good-for-nothing husband had finally thrown in the towel? Did she think that if she holed up in her room and never came out, she'd never have to face what her life had become? I admit that that might have worked, if it weren't for Darla. At nearly fourteen, I was old enough to take care of myself. Darla, however, needed help, and lots of it. Darla was not something Mother could opt out of.]

I got used to not seeing Ma. Ellie would bring me breakfast in the morning before she left for school, and I would spend the day in my room, walking back and forth, building up my strength. Ellie would cook me dinner when she came home, and we'd eat together in my room while she read me books. I don't know how long we went on like this until things changed. [Scribe's note: It was only a week. That's how long it took to run out of food in the pantry. That's when I knew I had to say something to Mother. I could do a lot, but I couldn't get a real job. I couldn't make the kind of money we needed to support ourselves. I hated to admit it, but we needed Mother, and I had to be the one to get her moving again.]

One day, Ma came and stood in my doorway. "Darla," she said, and she stared at me for a bit, as though she didn't recognize me. I think she'd been crying, because her face was puffy and there were big black pillows under her eyes. "Darla," she said again. I sat in my bed, waiting for her to say something else. Finally, she took a step towards me and said, "Mama has to go to work now." [Scribe's note: The confrontation needed to get Mother to this point was excruciating. While Darla was still in bed, I'd knocked on Mother's door and let myself in. She was, as usual, burrowed into her bed, sobbing into her sweat-stained pillow. She didn't look up as I entered, only batted her arm at me in a gesture that clearly meant I should leave. I ignored it, and walked right up to the foot of her bed. Without any warning, I gripped the bottom of the quilt and ripped it off of her, leaving it to puddle in a dirty heap on the floor. Mother hissed, as if she'd become some subterranean creature unused to sunlight. Her previously white nightgown was yellowed with the cigarette smoke she was almost always exhaling. "Leave me alone!" she yelled, but again, I ignored her.

"Get up, Mother," I said, moving to the side of the bed where she lay. "It's time to get up."

"No!" she wailed, and I began to find it difficult to ever remember a time when mother had been nurturing to me, when she was the responsible adult and I was the child in need of guidance and a firm hand.

"Yes," I said, grabbing her arm. "I know you're sad Father's gone. But you can't stay in here forever."

"Why not?" Mother said, trying to push my arm away.

I sighed, doubling my efforts to pull her out of the bed when it was clear she wasn't going to come willingly. "Be reasonable, Mother," I said. "The fridge is empty. I have to go to school. We're running low on everything."

"I don't care," she said, pressing her face back into the stinking pillow.

My face grew hot with anger. "I can't do this all on my own, Mother!" I yelled, and yanked her arm with as much strength as I could muster. It worked, and Mother crashed to the floor with a shaky rattle, like a bag full of buttons.

"Ow!" she cried, curling into a ball.

"Stop it!" I said. "Father is gone, Mother, and he's never coming back! I'm already taking care of Darla. I can't take care of you, too."

At this, Mother finally looked me in the eye, as if seeing me for the first time. She took in my knobby knees, my gangly legs still throbbing with growing pains, my fuller hips, my thinner waist, the way my blouse stretched tight across my blossoming bosom. My skirt, hovering just above my knee, would barely pass the school dress code, but what was I to do? I had no time to sew an appropriate one, and no time to drive to the store to get a new one, much less any money of my own to purchase one.

I watched Mother process what she saw. At last, she uncurled herself and beckoned for me to help her up. I did, and she put her nicotine-stained hands on my shoulders. "My baby girl," she said, and I wanted to slither out of her grasp. I had never felt less like a baby. "I'm so sorry."

I prepared myself for the weeping to begin afresh, but Mother surprised me. She stayed composed, and when she still hadn't let go of me after several minutes, I said, "Mother. I need you to go to work. Darla needs you to go to work. We can't live like this anymore."

She removed her hands, and I let loose an inconspicuous sigh of relief. "You're right," she said in a small voice.

When she didn't move, I prodded, "Shouldn't you get dressed?"

"Yes. Yes, of course."

She walked unsteadily to her vanity, and I checked my watch. I had to leave right then, otherwise I'd be late for school.

"Will you be alright?" I asked, and a flash of hatred sparked in my heart. There was no one around to ask me if I would be alright, if I would survive the nuclear wasteland our family had become.

"Sure," Mother said, but I could tell neither of us was convinced.

There was nothing more to say, and no more time left to say it. I headed out, hoping Mother would sort herself out on her own and step back into her life, even though it was radically different from both the one she wanted and the one she used to have.]

I blinked, staring at Ma, standing in my doorway. She had never gone to work like Pa used to. She'd always been home. I guessed with Pa gone forever, Ma would have to do his job. I giggled at the idea of

Ma putting on Pa's pressed trousers and driving to work, trying to fit neatly into the hole he left. I didn't mean anything by it, but Ma's face went red. "We need the money," she said, but she didn't sound happy with me. "I'll be back later." She didn't say anything else, or tell me where she was going, but I didn't care. Since Pa died, she hadn't done much for me, and I was used to being on my own. Maybe things would be even better without me having to worry about her coming into my room and making me rest.

I didn't want to rest. I wanted to learn.

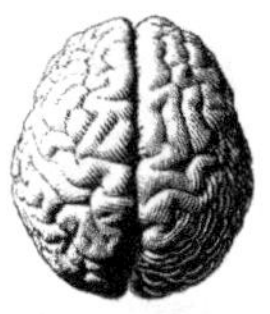

1 9 7 2

One day, as I watched Ellie read a new book, something shifted. I stared at the book's cover, and for the first time since the surgery, the letters didn't dance away from me. They stayed where they were and let me read them. I must have squealed, because Ellie stopped reading and looked at me. "Everything okay?" she asked.

"Uh-huh," I said, trying to nod. My muscles were getting stronger, but my movements were still a bit herky-jerky.

Ellie put the book down and leaned closer to me. "Then why did you make that sound?"

"Go," I said, and Ellie's nose scrunched up.

"You want me to leave?" she said.

Still, I studied the book's cover. "Ask," I said, and I started breathing harder.

"Ask who? For what?" Ellie looked more confused than ever, and it made me want to laugh, but I had to finish.

I took a deep breath. "Alice," I said, and I could tell I was smiling because my cheeks hurt.

"Who's Alice?" Ellie said, but it didn't take her long to understand me. Ellie was always the smart one. She gave me a big smile. "Oh my God, Darla, that's right! Did you just read the cover?"

"I don't know," I said, but I was nodding, and Ellie knew what I meant.

"This is huge," Ellie said, and she hopped off the bed and started pacing around the room. "Darla, do you know what this means?"

"I don't know," I said.

"You're starting to get better! Like, really better!" she said. "You might… " She looked at me, and her nose scrunched up again. "You might get to be normal again."

I was still smiling, and the serene pond of my mind felt the tiniest ripple.

Ellie rushed to my side and grabbed the book. "Read some more, Darla!"

She shoved the book into my hands and turned to the first page. "Read it!" she said again.

I looked down at the page, but something wasn't right. I don't know if the letters were too small, or too close together, or what it was, but I couldn't make sense of the words. I opened my mouth and tried to say something, but saliva dripped out and fell onto the book.

"Goddamnit," Ellie said, and ripped the book out of my hands. "This is a library book, Darla!"

Ellie picked up her book bag and left my room without saying goodbye.

[Scribe's note: I could hardly believe it when Darla managed to read the book's title. I had resigned myself to the idea that Darla would never be fully literate again, and hearing her sound out the words gave me the cruelest glimmer of hope. If Darla could read again, then maybe Darla could think clearly again, then maybe Darla could take care of herself again, then maybe Darla could… and on and on my mind raced through the possibilities. Without Darla to attend to, I could be free.

Seeing her drool onto the book lit a match to my newfound hopes. I didn't want to feel anger towards Darla, but she looked, in that moment, exactly how Father had envisioned her: Stupid. Idiotic. Incapable.

A burden.

I couldn't bear it. I left Darla's room immediately and resorted to Mother's chosen method of coping: I cried into my pillow until my eyes felt dry and my chest stopped heaving. It made me feel no better.]

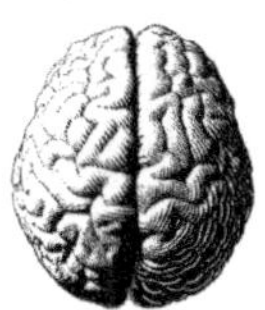

1 9 7 2

Ellie kept reading to me from the Alice book. Sometimes, she would gasp real loud. I supposed the story was surprising, but I couldn't really understand why Anonymous's life was so wrong. She used pills to feel better. How was that different from what the doctor had given me? [Scribe's note: I asked myself that same question over and over as I read *Go Ask Alice*. In hindsight, I probably shouldn't have been reading that book to Darla. She was only twelve, after all, and the subject matter was inarguably adult, despite its young protagonist. Drug abuse, sexual assault, homelessness, psychiatric breakdowns, suicide… it wasn't the sort of light fare Darla was used to me reading.

I have to confess—besides my own interest in the book, I also wanted to keep reading it to see how Darla would react. Ever since her surgery, nothing got a rise out of her. She was placid, maybe smiling simply every now and then whether it was warranted or not. She was hollowed out, like a jack-o'-lantern. The light was on, the face was smiling, but there was no real life there. At least, that's how she appeared to me.]

I found Anonymous fascinating. Here was a young girl, not so different from me, who had a rough start in life. And look what she'd done with herself! She'd escaped her home, she'd made new friends, she'd had new experiences, she'd fallen in love.

I wondered what that felt like.

[Scribe's note: I wondered what that felt like, too. Darla was stuck in the house, sure, and she was certainly stuck in her own mind. But wasn't I stuck, too? If I ever left Darla, who would take care of her? I spent so much time worrying about my sister, I didn't have time for friends or new experiences. And what was love to me? The teenager in Go Ask Alice was so obsessed with boys, it made me feel sick. I wanted to reach through the pages and grab her shoulders, shake some sense into her, tell her those boys weren't worth it, and she should focus her attention on something more productive and worthwhile.

Even as these thoughts skittered through my undamaged brain, I couldn't help but feel a deep yearning for something, anything. At least Anonymous's life was worth cataloguing in a diary. If I kept a diary, what could I possibly write? What would I want to record for posterity? I would certainly never want to reread my own thoughts and the monotonous, tragic drudgery of each day. There was nothing from this time in my life that I would want to remember. I'd be lying if I said I didn't resent Darla for making me relive it as I write this.]

Every day she read to me, Ellie would try to get me to sound out a few words. Some days I could, some days I couldn't. Without Ma around, Ellie decided she would teach me. I wanted to be able to read things for myself, so I was grateful. [Scribe's note: Mother couldn't have cared less about Darla's education. She'd found a job as a waitress at a nearby bar, and she was gone most nights, not getting home until after Darla and I had gone to bed. She slept during the day, and weeks would go by where the only evidence I saw of her was a scantily restocked fridge. This was fine by me. What was not fine by me was her neglect of Darla. In her grief, Mother had slipped into Father's way of thinking—that Darla was a lost cause, an eternal burden, a house pet.

I no longer wanted a house pet. I wanted a normal sister, someone who would eventually be able to live her own life. Someone whose presence wouldn't follow me everywhere like a dark, sticky shadow. So, beyond feeding her and helping her bathe, I tried to teach her.]

One day, I was able to read a full sentence. Ellie clapped so hard for me I thought she was going to break her fingers. "Smile, Darla!" she said, and I did, but I could tell by the way she looked at me that she wasn't happy. "Why can't you be happy?" she asked, and I tried to smile harder. Ellie just dropped her eyes back to the book and told me to try another sentence. [Scribe's note: Darla's smile was that same vapid, soulless upturning of the lips that she'd had since the surgery. There was no light in her eyes, no joy. No recognition of the progress she was making, and that lack of recognition rendered her reading achievement essentially moot, in my opinion.]

Eventually, I could read a whole paragraph. As my muscles got stronger from pacing my room, my mind was coming back, too. I still needed Ellie's help, but she seemed happy to give it. [Scribe's note: Even though Darla was improving, my grades were suffering. Instead of doing my homework after school, I poured myself into teaching Darla. At night, I dreamt of Darla as she could have been—vibrant, competent, *normal*. But when I woke, I knew the dream was just that—fiction. Darla was never destined to be that girl. Sometimes, before the sun had risen and the reality of another day had hit me, I wondered if this version of Darla wasn't better after all. I didn't have friends, but at least I had someone to talk to, a captive audience to listen when no one else would, when no one else cared.]

We kept reading, and I kept listening and learning. The Alice book made me feel excited, I guess, like maybe life wasn't over for me at all, but just beginning. I tried to understand Anonymous's feelings, and how they went up and down like a rollercoaster. I think I had been like that, once, and reading about Anonymous made me wish for that again. I was still that serene pond—my feelings were shallow, nothing went too deep. Any highs were just little bumps, and I could barely sense the lows. I knew from reading about Anonymous's life that the lows could be horrible, but at least she was feeling something, really feeling it in her soul. The surgery had taken my lows away from me, but they'd also taken away my highs. I was starting to better understand how to react to things, what emotions might be proper for a situation, but I couldn't access them like Anonymous could. Anonymous made me want things again.

[Scribe's note: Anonymous made me want things, too. I could understand how someone could feel like they never measured up, like they wanted to be anyone but who they were. At the same time, I wanted to be completely different from Anonymous. I felt death would be preferable to being so pathetic, whiny, and self-indulgent. And the obsession with sex! It lurked around every corner of *Go Ask Alice*. What teenager wasn't curious, I'll admit that, but the single-minded focus was laughable. In my case, all it did was raise questions I couldn't answer myself, nor could I ask Mother. Without a friend to talk to, I ended up spilling more of my soul to Darla. I let some of myself pour into her barren cup. As I became half-empty, she became half-full.]

When Anonymous started talking about dieting, and then about how she should just throw up after eating, I started to laugh. I couldn't help it. Here was this thing I'd been so afraid of, the reason I was now the way I was, and it was an act that some people would do on purpose! How could something that people might do willingly be the very same thing that terrified me to the point of madness? I couldn't stop giggling, and I could tell Ellie was bothered by it. She stopped reading and told me we could be done for the day. I didn't want her to go, but I was too busy laughing to stop her. [Scribe's note: I was concerned that the laughter signaled a sharp mental decline. We'd been making so much progress, and I didn't want to push Darla to a breaking point by giving her too much, too soon. Hearing Darla's recounting of that situation, I can better understand her reaction, although I don't share it.]

Anonymous cared so much about finding love and being accepted. I felt that way before the surgery, but now I was different, and I still didn't have that love. I still wasn't accepted—I knew that, even then. I just didn't care like I should have. I suspect it was better that way. [Scribe's note: I cared enough for the both of us. I wanted that love for myself, even though it felt frivolous and stupid. After all, if Mother and Father, two grown adults, couldn't find it, where was the proof to show it was even real?]

When Anonymous starting getting into drugs, I could tell Ellie was upset, but I was confused. Anonymous wanted to be like the other kids; she wanted to fit in. Ma and Pa put me on the Thorazine for the same reason—they wanted me to be normal. Why was Anonymous so bad for doing on her own what Ma and Pa asked a doctor to do to me? [Scribe's note: Yet another question Darla and I shared. I could understand things better than Darla could, though. I knew Anonymous wanted escape just as much as she wanted to fit in, and I hated her for it. Even if I craved it, I couldn't have indulged my drive for escape—otherwise, I would have ended up like Father. Too much depended on me... but, at the same time, I couldn't help but wonder if I would choose escape if I could. Darla needed me, yes, but did her needs save me from oblivion, or damn me to it? I still don't know the answer.

Maybe if someone had needed Anonymous like Darla needed me, she wouldn't have spent so much time scribbling that angsty, puerile drivel into her silly little diary. She wrote about her shallow experiences because she didn't have anything real to worry about. She could try drugs, run away from home, sell marijuana to school kids, have unprotected sex, and then just come back into the loving embrace of her family as though none of it happened. That was a level of security and privilege I couldn't understand anymore.]

I tried to remember what it felt like to take the Thorazine, but it was too fuzzy. I suppose that was the point: to blur my senses. Was it hurting me? I still don't know. [Scribe's note: Not much could have damaged her further.]

When Anonymous started trying different kinds of drugs, and then selling drugs to little kids, I felt a little sad, I think. With that feeling came some bit of excitement, because feeling anything make waves in my serene little pool meant I was getting better. [Scribe's note: Darla showed minimal outward signs of these supposed feelings. Even now, I am not convinced she was ever able to experience deep emotion after the surgery. Much later, I learned that frontal lobe damage of the kind Darla received in the lobotomy can blunt one's emotions to the point of sociopathy.]

Listening to Ellie read about Anonymous's adventures with boys made me feel curious in a way I hadn't before. What was Anonymous really doing with those boys? And why was she doing it? Did other people want to do that? Did Ellie? When I looked at my sister, I could see that she was starting to change. Her hips were getting wider, and the fabric of her skirt was starting to pull tight. Her chest was growing, too, and her skin, which was always so clear, was spotted with pimples. Something was happening to her, and I figured it would come for me, too, one day. [Scribe's note: I was indeed changing, and I wasn't sure I wanted to. Anonymous made being a teenager sound soul-crushingly exhausting, and every new experience she had made me cramp up with anxiety. One kiss from that boy Roger sent her into an absolute tizzy. How could a single brush of the lips hold so much meaning? To me, it seemed that something like that, which had so much power to lift you up, would have just as much power to knock you down. Looking back, I now know just how correct I was.]

Ellie came into my room after school one day wearing a new skirt and a new blouse. They were both pink with green trim, and they didn't pull across her chest or hips like her old clothes had. I didn't say anything, but Ellie must have noticed me looking, because she told me she'd borrowed some money from Ma and bought herself some new clothes. I managed to tell her she looked pretty, and she smiled at me the same way Ma used to when I helped her clean up after dinner. I felt warm inside, and I didn't want that feeling to ever go away. [Scribe's note: Darla wasn't the only one who noticed how ill-fitting my old clothes had become. Troublesome boys at school had started to point at me and snicker, and I hated it. Things got so bad that Mrs. Truman, the guidance counselor, called me into her office during lunch and told me that I was becoming a woman, and it might be best if I asked my parents to buy me some clothes that fit my new body. I've never been so embarrassed in my life. After school, I stopped at home just long enough to grab a fistful of cash from Mother's secret stash in the kitchen cookie jar (luckily Father hadn't plundered it completely before his death). At the department store near school, I spent every penny on four matching sets in four different colors. I'd have to do laundry mid-week, but that was okay. No one would snicker at me anymore—at least, not because of my clothes.]

We kept reading the Alice book, and Ellie kept helping me sound out the words. When we got to ones I didn't know, I'd stop and look at Ellie. Sometimes she could tell me what they meant, but other times, she had to run into the living room to look something up in our encyclopedia. Pa had bought it three years ago, and he was so proud of it, back before things got real bad. He'd come home from work and flip through the pages until he found something interesting, then he'd tell us all about it. I missed learning new things, but when Ellie finally told me what 'Dexies' and 'Bennies' and 'Heroin' were, I wasn't so sure that was what I wanted to learn about. [Scribe's note: I don't blame Darla. Reading about Anonymous's life was a constant rollercoaster, and even though I was ready to get off, I wanted to know how things ended. The diary would have been much shorter if Anonymous had simply had a lobotomy—from what I could tell, she could have used one much more than Darla.

Anonymous was so easily manipulated, it was pathetic. I decided that would never be me... too bad we can't control everything that happens in our lives, now can we?]

Things got even stranger when I had to ask Ellie what a blowjob was. She looked just as confused as I felt, and she didn't have an answer for me then—but the next day, she came home from school and told me it was something boys and girls did when they liked each other very much. I wondered if that was something I'd ever do. It sounded silly, and I thought of girls blowing bubbles onto the boys they liked, which made me giggle. [Scribe's note: I had an idea of what a blowjob was, but I wasn't clear on the mechanics or the intricate details. Darla's question had stoked my curiosity, though, so I waited in the bathroom during lunch period, when I knew Nancy Foster would be in there, cracking the window and smoking a cigarette. Nancy was alright, but she was fast, and everybody knew it. I figured if anyone would be able to answer my question without too much fuss, it would be Nancy.

I was right.

She told me more than I ever wanted to know, and then she frowned at me. "Now don't go getting into that if you don't have to," she said.

"What do you mean?" I asked, trying not to cough as she exhaled smoke into my face.

"Once people know that's something you'll do, they'll never leave you alone," she said. For a second, I thought she might cry, but she didn't, just took another drag from her cigarette. Her fingers were stained yellow, like Mother's. Nancy was pretty now, but I could tell she'd lose her luster quickly. She was already getting used up.

"Okay," I said, then I left the bathroom.

For obvious reasons, I wasn't going to tell Darla the truth, but I had to give her something when the word came up again in our reading. She wasn't quite old enough to understand—and with her damaged brain, I didn't know if there'd ever be a time she'd be ready to hear it. I also knew, however, that Darla's body would grow and mature whether her mind was ready for it or not. At some point, I'd have to tell her about the birds and the bees, because Mother sure as hell wasn't going to do it. Mother had become more of a mosquito in our lives, flitting around, stopping every now and then to feed on us in some way, then flit back into her own dimension of time and space. That's what it felt like, at least. Like she wasn't fully there, she didn't really matter, and she only kept us around because there was no other option.]

Ellie kept on reading, and I kept on listening. I loved hearing about the things Anonymous got to do, and wondering if I'd ever do them, too—if I'd ever get out of my little room, my little life. Her life felt so distant from my own, but sometimes, it also felt way too close, like an itchy sweater I couldn't wriggle out of. The drugs—there were so many drugs. Anonymous seemed to love the drugs, but also to hate them. It confused me, and when I asked Ellie about it, about why Anonymous just couldn't seem to make up her mind, Ellie shook her head and told me she didn't really understand it, either, but that maybe Anonymous was using the drugs to escape. I asked her what Anonymous would want to escape from, and Ellie told me some people have aching holes inside them that they keep trying to fill, and that maybe drugs were Anonymous's way of trying to fill herself up.

"But it doesn't work," I said, almost growing angry at my failure to understand. I desperately wanted to see what Ellie could see.

"No, it doesn't," Ellie said. "Maybe nothing does."

For a moment, I felt unbearably sad, but then it passed, another ripple within my serene pond that quickly settled.

[Scribe's note: I could understand Anonymous's attraction to drugs more than I wanted to admit, especially to Darla. I started to wonder if the pills—like Darla's Thorazine—could be an escape, rather than a prison. After all, my classmates at school frequently talked about their mothers popping Valium like they were candy, how they were much calmer afterwards. Mother could certainly use something like that, I thought, and it would be much easier to get than heroin or marijuana. These thoughts did not leave my mind, and I continued ruminating on them until the urge to act on them was so strong I could not resist.]

After all that Anonymous went through, I felt a new ripple in my pond when Ellie read the ending. I was happy, or something like it. Anonymous made things right with her family, she stopped taking the drugs, she went to school and worked hard, and she lived a good life. Her story gave me hope, made me start to want things I hadn't knew I wanted—a life outside of this house, people to talk to that weren't only

Ma and Ellie. Something to do with my days beyond pacing my room and trying to read and staring at the walls for hours upon hours. [Scribe's note: I couldn't tell Darla the truth. I just couldn't. I didn't read the real ending to Darla—about how Anonymous was found dead of an overdose shortly after we're led to believe all will be right in her world. Instead, I made up the last few passages, and when I saw some new light shining in Darla's eyes, I knew I'd done the right thing. Anonymous was a selfish, self-indulgent, weak, simpering girl, whose life read more like a pulp story than a real diary. Far too many unfortunate and cruel things happened to a single girl… but then, when I looked at my own unfortunate and cruel life, I couldn't help but laugh—the sort of laugh that could turn into a scream and threatened to never end.

Much later, when I, along with the rest of the world, discovered that the diary was, in fact, a fake, I laughed again. I laughed so hard one of my interns knocked on my office door to investigate my state of mind. I had no suitable explanation to offer him, so I dismissed him curtly with a wave of my hand, laughing all the while.]

Ma came into my room one morning, not long after we finished the Alice book. Her eyes looked so tired, but at least they weren't red anymore. She was smoking a cigarette, and the smell made me cough. "How are you doing?" she asked me.

"Okay," I said, and Ma was so surprised that she dropped her cigarette onto the carpet and had to stomp it out with the heel of her shoe.

"You're okay?" she said, and when she smiled, I saw her teeth were yellow. Had they always been that color? I couldn't remember. She picked up her crushed cigarette and walked closer to me. She had her work uniform on, and it smelled like grease and stale coffee.

"I don't know," I said, and Ma's face crumpled back in on itself.

She let out this big sigh, and then she ran all the way to my bed. She grabbed the Alice book off of my bedside table and held it up in my face. "What is this?"

"I don't know," I said, even though I knew perfectly well, I just didn't want to say. Why was she so angry?

"Did Ellie bring this to you?" she yelled.

"Yes," I said, at ease being able to answer a question I understood.

"Goddamnit!" she said, and I laughed. Ma cursed!

Ma stomped out of my room, still holding the Alice book. I wanted it back, but it was okay. I could read it again later when Ellie came home.

[Scribe's note: When I arrived home from school, Mother was sitting at the kitchen table. She called for me to come in and join her. I hadn't seen her in a few days, which was fine by me. I could never predict if she'd be weepy and morose or edgy and frustrated. Neither mood motivated me to seek out her company.

I put my book bag on the ground and joined her at the table. From her lap, she pulled out a book and slid it across the table to me. It was *Go Ask Alice*.

"What is this?" she asked me.

"It's a book," I said, suddenly feeling very tired.

"Do you know what this is about?" she demanded.

"It's about a girl named Alice," I said. I know I was being cheeky, but I hardly deserved the slap she delivered to my face.

"Don't you sass me!" she shouted, spittle flying onto the table's surface. "This is not appropriate!"

My cheek stung, but I didn't want to show any weakness in front of her. She didn't deserve my vulnerability. "And why not?" I asked, girding myself for another slap.

She didn't hit me again, but her eyes narrowed to slits. "This book is full of hippie drugs and sex and all sorts of things you don't need to know about. And you know what's worst of all? Do you know where I found this book?"

My heart sank, but I didn't give her an inch. "At the library?"

She sneered in disgust. "In your sister's room," she said. "Is this the kind of filth you've been reading to her?"

There was no sense denying it, so I tried to present the situation in a more positive light. "It's not just me reading it. Darla can read it, too.

We've been practicing."

I could see the confusion, then the shock, then the disbelief pass across Mother's face. "I don't believe you," she said.

"It's true!" I shouted. "You think she can't do anything, but you're wrong! She's getting better, and you wouldn't know, because I'm the only one helping her!"

I had struck a nerve, and I knew it. Mother stood up, her chair screeching across the linoleum. She came around to my side of the table and grabbed my arm, hauling me to Darla's room with surprising strength.

Darla glanced up at us when we came in, looking totally uninterested. Mother dragged me to Darla's bedside and pushed me closer to her. Then, she opened *Go Ask Alice* to a random page in the middle and shoved the book into Darla's hands.

"Read it," she said, pointing at the page.

Darla looked from Mother to me, then back to Mother. Her mouth was open, and I knew if I didn't reach forward soon, she'd drool on the book again. I moved to close her mouth, but Mother blocked me. "Don't you help her," she said. "If you say she can do it, let's hear it."

Amazingly, Darla closed her own mouth and swallowed. She looked down at the page, and I could see her eyes flitting over the paragraphs. I looked away, crossing my fingers that Darla would read the damn words. More than anything in that moment, I wanted to feel triumphant. I wanted to have something to show for all the hours I'd spent with Darla, painstakingly sounding out letters she'd forgotten she ever understood.

"Read it!" Mother repeated, nearly screaming the words.

Darla, never losing her placid expression, stared at the page. She looked back up, at Mother, then at me.

She said, "I don't know."

Mother yanked the book out of her hands, nearly ripping its cover in the process. She whipped around to face me, her cheeks red and glowing. "You filthy little liar!" she yelled, and I took a step back. This was not the mother

I'd known for thirteen years. This was someone else, someone who had invaded my mother's body and turned her into a person I didn't recognize.

It was then I saw how much the surgery had changed more than just Darla.]

I didn't want to read the book in front of Ma. It felt like my secret with Ellie, and I didn't understand why Ma was so angry. It seemed safer to stay quiet. If Ma didn't like me getting out of bed and exercising, I didn't think she'd like the idea of me reading, either.

Ma was so angry at Ellie, I thought she was going to push her to the ground. She didn't, but she did stomp out for the second time that day with the Alice book in her hands. Ellie stayed behind, staring at me, until Ma called for her.

[Scribe's note: Mother threw *Go Ask Alice* into the trashcan, then covered it with leftover coffee from the pot. She knew it was a library book, but she didn't care. After this display, she told me I was forbidden from reading to Darla anymore.

What kind of punishment was that? It would hurt Darla far more than it would hurt me. Without me to read to her, Darla wouldn't make any more progress. Beyond that, she'd be alone almost constantly without me to come keep her company. Did Mother, like Father surely had, hope that Darla would shrivel up and die without attention?

I want to think Mother was just appalled by the book's subject matter and overcome with emotion, combined with her unresolved grief over what Father had done to himself.

But, if I'm being honest, I think it was more than that. I think Mother wanted to keep me from Darla because my caretaking made Mother look uncaring and cold in comparison. If she wasn't able to help Darla recover, then she didn't want me to have any sense of accomplishment, either. It was selfish, it was perverse, and it was sadistic. I didn't have the words to describe the situation then, so all I did was turn around, leave the kitchen, and lock myself in my room until Mother left for work.]

I thought Ellie would stop coming to my room for awhile after Ma got so angry, but she was back the next day with a new book. This one wasn't as interesting as the Alice one, but my eyes were getting stronger, and I could read whole pages. I thought Ellie might try to bring Ma in again and show her what I could do now, but she never did. Ellie even told me to keep our reading a secret, and she took her books with her when she left instead of letting me keep them in my room. That was fine with me, since I spent most of my day walking back and forth. I could even go to the bathroom by myself now, even though I sometimes still made little messes.

I even started to think I might go back to school one day, just to be able to get out of the house. Most of the time, I was okay living in my small world, but as I got better at moving around, I wanted desperately to go outside, to get some fresh air.

Ellie was at school and Ma was still asleep when I decided I couldn't wait any longer. I put on a dress I hadn't worn in a long time and tried to put my shoes on, but I couldn't get the buckles to clasp. I did the best I could, then I walked out into the living room and opened the front door as quietly as I was able. It was a bright sunny day, warmish, and I could hear a lawnmower a few streets over. The grass was greener than I ever thought possible, and the sky was so blue it hurt my eyes. The trees were covered in red and gold leaves. I stepped onto our front porch and closed the door behind me.

I was halfway to the sidewalk when I heard Ma. "You get back here this instant!" She was whispering, but it was also like a yell.

When I didn't move, she ran over to me and grabbed my shoulder. "You get back inside. Now!"

She pulled me into the house, then slammed the door behind us and locked it. When we got back to my room, she took a sheet and tied my wrists to the bed. She only untied me later because we were going to have company, she said.

The next day, a man came to our house and changed my doorknob. My old one was shiny and clear, like a crystal. The new one was a too-bright brassy color, and there was a hole in the middle, on the outside. When he was done, he handed Ma a key and told her that should do it. He didn't even look at me. Ma paid him and he left.

Ma closed the door, then I heard a clicking sound.

[Scribe's note: In Mother's words, Darla had made an 'escape attempt' and could have 'seriously hurt herself.' We were all so lucky that Mother 'had been there' and that she had 'found Darla in time.' She didn't say it, but I knew Mother was terrified a neighbor had seen the daughter she'd supposedly sent away months ago. After Mrs. Knowles had spread the word about Father's suicide (thank goodness Darla was unconscious among the bushes and therefore went largely unnoticed), Mother was far more afraid of becoming the topic of neighborhood gossip yet again than of anything harmful happening to Darla. If she'd had more foresight, she probably would have let Darla leave. If Mother was lucky, Darla would walk off into the sunset and never darken her doorstep again.

I'd seen Mother's homemade restraints the day before when I came home from school, and I was shocked. It seemed barbaric, but then again, the entire process was barbaric. I didn't protest too much when Mother told me shortly thereafter that Darla's room was to be locked at all times, and that when she wasn't home, it was my responsibility to listen for Darla and escort her to the bathroom as needed. Except for toileting, Darla was not to leave her room. At least she wouldn't be restrained anymore.

I was Darla's cook, her laundress, her groomer, her teacher, and now, Mother expected me to be her jailer, too.

As with the reading lessons, though, I didn't listen. When Mother was gone, I left Darla's door wide open.]

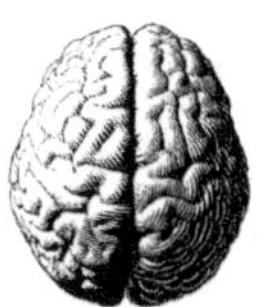

1 9 7 2

Ellie came home from school one day and sat on the end of my bed. I'd just finished walking around the house, and I was sweaty and tired. Instead of reading to me, Ellie started talking, and I was so caught up in what she said that I forgot to close my mouth. Ellie didn't miss a beat— she just closed my mouth for me and used my nightgown to wipe the drool from my chin. She was telling me all about her life at school, but instead of talking about all the good parts, like the nice teachers and the fun playground and what she was learning, she told me about the bad parts. About the way mean girls sneered at her and made fun of her clothes, or about how the teachers yelled at her for falling asleep in class, or about how the boys pulled her ponytail and told her Pa killed himself because he was so disappointed to have a daughter like her. It was horrible. For once, I was glad to be safe at home, where nobody could say such nasty things to me. When Ellie stopped, she started to cry. I put my hand on her shoulder and tried to tell her that everything would be alright, but the words didn't come out quite the way I wanted. Ellie just cried harder, which made me nervous, because I hadn't seen Ellie cry in ages, not even when Pa died.

[Scribe's note: There was no single incident that broke my emotional dam. Maybe it was all of the feelings *Go Ask Alice* had kindled in me, combined with the wretched treatment I got from the vile miscreants at school. I've come to realize that children can be impossibly cruel—after all, who would berate a little girl who'd just lost her father? Who would make such a girl feel smaller than she already did? Even though I still longed for the same kind of love Anonymous was always going on about, I knew I would never want children of my own. They were just as apt to rip your heart out and eat it as they were to give you purpose and meaning. The only purpose and meaning Darla and I had given our parents was a reason to work and a reason to die. I didn't like those outcomes.

I was tired of holding everything inside. I wanted to get it out, even if Darla didn't comprehend what I was telling her. That would be better, actually.

It wasn't until much, much later that I realized just how much Darla did understand. But by then, it was too late.]

Ellie reminded me a lot of Anonymous, how the kids at school were so mean to her, in so many different ways. I tried to remember a time kids had been mean to me, but I couldn't. I wanted to believe there were good people out there, people who would be kind to me and Ellie. I was starting to understand that I was different, but not in the same way I'd been before. I still felt hollow, but it was starting to become a hollow ache, like hunger pains. I wasn't sure what I hungered for, but I knew it wasn't the life I was currently living. I wanted to tell Ellie all of this, but the words crowded on my tongue and pushed each other out in ways that didn't make sense. Ellie was never mean to me about it, though. She smiled at me and never locked my door like Ma did. Ellie made me feel like a real person, not a dirty secret.

I started thinking about Anonymous's diary, and how it was her only friend for awhile, the one thing she could talk to openly and honestly. One day, when Ellie was sitting on the edge of my bed, telling me about Pauline Akroyd's new puppy, I managed to ask her something.

"Can I write?" I asked, and Ellie's eyes opened wide.

"Well," she said, "I think so?"

I wasn't asking it the right way. I'd been able to write before the surgery. I tried again. "Can you help me?"

Ellie looked startled again, then she smiled. "Sure," she said, and she hopped up from the bed and ran out of the room. A few minutes later she came back, carrying a pink notebook and a sharpened pencil. She handed them to me, then sat back down on my bed. I fluffed my pillows and scooched into a sitting position, then opened up the notebook.

"I'm so sorry I didn't think of this before," Ellie said. "Of course I should have tried to get you writing right away."

I wanted to tell her it wasn't her fault, nothing was, but the words wouldn't come, so I stayed quiet, wrapping my fingers around the warm wood of the pencil. It had been so long since I'd held one.

"Well?" Ellie said. "What do you want to write about?"

"I don't know," I said, but that wasn't true. I knew what I wanted to write, but I didn't know how to tell Ellie about it. My speech was getting better, but it still wasn't good enough.

Ellie shrugged. "Just start going, then. It doesn't have to be anything important."

I brought the tip of the pencil to the paper and pressed down. The pointy tip broke instantly, and Ellie flinched at the snapping sound.

"Let me get you a pen instead," she said, and flitted out of the room again. She came back with a black pen and fitted it into my hand, sliding the pencil out. "Try this."

I pressed the pen into the paper, and a black dot appeared.

"Try to write your name," Ellie suggested.

"Okay," I said, pressing down into the paper again.

My brain was telling my hand to write, to move, to do something—but nothing was happening. I was concentrating so hard I started sweating. My fingers would not budge, not even to scrawl a single line. At last, I tried to use my left hand to drag my right one around the page, but I only ended up with a crooked spiral that meant nothing.

Before I knew what was happening, the pen was stabbing through the notebook, going through pages and pages of paper.

"It's okay," Ellie said, pulling the pen from my hand. "We'll try again another time."

"Okay," I said, letting the anger spill away.

[Scribe's note: Darla's violent outburst didn't surprise me, but it did make me wary. Please understand, I wanted desperately for Darla to be able to write again. Writing would have opened up her world considerably— she would have been able to communicate better, not just with me, but with others. She would be able to carry on a correspondence, to learn, to make some sort of mark in the world—to make others, outside of Mother and me, aware of her existence. More selfishly, I wanted her to be able to write so that she could one day live a productive life on her own. I was young, but I wasn't stupid. I knew very well what could happen when Mother died if Darla wasn't better, or if Mother decided she didn't want to care for Darla anymore, even though she was doing less than the bare minimum at that time. She was my sister, of course, but I yearned for a life free of the shackles that bound me to her, to Mother, to that lonely, dismal house. Without literacy, without proper exercise and improvement, I knew Darla would be shackled to me for life.

Call me selfish if you want, but don't tell me you wouldn't feel the same.]

We tried again the next day, and the next, and the next after that. I didn't get so angry the more we practiced. We tried so many times I lost count. One afternoon, I managed to make something that looked like a 'D,' and Ellie got so excited she squealed like a piglet. I didn't tell her that the D was a happy accident, not something I was able to do on purpose. Ellie realized that on her own when, the next day, I couldn't do it again. I threw the pen at the wall, leaving a black mark.

[Scribe's note: I pushed Darla hard, even begging for mother to get her a tutor, someone with more skills than I had, someone trained in successful teaching methods. Mother looked at me, eyes narrowed, cigarette clamped between her yellow teeth, and laughed. "Yeah, right," she said. "I'm not going to waste money on a moron."

That's what Darla had become to her. Not her daughter, not her baby, not even her ward—just a moron. Mother was no better than Father. I was so angry I had to remove myself from her presence immediately, lest I do something I'd regret.

I had to remind myself countless times that Mother's miserable life was penance for the evil she'd brought on her daughter. She was living in her own personal hell—but that still didn't give her the right to drag us into it with her.]

I still had these thoughts that I wanted to get out, and I felt this dull anger, like a drum beating far away, every time I failed at writing. I tried to tell Ellie what I was thinking, but the words never wanted to come out right, or even if I managed to say something, I'd forget what I was talking about halfway through. Ellie was kind to me, though. She didn't laugh or yell like Ma probably would have. Ellie thought I didn't know much about how Ma felt about me, but I did. I'm glad it didn't hurt like it should have, like it would have if I hadn't had that surgery. [Scribe's note: I hurt enough for the both of us, I'm sure.]

I kept trying to do a little bit more every day—a little bit more walking around the house, a little bit more reading, a little bit more writing, although that never really worked. Every day was the same as the one before it, and the one after it. I wondered maybe if I would go crazy, but then I remembered I'd already been cured of that, so how could it happen again? [Scribe's note: I never believed Darla was crazy in the first place, so I was increasingly concerned about her rather sedentary life. I knew, were I in her position, I would have let insanity take me easily, just to escape any awareness of that hellhole.]

Time passed.

Ellie started to change.

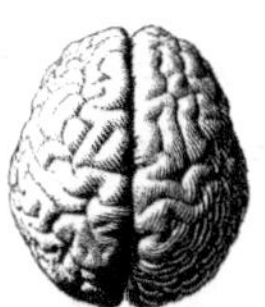

1 9 7 3

I felt like Ellie was leaving me behind. She still came to my room almost every day, but she didn't feel there in the same way she had before.

[Scribe's note: I tried to hide my descent and my inappropriate behavior from Darla as much as possible, but I was no actress.

Those years were the hardest of my early life. Sure, harder years were to come, but puberty beat me like an unwanted stepchild, leaving me gasping for relief that never came.

I hated the psychiatrist for the path he'd put Darla on, the one that led straight to her lobotomy. Even through my hate, though, I wondered. I wondered about those little orange-brown pills, the same color as the shag carpet in our living room. On the nights when I couldn't sleep, which were often, or the days I came home crying from school, which were also very often, the half-empty bottle of Thorazine in the medicine cabinet called to me. I wasn't stupid; I'd absorbed enough of *Go Ask Alice* to understand that drugs were tiny ministers of destruction, but I was also angry. I was angry that a girl like Anonymous could relinquish all of her responsibilities, escape her home, her family, her school, her entire goddamn life, and have an experience of pure freedom, even if it killed her in the end. Slowly, as my grades dropped and my classmates' cruel barbs dug deeper, my anger started to outweigh my caution. Why say no to drugs when oblivion could be so close at hand?

Why do we cling to ourselves at all? Even at that young age, I could see that there were people who hung looser in their skins than others—Father, for one. Darla, on the other hand, used to cling to her corporeality far too tightly, manifesting that desperation into the extremely physical fear of vomiting. The lobotomy had subsequently made her far too loose, to the point where she was rattling around in her own skin like a marble in a tin can. I often wondered what would fill up that empty space. After all, nature hates a vacuum.

My brain had remained intact, but I felt my own vacuum widening within me, every time a girl at school jabbed my shoulder with her pointy nail and told me I was a loser, every time Mother sneered at me when our paths happened to cross in the hallway, every time Darla failed to draw a straight line.

The Thorazine kept calling to me, telling me it could help me fill that void, on my own terms, before something else could take hold of me.

One day, I listened.]

I was in my room, staring at a library book I'd read over and over already, when Ellie came into my room. She was walking funny, like she couldn't quite keep up with her own feet. When she got to my bed, she fell onto the covers like she was exhausted, and when she pushed herself up, there was spit on my blanket. I'd never seen her like that before, and I was a bit scared. I knew she was changing, but this shift was too fast. I'd seen her only that morning, and she'd seemed like her usual self. Now, when I looked at her, I saw a little too much of me.

[Scribe's note: I took the Thorazine the moment I got back from a particularly terrible school day. Gina Fletcher had told everyone Father had killed himself because he was so ashamed of having a cow for a daughter, and everywhere I went, an ensemble of 'moos' trailed behind me like a bovine Greek chorus. I was feeling weak, defeated, useless. So I opened the medicine cabinet, shook one of the rust-colored pills into my palm, and swallowed it dry. At the time, I was looking for escape. For what I think was an entire day, I got it, but that escape didn't last long.

I quickly learned that the pill was nothing more than a prison.]

"Are you okay?" I managed to ask Ellie. She looked at me like she'd never seen me before, and then she started talking about my hair. She told me it wasn't actually hair, but a nest of brown recluse spiders, and if I didn't spray my head with hairspray and light it on fire, then I was going to die. A dark feeling started growing in my stomach, and I thought I might be sick.

"Ellie?" I said, hoping she'd say she was just kidding, anything normal. She didn't respond, and I could see her face turning red. Sweat started sliding down her face, more than seemed possible. The room wasn't hot. I was even a little bit cold.

She started breathing real funny, like she'd just run around the block and couldn't catch her breath.

"Ellie?" I tried again, and even though she was looking at me, I could tell she wasn't seeing me. Her body started to tighten, like all of her muscles were squeezing at once, and she fell off my bed onto the floor.

I knew this wasn't right, I knew it, but what was I supposed to do? I didn't know how to work the telephone, Ma wasn't home, and I wasn't supposed to leave the house.

On the floor, Ellie started to shake, and she kept asking where Papa was, and why wasn't he here helping her.

The terror I felt in that moment was the strongest feeling I'd had since the surgery. Somehow, I managed to run to the front door, unlock it, and go outside. I must have been screaming, because our neighbor, Mrs. Knowles, came out of her house running, wiping her hands on a dish towel. "Heavens, what's the matter?" she asked me, and all I could do was grab her hand and pull her into my room. She went with me, but she kept asking what was happening, and I couldn't answer her. I could only show her.

When we got into my room, Ellie was still shaking on the floor, and her face was redder than Ma's lipstick.

"Dear Jesus in Heaven!" Mrs. Knowles said, and then she told me to grab a towel full of ice and, for heaven's sake, call an ambulance.

I just sat on the bed and stared until Mrs. Knowles stopped fretting and took a good look at me. It looked like she wanted to say something, but just then, Ellie started screaming, and Mrs. Knowles ran into the kitchen on her own.

Ma still wasn't home when the ambulance came, and Mrs. Knowles didn't want to leave me by myself, so Ellie had to ride to the hospital alone.

I didn't see her or Ma for a few days after that. I probably would have started eating my sheets if Mrs. Knowles hadn't brought some food over for me.

"What's your name, dear?" she asked me, and it had been so long since I'd heard that question, that I almost didn't know how to answer.

"D," I started, then swallowed and tried again. "Darla."

Mrs. Knowles gasped like she'd seen a ghost. "Darla Gregory, my dear Lord!"

I didn't understand what she was all excited about. People were not excited to see me. Had I said something wrong?

"We all thought... we all thought you passed away," she said softly.

I was so confused, I said the first thing that came to my mind. "I'm not dead," I said. "I'm right here."

Mrs. Knowles laughed, but it wasn't a happy laugh. "I can see that, dear."

When I didn't say anything else, she asked me, "Have you been here, right here in this house, all this time?"

"Yes," I said. Where else would I have been?

"Even when your father died?" she asked.

I nodded.

Mrs. Knowles brought a hand to her chest like people do when they're going to cry, or they feel sorry for you. Mrs. Knowles was both. Tears started leaking out of her eyes, and she wiped them away with a handkerchief as fast as she could. "I'm so sorry," she whispered. "I should have known." I was starting to get upset because nothing she was doing or saying made any sense.

"Why?" I asked, but this only made Mrs. Knowles cry harder.

When she stopped and started sniffling, she told me, "I'm going to help you. I'm going to help you, honey."

Help me with what? Ma certainly wouldn't like that, I was sure.

Mrs. Knowles left my room and came back with a plate piled high with meatloaf, canned green beans, and a roll with butter. I had gotten used to eating on my own, but I still wasn't great at it, and Mrs. Knowles stared at me as I ate my dinner. She made me nervous, and I wanted to yell at her. She must not have liked what she saw, because she said, "Dear child, what has that woman done to you?"

I wanted her to stop acting so strangely, so I told her I was fine.

I didn't think much more about it until Ma stormed into my room like a thundercloud the day after Ellie finally came back from the hospital.

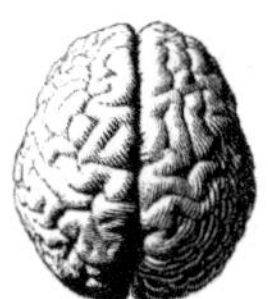

1 9 7 3

[Scribe's note: I don't remember the ambulance ride, but Mother sure as hell made sure I didn't forget it. The first thing she said to me when I regained consciousness at the hospital was how irresponsible I'd been for requiring an ambulance. "How do you think I'm going to pay for that?" she said, pounding her fist on the iron frame of my hospital bed. "Ambulances are expensive, Ellen!"

I was glad Mother's anger was the first thing I experienced while lucid. It made the transition back into my body easier, in a way—I was distracted, even if only briefly, from the pain. My muscles felt cramped and achy, as though I'd run a marathon. I had a blistering headache, made all the worse by Mother's loudness and the harsh fluorescent lights overhead. There were ice packs around my head, which crunched and sloshed as I struggled to sit up. The IV in my arm itched.

A nurse came into the room, likely alerted by Mother's tantrum.

"How are we doing today, sweetie?" she asked.

I wanted to cry. Not because I was particularly sad, and the pain wasn't anything I couldn't handle. It was the way she so casually called me 'sweetie,' as though I was a person worthy of compassion, a person she wanted to play a role in healing rather than hurting.

"Fine," I managed to say. "My head hurts, though."

She frowned. "I'm so sorry. You'll probably feel a bit out of sorts for a few days."

"What happened?" I asked.

The nurse tilted her head, then glanced at my mother. "Best wait for the doctor, sweetie. I'll go get him for you."

With the nurse gone, Mother returned to berating me—for my stupidity, for my sickness, for my weakness. Part of me wanted to scream at her, but the other part of me knew Mother was projecting onto me, taking out her anger on me while I was at my weakest.

Rage bloomed in my gut alongside the pain, but I was careful not to let it show. Not yet, anyway.

"Miss Gregory?" A youngish male doctor entered the room, the kind nurse trailing behind him. "I'm Doctor Radford. Nurse Kent tells me you're feeling a bit woozy?"

I swallowed, my throat still feeling parched. "Yes, sir," I said. "What happened to me?"

The doctor and Nurse Kent exchanged a look I couldn't read, and he nodded his head slightly at her.

"Mrs. Gregory," Nurse Kent said brightly. "Would you mind stepping out into the hall with me for a moment? I have some forms I'll need you to sign."

Mother grumbled the whole way out of the room, but finally, she left, the door swinging closed behind her.

Doctor Radford leaned in closer to me. "Miss Gregory, are you currently taking any prescription medications?"

"No," I said automatically.

Doctor Radford sighed. "What about any… non-prescription medications?"

I didn't want to tell him about the Thorazine. It was too stupid, too pathetic, too reckless to admit, even to a doctor—but I didn't see another way out. At least Mother wasn't in the room to hear my confession.

"I… I took some Thorazine," I said in a tiny voice.

Doctor Radford's eyebrows shot up into his thick brown hair. "Thorazine?"

I nodded almost imperceptibly.

"There's no record of psychiatric illness in your medical chart," he said, more to himself than to me.

"I'm not crazy," I said quickly. "It... it was my sister's medication."

"Ah," he said, frowning. "I see. And why did you take your sister's medication?"

I would tell him what he needed to know that pertained to my physical health, but he was asking too much of me. There was only so much humiliation I could suffer, and I wouldn't let this doctor touch that vulnerable part of my soul. I couldn't.

"I thought it would help my headache," I said, and it must have convinced him, because he smiled.

"Never take a pill if you don't know for sure what it is," he said, patting my knee. "Try to be more careful next time."

He turned to leave, but I grabbed at his hand. "Why, Doctor? What happened?"

He faced me again. "Well," he said. "It's rather complicated."

"Just tell me, please," I begged.

"Alright. I believe you had a bad reaction to the Thorazine," he said.

"Bad how?" I asked.

"It's called Neuroleptic Malignant Syndrome, or NMS for short," he said. "I used to work in the psychiatric ward, so I recognized the signs fairly quickly—your high fever, your muscle spasms, your delirium."

Thoughts of winding up like Darla swirled through my head, and I fought back the panic rising in my gullet. "Will I... will I be okay?" I stammered.

The doctor smiled. "As long as you stay away from the Thorazine, or any more medications that aren't yours. NMS is a side effect of pills like Thorazine. The pills aren't toys, or something to take to impress your friends."

I resented the doctor's patronizing comments—I was a teenager, not some stupid child who couldn't tell a Valium from an M&M (although, that was quite close to what I was expecting him to believe, I know that). Also, I didn't have any friends, so the joke was on him.

He continued, "With a bit of rest and hydration, you'll be right as rain in a few days. You're lucky your neighbor called the ambulance when she did. If NMS isn't treated quickly, it can be very dangerous indeed."

With that, he patted my knee once again and left the room.

"Fuck," I said aloud, relishing the curse on my lips. I had escaped death by the skin of my teeth, and for what? A few hours of bliss I couldn't even remember? It wasn't worth it.

I vowed then and there to never touch another drug like that—one I hadn't been prescribed and didn't need. I expect you to take a similar vow, because you'd be an ignorant, idiotic fool not to learn from my mistakes. And before you can say marijuana or cocaine are nothing like Thorazine, let me share something with you. During my residency, I was working in the Emergency Room when a patient erupted through the front doors, a bucket clutched in his hands, vomiting profusely and screaming in between retches. This wasn't a virus, or a bacterium, or a bulimic psychotic episode—this was Cannabinoid Hyperemesis Syndrome. This doped-up patient had consumed so much marijuana over so many years that his body was fighting against the drugs. I saw this referred to later in the news as 'scromiting,' a term I actually found quite amusing. What's anything but amusing, however, is the way drugs can rip you apart from the inside. They're no better than a chemical lobotomy.

Even now, in times of extreme stress—which, mercifully, are few and far between nowadays—I feel my memory become… shaky, and I'm brought back to that feeling of stiffness, of helplessness. Thank the God I do not believe in that I have suffered no long-lasting physical effects—I could never have been a surgeon otherwise. I can't be certain my occasionally blurred memory is due to the NMS, but any time I forget a patient's name or have to recheck a medical history, my chest aches with anxiety. Luckily, you know better than to cause me undue stress. Right?

When Mother came back in my room at the hospital, still griping, she sneered at me. "Guess that's the last time you eat walnuts, huh? Damn allergies."

I was confused, but I was smart enough to recognize when to keep my mouth shut. I just nodded and let her think whatever she wanted to think. I silently thanked Doctor Radford and Nurse Kent for distracting Mother from the truth, which surely would have earned me a harsh punishment, and who knows what that could have meant for Darla.

Just as I was sighing with relief over the secret I would get to keep, something stuck in my mind. Nurse Kent had said a neighbor had called the ambulance.

That meant somebody else knew about Darla.]

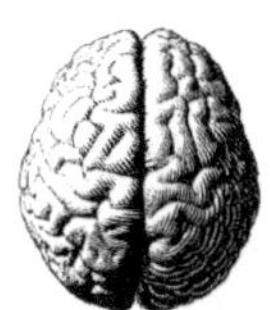

1973 - 1974

The first person I saw after Ellie came home wasn't Ellie, but Ma. I was sitting in my bed, trying to read a newspaper. The words were too small, and the paper felt too fuzzy in my hands, and nothing made sense.

"Darla Marie Gregory!" Ma stampeded into my room like a wild bull. Out of shock—not fear—I sat up ramrod straight, because Ma never used my full name.

"Ma?" I said, looking up into her face. She looked angrier than the time the neighbor kids ripped up her flowerbeds while playing baseball in the street. At least she didn't have to worry about that anymore—she had let those flowers die a long time ago, according to Ellie.

"How could you do this?"

I didn't understand what she was asking. How could I do what? How could I try to read a newspaper? How could I sit quietly in my room day after day? How could I exist? I wondered these questions myself, often.

When I didn't answer, just shrugged, she started yelling. "Belinda Knowles of all people just stopped me in the driveway and talked my ear off about you. About how she didn't even know you were here, about how I really should be taking better care of you, about how you should be in school. In school, Darla, can you imagine it? You?" She laughed, but it was a mean sound.

In fact, I could imagine it. If I squinted really hard and used all my concentration, I could picture myself at school, in the same class as Ellie, writing notes in a composition book and listening to the teacher talk about how the world worked. Sometimes I dreamed about this, and I would wake up with a wet pillow.

Ma wasn't finished. "You know what that awful woman said? The same one who flapped her tongue about your father? She dared to tell me how to raise my own child. She told me this was no kind of life for you. What the fuck does she know? I'm sure you couldn't even tell her about your motherfucking lobotomy, about how you're an imbecile with half a brain now. A woman like Belinda could never understand, with her perfect children and her perfect husband and her perfect home." Ma stopped, panting. I'd never heard her curse so much, and it was thrilling, in a way. If I'd been younger, before the surgery, I probably would have been scared. Instead, I felt numb. Sometimes being a serene pond had its advantages. This woman who looked like Ma—but didn't act like Ma— couldn't hurt me, however hard she tried.

Ma kept going, like a whistling teakettle that nobody would take off the burner. "Are you getting this, Darla? Are you getting this through that tiny little broken brain of yours? Belinda over there... that should have been me. I did everything right! I married the right man, he bought the right house, I birthed his children, and what happens? I get an idiot daughter, and my husband takes the easy way out and leaves me to clean up his mess, as usual."

Ma slumped against the wall. I didn't know what to say, so I kept silent. That, at least, was something I was very good at.

"Do you know what I have to do now, Darla?" Ma asked in a small voice.

She didn't expect an answer, but I spoke anyway. "What?"

She acted as though she hadn't heard me, but I was used to that. "I have to work even harder to make Belinda Knowles think you're living a normal life. She didn't come right out and say it, but she basically threatened me with the authorities if I didn't 'shape up,' as she put it."

Ma pulled a cigarette and lighter from her dress pockets. She stuck the cigarette between her wrinkled lips and lit it. She took a few puffs before sighing. "Meddling bitch."

She blew smoke into my room, then walked out. The fumes filled the air, making me cough. I wished Ellie had been there to see Ma's tantrum. I wonder what she would have made of it.

[Scribe's note: I didn't need to be there to hear it. Mother screamed loud enough for the whole neighborhood to hear. Maybe that's what she wanted— to let Mrs. Knowles know just how much she had fouled things up with her 'helping.' All I knew was that if Mrs. Knowles hadn't been there, I very well could have died. Some days, I'm grateful for her intervention. Other days, I wish she'd have stayed away.

While Darla might have been intrigued by Mother's outburst, I was disgusted. How could she speak to her own daughter like that? Especially when she knew nothing of Darla as she was now. She never bothered to find out. She treated Darla like the unwanted ghost of the daughter she felt she'd been promised, a girl as perfect as Belinda Knowles' sons. Every day, Mother grew more bitter, more sucked dry by her resentment.

With Belinda Knowles' meddling, I wondered how things would change for Darla, if they would at all. Would Mother finally cough up the cash to get Darla a tutor? Would she spend more time with Darla, maybe find a way to reconnect with her?

I didn't know what to expect—or what to hope for.]

Nothing much changed for me for awhile, but then, one day, Ma came into my room. Her mouth was a tight line, and she fiddled with the pack of cigarettes in her pocket. She was dressed in her waitress uniform.

"Darla," she said, her voice higher-pitched than usual. "You have a visitor."

A visitor? Besides Mrs. Knowles, I'd seen no other person besides

Ellie and Ma for years. My pond rippled with excitement, as though a frog had jumped right into the center, then frothed the water with his kicking legs.

I stood up from the bed, and Ma raised her eyebrows at me. There was a shadow behind her in the hallway. When she moved aside at last, I could see the shape of a woman.

"Hello, dear," Mrs. Knowles said, stepping in to my room. "How are you today?"

Behind her back, Ma rolled her eyes. "I have to go to work," she said, and a few seconds later, I heard the front door slam and the car engine growl.

Mrs. Knowles took a few steps closer to me. "Your mother told me about your medical history, dear," she said.

My mouth must have dropped open, because Mrs. Knowles smiled. "It's okay, I promise. I had an aunt, many years ago, who underwent the same procedure." She closed her eyes for a long moment. "I wish our families were closer. Maybe if I'd known what had been planned for you…"

She trailed off, staring at me. I stared back at her, but she didn't finish her sentence.

Mrs. Knowles clapped her hands together. "Alright," she said. "I've worked out a deal with your mother. I can understand now why you haven't received regular schooling. While I might not agree with your mother's actions, I can understand them. But that doesn't mean we have to perpetuate our mistakes."

I tilted my head, trying to understand what she was talking about.

"I'm going to teach you," she said, speaking more slowly.

A smile broke over my face before I could stop it.

"Would you like that?" she asked.

I nodded. I would like that very much.

[Scribe's note: I was still recovering in my bedroom when Mrs. Knowles came over to tutor Darla for the first time. For years after this, I was both grateful for and angry at this woman. My gratitude was simple—by taking over my didactic duties with Darla, Mrs. Knowles freed up my time. She was also able to be present with Darla far more often than I was, and I figured the social interaction could only be good for my sister.

My anger was more complex. For so long, my toxic little family had clung to ourselves, not letting outsiders near. The arrival of Mrs. Knowles—whom Mother positively loathed—was a breach, and it made me uncomfortable. What made me more uncomfortable than what she did do for us, however, was what she didn't do. She understood Darla's situation. She could see how we'd been living, but she didn't call the authorities like she'd threatened to do. It's complicated, I know, and you have to understand—back then, nobody wanted to spread their family secrets around, to lay their souls bare for all of the neighbors to see and judge. Suzy Coplin's mother routinely used heavy pancake makeup to conceal the bruises she got from her drunk husband's fists. Jade Andrews got pregnant in the ninth grade, but instead of being open about it, her parents sent her away for the summer. When she returned, she was thin again, but she looked like she'd lived a lifetime. Nancy Foster's father was a drug addict, but everybody pretended he was an upstanding citizen. The duality was painful and incongruous. Nobody wanted to call out anybody else's faults outside of the family unit for fear of having their own exposed—yet, at the same time, every vulture was hungry for gossip, for a way to measure their own lives and progress against those of their friends and neighbors. It was sickening.

So, it was no surprise that Mrs. Knowles hadn't called a doctor for Darla, or the police, or even a social worker, although Mother certainly believed she'd told just about everyone else in our neighborhood. Not that I wanted yet another person meddling in our lives (I was a product of my generation, after all), but I can't help thinking Darla's life would have been better outside of that house. Maybe I'm naive—in fact, I'm sure I am—but at the time, I saw Mrs. Knowles' inaction as a failure. Yes, Darla needed tutoring, but she needed medical attention even more. If medicine had made her this way, then medicine should be able to undo it.

As I said, I was naive. I know better now.]

Mrs. Knowles started coming over most mornings, while Ma was sleeping in her room. They never spoke to each other, as far as I could tell.

It started getting hot outside, and my days took on a new pattern. When I woke up, I walked into the kitchen and got a piece of bread from the breadbox, then put some jelly on it. Ellie would usually come into the kitchen, too, and sometimes whisper-shout at me for leaving the fridge door open again. I ate my bread and jelly at the table, and it was just fine. I wasn't allowed to use the toaster, Ellie said it was too dangerous, and she said I was only allowed to have one piece of bread. She poured me a glass of milk when we had it, water when we didn't. She sat at the table with me, drinking coffee that smelled like the cleaning wipes they used on me in the hospital. [Scribe's note: What can I say? I like my coffee black. Plus, if there was any milk in the fridge, Darla needed it more than I did. That summer, I focused mostly on rereading the texts I'd been neglecting for the previous year, a sort of self-directed course correction that I so desperately needed.]

Most mornings, Ellie would open up her schoolbooks and study at the table with me. She'd get annoyed if I asked questions, so I tried really hard to stay quiet. Her textbooks were full of diagrams I couldn't understand and words I didn't know. I tried to sound them out in my head, but nothing worked. One time, I accidentally tried to sound out a word with my mouth, and I ended up spraying bread-and-jelly crumbs all over Ellie's books. She didn't yell at me, like I expected her to, but she did stare at me, looking like she was about to cry. That was worse.

After Ellie left for the library, I would do my best to comb my hair and get dressed so I could be presentable for Mrs. Knowles. I had trouble with the buttons on my blouses, and my hair was always flat on one side, but Mrs. Knowles didn't seem to care. She'd come into the house without knocking and bring me from my room into the kitchen, where we'd sit at the table and she'd help me read, or try to do my numbers, or color a picture inside the lines with big fat crayons. I liked Mrs. Knowles, and I was grateful for her help, but I missed Ellie—especially when we sat at the kitchen table, Mrs. Knowles squatting in Ellie's chair.

I was no good at numbers. Mrs. Knowles tried every day, and she never lost patience with me, even when I told her the numbers made no sense. Eventually, we stopped trying, and she helped me get better at the things I could do, like read and color.

Writing was another story. I managed to tell Mrs. Knowles that I wanted to write a diary, and she smiled at me. "I'm sure you've got quite the story to tell!" I didn't really know what she meant by that, but I nodded anyway. The next day, she brought me a clean composition book and a box of sharpened pencils.

"Let's get started," she said.

Weeks, maybe months, went by. It got hotter, and then the weather got better again. Ellie started back to school. Every day except weekends, Mrs. Knowles sat with me in the kitchen, moving my hand, pointing at letters, helping me trace—doing everything she could think of to help me do what I wanted to do.

Even after those long months of work, I couldn't really write anything readable. The few letters I could force my hand to make looked like a toddler's, and even though I could read okay, spelling on my own was another matter.

Mrs. Knowles never gave up on me, though, even when I gave up on myself.

[Scribe's note: I was devastated when Mrs. Knowles couldn't help Darla with writing. I thought, for sure, with the focused attention and patience Mrs. Knowles could provide, Darla would surely make leaps and bounds, more progress than I could ever hope for. Darla did get better at reading and her fine motor skills improved, but writing was still beyond her. If Mrs. Knowles couldn't help her, then, yet again, I resigned myself to the patent fact that Darla was simply beyond help.]

After lessons, Mrs. Knowles would fix me lunch. Sometimes it was leftovers from her dinner, usually tasty things like meatloaf or brisket and mashed potatoes. Once in a while she brought a slice of pie, but I could tell it troubled her to see me have a hard time eating the gooey stuff on my own. She'd wipe my mouth and tuck my napkin into my collar, and she'd tell me stories while I ate. Most of the stories were fairy tales, and as I chewed my chicken casserole or spooned peas into my mouth, I'd dream I was a part of a fairy tale, and that the life I was living now was just the moment before my prince took me away and we lived happily ever after.

Mrs. Knowles left after lunchtime, after cleaning the kitchen so there'd be no extra work for Ma. Ma would usually come out of her bedroom around that time, her hair tangled and her eyes dark. She wouldn't usually talk to me, but if she did, it sounded more like she was talking to herself. She'd say things like "Uppity bitch," or "She doesn't think I can take care of my own children." If Ma was in a talkative mood, I'd stay to listen, even though she didn't seem to care or even know if I was there or not. If she was quiet, I'd go back to my room and take a nap.

Ellie started getting home from school later and later. Usually, there was no time to visit. She'd just come into the kitchen and start making dinner. Her cooking wasn't nearly as tasty as Mrs. Knowles's, and the one time I told her that, she threw a plate of watery macaroni on the floor. It broke into a million tiny sharp pieces, and Ellie spent the rest of the evening picking them up. We went to bed without food that night.

[Scribe's note: With Mrs. Knowles teaching Darla, however slow or nonexistent their progress was, I rededicated myself to my schoolwork. After a summer of studying and languishing in the empty library, I was ready to hit the ground running in the new school year. Mother's trajectory in life had plateaued at a very low point, and I knew I would never be able to rely on her to function as a safety net or a security blanket in any sense. After my scare with the Thorazine, I wanted nothing more than to understand what had happened to me. It fascinated and repelled me, but my fascination won out. If I was going to make something of myself, and have a bigger life than Mother's, with even the smallest scrap of happiness given the shitty hand I'd been dealt, I knew I'd have to rely on my own intelligence and grit, both of which I had in spades.

I put my head down, tried to ignore the evil jokes my classmates continued to make at my expense, and studied as hard as I could. I stayed after school to work in the library, where it was quiet and nobody needed me. I could escape there in a way I never could at home.

When I did open our front door and enter our dreary house, Darla was usually waiting for me at the kitchen table like a loyal puppy dog. I felt more like a working mother than her sister; I went right into preparing dinner. Darla's not wrong, I was no cook—I'm still not, as I'm sure you know. Food didn't need to taste good, it just needed to keep us alive for another day. The day I broke the plate, I'd endured one of the worst days of bullying yet—Trudy Winthrop had stuck a 'Spit on Me' sign to my back, and I didn't realize until the day was over and I was scratching my shoulder blade in the library and felt something crinkling. As a result, I had spent the entire school day dodging loogies, mostly unsuccessfully. I was at my wit's end by the time I came home, and when Darla told me I was a shoddy cook, I'd had more than I could take, so I exploded. Who can really blame me? I didn't hurt anybody, after all.]

When Mrs. Knowles wasn't with me, I was trying to study on my own, like I watched Ellie do every day. After dinner, Ellie would take her books into her room, and sometimes, if I was quiet, she would let me sit on the floor next to her bed and try to read my own books. What Mrs. Knowles brought me from her home wasn't nearly as exciting as *Go Ask Alice*, but I made do with things like *Are You There,*

God? It's Me, Margaret and *Bridge to Terabithia.* Ellie snorted when she saw the Margaret book, and when I asked her why, she just shrugged her shoulders and went back to staring at her textbook. [Scribe's note: The book was absolutely absurd—it was all right there in the title. Hadn't Darla lived long enough to see that God was not there, had never been there? Darla asked me if I wanted to read it, and it took all my strength to keep from slapping it to the floor.

A few weeks later, when Darla started asking me nonstop about her 'changing body,' I wondered if I should have read the book, after all, just to get an idea of what Darla had been absorbing. Really, what did Mrs. Knowles expect, giving Darla a story like that? She didn't need those questions in her head, not yet.

Even as I say that, I know I was wrong, but I can't change the past, I can only recount it, as painful as that is.]

I learned a lot from the Margaret book, and it made more sense to me even than the Alice book. I could understand Margaret, and I wondered mostly about the 'changing body.' I looked at Ellie whenever I could, and she had certainly changed, anybody with eyes could see that, even someone like me. But even though I could see it, I couldn't understand it. Why did it happen? What did it mean? Would it happen to me? That last question is what bothered me the most, but when I asked Mrs. Knowles about it, she told me it was really a conversation I should have with my mother. When I asked again the next day, and the day after that, Mrs. Knowles finally told me that, as a girl, I would go through changes in my body that would make me a woman. She wouldn't be more specific than that, so I had to ask Ellie.

"What's going to happen to my body?" I asked one afternoon while we were sitting in Ellie's room.

"What do you mean?" she asked.

"Am I going to look like you?"

Ellie paused and looked at me. "Maybe," she said after a moment.

"I don't understand," I said, my mouth slow. I still struggled with long words, having to sound them out as slowly as possible to keep them from turning to mush on my tongue.

"You'll look like me in that you'll grow breasts, and you'll probably get taller, and your armpits will grow hair, and so will your legs and other places, too. And your hips will get wider."

I was stunned. I'd been different for so long, it was hard to wrap my mind around the idea that my body would go through something normal, just like everybody else.

"Does it hurt?" I asked.

Ellie's eyes shifted around before she answered. "No."

[Scribe's note: What was I supposed to tell her? That menstrual cramps are the gift of a sadistic god? That she'd bleed like a stuck pig every month, and she'd need to either insert a glorified cotton ball inside of herself or wrap her undercarriage in a pad no better than a child's diaper, and if she failed to perform properly, she'd be subject to ridicule simply for undergoing a natural bodily experience? That her legs would grow furrier than a field mouse? That she'd start to stink, even without sweating, and would need to apply deodorant and perfume and makeup and fix her hair and wear pantyhose and smile all the time just to be accepted as a woman in this world? No, I think I made the right decision, even though I had to deal with the bloody aftermath.]

Mrs. Knowles was working through a history lesson with me in the kitchen when I knocked over a cup of water on accident. She jumped up to clean the spill, then refilled my cup and brought it back to me. There was something about the way the water dripped onto the linoleum—I couldn't take my eyes off of it.

So I did it again. This time, I knocked the cup over on purpose, just so I could see the way the water fell to the floor.

"Now, Darla, that's not very kind of you," she said, pinching her eyebrows and shaking her head.

I had the odd sensation that I should feel upset with myself, but I simply wasn't. I could understand that what I had done wasn't necessarily good, but I couldn't wrap my mind around why it wasn't good.

When Mrs. Knowles refilled my cup for the second time and sat down again to talk about the French Revolution, I pushed the cup with one finger so slowly that Mrs. Knowles didn't notice what I was doing until water splashed onto her leg.

"Darla!" she yelled. I cocked my head at her—she'd never yelled at me before, not really. Her voice was sharp, but it didn't cut me. It didn't even leave a scratch.

Mrs. Knowles stood up again, staring at me with that pinch between her eyebrows. "This is not acceptable, Darla," she said. The water spot on her leg made it look like she had wet herself, and I started to giggle.

Mrs. Knowles scowled, which only made me laugh harder. She picked up her books and left the house without saying goodbye, leaving me alone in the kitchen, giggling to myself.

She didn't come back for a few days. The next time I saw her, she handled me differently, like I was at arms' length. She used a softer voice, but it was firmer. She sat farther away from me at the table. She never brought me water in a cup anymore, and she always looked at me out of the corner of her eye, like she was waiting for me to do something else she could call 'not good.' I don't think she thought she should explain to me why something was good or not. Nobody did.

[Scribe's note: Maybe you'll say I should have stepped in, or checked in with Mrs. Knowles once in a while, but I no longer had the capacity for Darla and her needs. I tried not to worry about her so profusely once she had Mrs. Knowles to look out for her. Instead, I buried my head into my studies as if my life depended on it—because, in a way, it did. Nobody was going to help me out of the hellhole our lives had become except for me, and if I wanted to do that, I would need money. I was still young, but I was far less naive than someone my age probably should have been. I knew money ran the world, and the best way to get money outside of stealing it from someone else was to educate your way to it. I absorbed myself in homework, in papers and textbooks and lectures, and ignored the evil little goblins who sat around me in school, wanting me to fail. Whether it was their perpetual taunting or my own subconscious desire to live twice as hard since Darla could barely live at all, I pushed myself to excel, no matter the cost.]

Mrs. Knowles warmed back up to me, at least I think she did. When the leaves started changing color again, she even began taking me on little walks around the neighborhood. With her arm around my waist, we strolled slowly along the sidewalk. The cool breeze was nice, and I'd forgotten what the air smelled like.

The walks stopped suddenly, and when I asked Mrs. Knowles to take me outside, she just shook her head. I probably did something 'not good,' but I couldn't fathom what it was. Like everything in my life, I accepted the change and we went back to studying indoors.

[Scribe's note: Darla did nothing wrong. Mother had been at work one evening when a neighbor sat in her section and idly commented on how lovely it was to see her 'other daughter' out and about, how he'd thought she'd been sent away. I've no idea how Mother reacted in the moment, but when she came home, she was so furious she began throwing things against the wall in her bedroom. Miraculously, Darla slept through the commotion. I crept to Mother's closed door to try to eavesdrop, but all I heard was the occasional sob and the glug of alcohol slipping down Mother's throat.

Mother must have confronted Mrs. Knowles while I was at school, and I can imagine it was ugly. Fortunately for Darla (and, frankly, for me), it wasn't ugly enough to scare Mrs. Knowles away for good, but it did bring a definitive end to the walks. Darla remained the dirty little secret Mother wanted to hide at all costs.]

Winter came, then spring, and things continued as they had. If there was a Christmas celebration, I don't remember it. [Scribe's note: There was not. On Christmas morning, Mother holed up in her room with a bottle of peppermint schnapps and didn't come out until the following day. I made Darla pancakes, which she drooled her way through, most of the meal ending up in her lap. We watched television together until Darla fell asleep, then I went back to my own room to study.]

Mrs. Knowles was very patient with me, even when I did more things she said were 'not good,' like rip up a few pages from her books, or throw a spoonful of macaroni salad at the refrigerator, or rummage through her purse looking for candy.

I tried to tell myself it wasn't such a bad life.

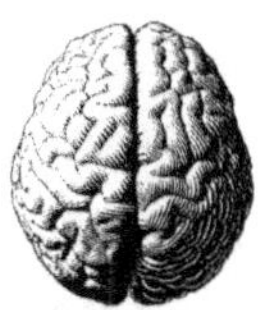

1 9 7 4

Ma was not doing okay, even I could see that. [Scribe's note: This is a major understatement. Mother had been regressing slowly ever since Darla's surgery, then more quickly after Father's suicide. Perhaps, if Father had stuck around longer, he might have been pleased with Darla's recovery (sluggish though it was) and could have halted Mother's decline.

After Mrs. Knowles's introduction into our home, however, Mother gave up even the tiniest pretense of being a loving parent. I suppose she figured Mrs. Knowles would be spreading lies about her anyway, so why even bother to put on an act. I had to steal money from her purse to buy groceries at the corner store on my way home from the library. I don't know what Mother ate; I assume she consumed her fill at her workplace, and supplemented the rest of her caloric needs with alcohol. Our garbage bags clinked with glass when I took them out to the curb.

I first noticed the orange prescription bottle shortly after our dismal Christmas. It was sitting on the kitchen counter next to the fridge, and I could only assume Mother left it out by mistake. The label read KELLY GREGORY, TAKE AS DIRECTED, VALIUM. Even though it wasn't Thorazine, holding the bottle made my fingers sweaty, and I set it back down on the counter with a rattling clunk.

I left the bottle where it was, but I wrote down the name of the medication and spent my afternoon in the library reading about diazepam, better known as Valium. There were articles touting its effectiveness against anxiety, insomnia, and alcohol withdrawal. This last made me pause—could Mother be considering sobriety?

I shook my head, chasing away the fanciful idea. Our garbage bags were heavier and louder than ever, the bottles clanging together like cymbals.

The articles I read also indicated that Valium should not be taken with alcohol, and that the medication could result in 'suicidal thoughts.'

For God's sake, I couldn't withstand another parent taking the easy way out. What was Mother thinking? Was she thinking at all? If she died, who would take care of Darla and me? We had no close relatives—Mother and Father were both only children, and all of our grandparents were dead. We'd be herded into the foster care system like sheep, where we'd likely be split up. Nobody would be able to care for Darla properly. She'd probably end up in a horrible institution somewhere, the one thing Mother had fought so hard against when she'd still had the will to fight, and I'd be in no position to get Darla out.

The thought was unfathomable. To tell you the truth, I didn't care about Mother's health. My mother, as I knew her, had died long before, and the person who barely kept the roof over our heads and the liquor cabinet fully stocked was no more than a useful ghost. I cared only about her role in our lives and the protection a living parent, however mentally absent, provided.]

Ma stayed away from me, for the most part, and that was okay with me. She smelled of cigarettes and sweat, and she often slurred her words worse than I still did.

"Has your mother ever hurt you?" Mrs. Knowles whispered to me one day during our lessons.

"What?" I asked, and Mrs. Knowles hushed me. Ma was still sleeping in her bedroom.

"Has your mother ever struck you?" Mrs. Knowles whispered again.

I stared at her, trying to figure out how to answer. I didn't want to be 'not good' again.

"No," I said.

Mrs. Knowles' eyebrows pinched again, and I prepared myself for her to be angry with me.

"Do you have enough to eat? Does she care for you properly?" Mrs. Knowles asked.

Between Mrs. Knowles and Ellie, I ate fine. As for the caring for me part, I didn't know how to answer, so I just nodded.

Mrs. Knowles' eyebrows were still all scrunched up, but she stopped asking me questions and stopped whispering.

[Scribe's note: Mrs. Knowles stopped me on the sidewalk at the corner of Beech and Sycamore on my way home from school one day. She looked sheepish and tired.

"Ellen, I'm concerned about your mother," she said.

I held my breath. I knew Mrs. Knowles's intentions were good, but her meddling made me uneasy. If Mrs. Knowles had a mind to call the authorities, Darla and I could be ousted from our home even while Mother was still alive.

"Why?" I finally asked, when the silence became awkward.

"She's... well, Ellen, she's unkempt," Mrs. Knowles said, and I tried not to laugh. That was her biggest complaint?

Mrs. Knowles continued, "I heard from Jason Crouch that your mother has been making mistakes at work. She brought him a chicken sandwich with a pickle instead of his brisket, and the whole town knows Jason is allergic to cucumbers. She may be trying to hide it, but people are starting to notice, Ellen."

I shrugged. What did she want from me? If I didn't have capacity for Darla right then, I certainly didn't have—nor did I want—capacity for Mother's issues.

"You know," Mrs. Knowles said, and she leaned even closer into me, gripping my wrist. She smelled of sugar cookies and lavender. "You and Darla can come stay with me whenever you need."

I stared at her. Could she be telling the truth? It was as though I was drowning and she'd thrown me a life preserver. "Really?" I said.

She nodded resolutely. "Really. David and Mitchell are grown and out of the house, and Mr. Knowles is at work far more often than he's home. I could use the company."

"Thank you," I said, for lack of anything better, even though her closeness made me nervous.

I tried to turn away, but Mrs. Knowles squeezed my arm, hard. "I'm serious, Ellen," she said, her voice raspy. "You and Darla can stay with me, if anything happens."

I wondered what she meant by 'anything.' Did she see Mother's decline as starkly as I did, even though Mother tried so hard to hide her true self just as much as she hid Darla?

"Thank you," I said again, and she finally released me.

"Take care of yourself, dear," she said, then continued on her way down the sidewalk.

It was nothing much—a hushed conversation on a neighborhood sidewalk—but it changed everything.]

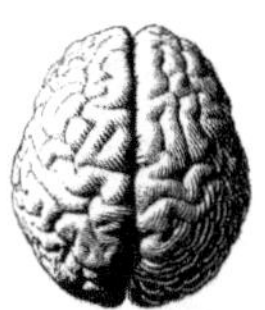

1 9 7 4

Ma found me at the kitchen table, finishing my bread and jelly. Ellie had just left for school, and Mrs. Knowles wouldn't come until later. Ma usually never got up this early; she didn't come home from the restaurant until I was already asleep.

"Close your mouth," Ma said. I didn't know my mouth had been open, but sure enough, when I poked my chin with a finger, it was hanging low, and some chewed bread was starting to slide past my bottom lip. I did as Ma asked, holding my jaw closed to finish chewing.

Ma shuffled past me and grabbed an orange bottle off the kitchen counter. She twisted it open and shook a few pills into her hand. They looked like candy, and my mouth started to water more, which made it hard to keep myself from drooling, which I knew Ma hated. She filled a glass with water from the sink, threw the pills into her mouth, and gulped them down. The sound was very loud in the quiet kitchen, and it made me want to laugh.

I couldn't hold it in, even though I knew Ma would be mad at me. She was always mad at me, so what did it matter? I let my laughter out in a little snort through my nose.

Ma whipped around to face me. "What're you laughing at?" Her eyes were slits, and her voice was low and mean, like a dog growling.

I shrugged instead of answering. I knew if I spoke, I'd spray breadcrumbs all over the table.

Ma walked past me to one of the cabinets in the living room and pulled out a bottle of something brown. She unscrewed the cap and took another loud gulp. I couldn't remember if she'd always been such a loud drinker. The thought brought another snort out of me.

"Shut up, you moron!" Ma yelled at me, slamming the bottle onto the coffee table. Liquid sloshed onto the wood. Ma used to get angry at me or Ellie when we'd put a glass on that table—she said it would leave a ring and ruin it, and we couldn't afford new furniture. I guessed the rules didn't apply anymore. I was more confused by her actions than the words, which floated over me like balloons.

Ma kept staring at me as she picked the bottle back up and noisily drank more. I couldn't help it—the laughter kept coming.

Ma capped the bottle and put it back in the cabinet. When she turned to face me again, her cheeks were red. "I'm so goddamned sick of this shit," she said, then walked back to her bedroom and slammed the door.

Ma had cursed! Again! I guessed this was just something she did now. I shoved my last bite of bread with jelly into my mouth, then ran to my room and pressed my face against my pillow. I could keep my food in my mouth and keep Ma from hearing my laughter, which, like vomit, just wouldn't stop, even though I wanted it to.

I know Mrs. Knowles came not long after that, and we did our lessons, and we had lunch, which was spaghetti with meatballs. Mrs. Knowles cut up my noodles into little pieces so I could eat them with a spoon.

That's the last thing I remember from the day Ma died.

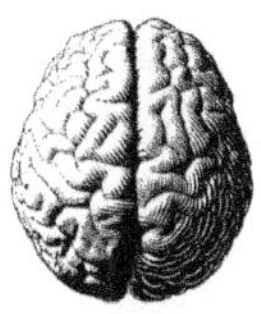

1 9 7 4

[Scribe's note: I'm glad Darla doesn't remember the rest of what happened that day.

After school, I'd planned to go to the library to study, as I typically did. When I arrived at the library and started unpacking my books, I realized I'd left my chemistry text at home. We had a quiz the following day, so it was the only book I really needed. I would rather have died than ask another student in my class to borrow theirs—the ridicule and mockery that would earn me would have been too much.

So, I repacked my book bag and headed back home, resolved to do my studying in my room.

It was pure luck that brought me home in time.

When I entered the house, I half-expected to see Mother at the kitchen table, drinking black coffee and smoking a cigarette. She wasn't there, but an empty mug in the sink and the ghost of cigarette smoke told me I'd just missed her, that she was still close.

The last thing I wanted to do was run into Mother. I found her unbearable to be around, with her violent mood swings, her anger, the way the events of our lives had completely hollowed her out, left her more of a shell than Darla ever was. It's safe to say I resented Kelly Gregory, because she'd so willingly given up everything that made her my mother. What she was now was nothing more than a husk, the bits and pieces of her shattered soul clattering around inside.

I grabbed a brown-spotted banana from the pantry and scurried toward my room, tiptoeing past Mother's closed bedroom door. If I were lucky, she'd still be sleeping, and our paths wouldn't have to cross today.

As it happened, luck is a fickle thing.

As I passed Darla's door, something gave me pause. Her door was shut, even though those days, it was typically wide open. Ever since Mrs. Knowles had started coming around, Mother had eased up on locking Darla in. What would be the point? Darla's existence was no longer a secret confined to the four walls of our home.

I set my book bag on the ground and crept closer to Darla's door. I pressed my ear to the cheap wood, and that's when I heard it.

Muffled groans. The shake of the bed frame hitting the wall. And then—a voice.

"Hold still, goddamnit!"

It was Mother. Of course it was.

I didn't waste any more time. I twisted the knob and burst into the room, where I found Darla supine on the bed, Mother straddling her. Mother's gnarled fingers were gripping a fat pillow and pressing it over Darla's face. Sweat dripped off her forehead from the effort, as Darla thrashed like a hooked fish at the bottom of a boat.

"Mother!" I screamed, but she didn't seem to hear me—or if she did, she didn't care.

I crossed the room in two strides and grabbed Mother's upper arms, the stringy muscle barely covering her fragile bones. If I squeezed too hard, I felt I'd be able to snap them into pieces.

I considered it, and I'm not ashamed to tell you that.

Instead, I sunk my fingers deeper and pulled, putting my entire body weight into the movement. Finally, I managed to wrench Mother to the floor, hurling her with as much force as I could muster. Without Mother holding her down, Darla sprang up like a jack-in-the-box, the pillow, a would-be murder weapon, falling to the floor with a soft thud.

Darla wailed, in between sucking in huge lungfuls of air. Her eyes were red. If I had gotten there even a few seconds later, Mother probably would have succeeded in killing her daughter.

Mother lay sprawled on the floor, her housedress having flown up to her upper thighs, which were nearly as sticklike as her arms. Like Darla, she was heaving from exertion.

"What have you done?" I yelled, throwing my arms out wide, as if to increase my volume.

Mother pushed a wisp of gray-brown hair out of her face and turned to spit on the carpet. "What I should have done a long time ago," she said, the venom in her voice pungent and deadly, even as she slurred her words.

I shook my head, angry at Mother for her monstrousness, angry at Darla, as unfair as it was, for her helplessness, and angry at myself most of all, for my lack of foresight. How had I not seen this coming? Mother was a ticking time bomb, descending ever deeper into alcohol and substance abuse. Deep down, I knew I never intervened or told anyone because I hoped Mother would quietly die at a convenient time, such as when I was over eighteen and fears of the foster care system couldn't hold me hostage anymore.

Clearly, Mother had no intention of fading quietly away... on her own, at least.

I turned to Darla, who had managed to catch her breath, and was staring at Mother with her usual placid expression on her face.

"Are you okay, Darla?" I asked, laying a hand on her cheek. It was hot to the touch.

"I don't know," she said, and even if it was her automatic response, it was probably the truth.

Mother snorted angrily from her position on the floor. At last, she tugged her dress down, so we would be spared the sight of her wasted legs, the purple veins crisscrossing like highways under her lily-white flesh. "She hasn't been okay for years," Mother said, rather petulantly. "Fucking idiot."

Something snapped inside of me, and in that moment, a plan formed in my mind, whole and complete and perfect.

"Darla, I'm going to get you a glass of water, okay?" I said. Darla nodded, as if she didn't care one way or the other.

I looked toward Mother. "Get out of this room," I snarled. Mother stared at me, as if seeing me for the first time.

"You ungrateful little bitch," Mother said, beginning the laborious process of hauling herself up from the dusty carpet.

"Apple doesn't fall far from the tree, huh, Mother?" I said, surprised at my own cheekiness. Mother's attempted murder had unlocked a nastiness inside me, and I was happy to let it take me over. It made me feel strong, invincible.

Mother regained her feet and scuttled out of the room like a spider, hissing as she went. A few moments later I heard the creak of a cabinet being opened, the clink of a bottle, then the slam of Mother's bedroom door.

Perfect.

With Mother out of the way, I rushed to get Darla some water, then brought it back to her bedside. She took it from me without a word and drained half the glass in one go, runnels of it streaming down her chin. She wiped her mouth on the sleeve of her blouse, then laid back down against her pillows.

"Get some sleep, okay?" I said. Darla nodded, the ghost of a smile on her lips, as though she knew what I was planning and heartily approved.

When I left Darla's room, I reengaged the lock on the door. I didn't want Darla wandering out while I was doing what needed to be done. I didn't want her implicated, but I also didn't want her bearing witness.

What would I have done if Mother had actually killed Darla? Would our lives have been any better? I thought not. Darla was like a dog, something that didn't cause too much trouble, didn't ask for much, and, most importantly of all, offered an unconditional human warmth that was so hard to come by in this world. Even though I'd pulled away from her over the past few months, letting Mrs. Knowles take my place, Darla still gave me purpose. She kept me from sliding into the same oblivion that had swallowed Father. The same oblivion that was about to swallow Mother.

I refused to be swallowed.

In the kitchen, I pulled a tumbler glass from the cabinet. Mother's orange bottle of Valium was still on the counter near the refrigerator. According to the dosage information printed on the side of the bottle, each pill contained ten milligrams of the diazepam drug, and Mother's doctor had directed her to take two pills per day. I already suspected she was taking more than that, and had possibly developed a tolerance for it. To be safe, I poured every last pill—some fifty or so—into a plastic bag, pulled a rolling pin from a drawer, and began crushing the pills into powder. I worked as quietly as possible, not wanting to alert Mother.

Finally, all that remained in the bag was a light blue dust that looked like tainted baking soda. I poured all of it into the tumbler, then retrieved a bottle of Jack Daniel's from the liquor cabinet. It was already half-empty, but it didn't matter. I filled the glass nearly to the brim, then used a spoon to stir until the powder had dissolved.

I didn't bother knocking on Mother's door. When I entered, she was curled on her bed, weeping and mumbling incoherently. It was possible she'd already had several doses of Valium that day, and who knows how much alcohol on top of it. I was only doing her a favor, after all—bringing her her two favorite medications of choice.

"Mother," I said, when she didn't react to my presence.

"What do you want," she mumbled, head still pressed into her dirty blankets.

"I'm sorry," I said, the lie rolling off my tongue smoothly. "I shouldn't have grabbed you so hard."

Mother looked up at me, her face sallow and tearstained. "No, you shouldn't have," she said, as if trying to regain the maternal authority she'd relinquished many years before. "I should punish you."

With difficulty, I managed not to roll my eyes. "Here," I said, offering her the glass. "I brought something for you."

She squinted at me, suspicious, and for a second fear gripped my heart. What would I do if she wouldn't drink every last drop willingly? I could hold her down and try to force the liquid into her mouth—after all, she was so thin and weak she would be no match for me—but I didn't want to have to do that. It felt... inelegant.

"I'll take it," she said after a pause, and relief flooded my veins like saline. She yanked the glass from my hands, spilling some on her blanket in the process. Hopefully there was enough left to do the job.

She tipped it back, her lips parting like writhing worms. I hadn't tested it, of course I hadn't, and I wondered if she'd notice the bitterness.

She didn't. She chugged the entire glass, then slammed it down on her bedside table, which was already cluttered with half a dozen other empty glasses, most rimmed with brown grime.

Mother belched, then collapsed back against the bed. Her snores echoed through the room just as I reached her door. For a moment, I stood in the doorway, drinking my mother in. I'd tried hard to ignore her, to be anywhere but where she was, to avoid her at all costs. As a result, I hadn't gotten a good look at her, hadn't seen the physical evidence of her decline up close. I would have pitied her if the hate didn't burn away all other feelings.

As I looked at her, I was reminded of my Thorazine haze, the way the drug had left me seizing, gasping, imprisoned, and suffering. The way it had given me Neuroleptic Malignant Syndrome, colored me with death like a painter with a fat brush. Thorazine had been a prison for me, and now Valium would be both Mother's prison and the source of her ultimate freedom. The poetic justice of it all comforts me to this day.

I nodded, my last salute to the woman who gave birth to me. Then I closed the door and went to my room with my chemistry textbook to study.

Before you cast judgment on me, or think you can use this against me in any way, remember that I didn't kill her. She killed herself—she made the choice to drink the alcohol, to swallow the pills, to try to murder her own child.

And if that doesn't convince you, remember this—Mother's death happened long before I took my oath to 'do no harm.' And is euthanasia really considered harm, anyway? Some doctors would say yes. I am not one of them.

In fact, Mother's death was the only real way to keep more harm from being done to Darla. I believed that then, and I still believe it, to this day, despite everything that came after.]

1974

DEATH INVESTIGATION REPORT

Reporting officer: Mark Beechum

Date of report: November 4, 1974

Case number: 0005612

Incident Details

Decedent: Kelly Gregory

Date and time of death: Estimated November 4, 1974, approximately 3:30 p.m.

Location of death: Decedent's bedroom at her home, 1560 Dogwood Lane

Date and time body discovered: November 4, 1974, around 4 p.m.

Circumstances surrounding death: Decedent was an adult female. The body was discovered by the decedent's daughter, Ellen Gregory, aged 16. Ellen stated that she checked on her mother when she returned home from school, and found her mother unresponsive. She called 911. Paramedics arrived at the scene approximately ten minutes later. Decedent was declared dead at the scene. When Ellen discovered the decedent, the body was prone on the bed, above the covers. An empty glass was on the bedside table, along with an empty bottle of Jack Daniel's. There was also an empty bottle of prescription Valium, prescribed to the decedent. Ellen Gregory stated that her mother had recently been depressed. There is no evidence of foul play. Another daughter, Darla Gregory, aged 14, was also in the house, but did not witness the death or view her mother's body.

Apparent cause of death: Suspected prescription drug and/or alcohol overdose.

Decedent Information

Full name: Kelly Ann Gregory

Date of birth: February 21, 1937

Age: 37

Race and sex: Caucasian female

Home address: 1560 Dogwood Lane

Identifying features: Decedent had shoulder-length brown hair and gray eyes. She was roughly 105 pounds, five foot five inches in height.

Clothing/personal effects: Decedent was dressed in a stained nightshirt and appeared unkempt.

Medical history: Decedent was legally prescribed Valium for anxiety.

Medications: Valium.

Additional Information

Next of kin notification: Ellen Gregory, decedent's daughter.

Other relevant details: Decedent's husband, John Gregory, died by suicide in 1972. Daughters Ellen (16) and Darla (14) will require follow-up care and will need to meet with a social worker to determine a temporary housing solution.

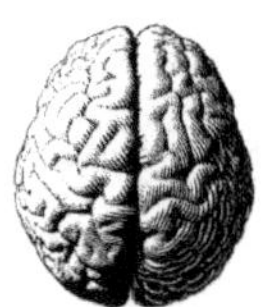

1 9 7 4

I don't really remember Ma's funeral. I guess there was one, but since Ma didn't have lots of friends, and her only family was me and Ellie, I can't imagine there were many people there. If I'd died when Ma did, I bet the only person at my funeral would be Ellie. And maybe Mrs. Knowles. [Scribe's note: The service for Mother was short and uninspired. Luckily, Mother had a life insurance policy set up for us by Father before he killed himself, so the funeral expenses were paid, along with some left over for me and Darla. The responsibility for planning the service fell to me— after all, there was no one else left, and Darla was not capable. I picked the cheapest, plainest coffin I could find. I would have had Mother cremated, but her last will and testament expressly stated she wanted to be buried next to her husband in the family plot at Richmond's Hollywood Cemetery. Father's family had bought the plot decades ago, a way of flashing their meagre wealth around, back when they had it. I don't know why they bothered; their plot was far away from the much more illustrious cemetery guests, like President Tyler and President Monroe. The ridiculous clutching at social cache felt more pathetic than noble, in my opinion. Apparently, though, Mother did not agree, so instead of scattering her ashes in the garbage heap where they belonged, Darla and I, along with Mrs. Knowles, stood side by side next to the gaping hole in the earth, shivering in the early winter cold, as a preacher offered some pitiful eulogy and Mother's coffin was lowered into the ground. I wore a black dress, as did Mrs. Knowles, but Darla barely had any clothes, so a floral blouse and pair of my old jeans it was. Mrs. Knowles had made a brief fuss about Darla's attire, but she shut up when she mistook the fake tears in my eyes for real ones.

Mother's gravestone was as spare as her coffin. Her name, Kelly Ann Gregory, and her birth and death dates. Father's proclaimed 'Beloved Husband and Father,' a rather blatant lie, but it was Mother's choice. Now that things were up to me, I wanted to tell the truth, and the truth was that Kelly Gregory was nothing to me, and had been nothing for some time.]

"Who would like a nice glass of milk?" Mrs. Knowles asked me. It's the first thing I think about when I try to remember Ma's death. Mrs. Knowles and Ellie were both wearing black, but I wasn't. It had started to rain outside, and Mrs. Knowles pushed Ellie and me into her kitchen, which was much bigger and cleaner than ours. Her refrigerator, a lovely robin's egg blue, was covered with family photographs. Mrs. Knowles and Mr. Knowles, along with their two sons.

I raised my hand, and Mrs. Knowles placed a big glass in front of me. I was about to pick it up when she put a straw into the milk. She'd been a part of my life long enough to know swallowing from an open cup was still hard for me.

I took a sip, and then, before I knew it, Mrs. Knowles was showing me to a bedroom that was not mine, telling me that me and Ellie would be happy here, she just knew it.

[Scribe's note: After the service, Mrs. Knowles, our newly appointed guardian, drove Darla and me back to her house. I'd already discussed the arrangements with her. If she found my brusque businesslike manner in the wake of Mother's death off-putting, she didn't say anything. She probably assumed that people grieve in many different ways, and this was mine. What she didn't understand was that I wasn't grieving at all. I was ready to move on, to restart Darla's and my lives without the heavy emotional weight of our sick mother dragging us down. If Mother had had it her way, it would be Darla rotting in a coffin instead of her. The thought made me inordinately angry, but I disguised my rage as anguished grief for Mrs. Knowles's benefit.

While Darla got used to her new room, which used to belong to David, the elder Knowles boy, I went to work ferrying our few important belongings from our deathtrap of a home to Mrs. Knowles's far more welcoming abode. The woman was eager for us to join her. As she told me, in no uncertain terms, Mr. Knowles was often busy with work, and with her boys out of the house and living their own lives, she was often lonely. Having Darla and me around would be a favor to her, not an imposition. I chose to take her words at face value, putting far more trust into her than I ever had in my own parents.

I wouldn't be difficult for Mrs. Knowles. All I wanted to do was keep my head down, work hard in school, and build a better life for myself, far away from the tragedy of our family. I wanted Darla to be okay, of course, but I wanted my own identity. For too long, I'd clung to the idea that I was Darla's lifesaving flotation device, and if I sunk, we'd both be worse than dead. I didn't want to be her buoy anymore. I wanted to be my own.

Darla and Mrs. Knowles were already extremely well acquainted, and I had no doubt that Darla would be easy for her—or as easy as she could be, given the abrupt change in environment. Were Mother still around to see the new arrangement, she probably would have insisted that a move like this would damage Darla's already fragile mental state, sending her into a tailspin from which she would never recover. But, of course, as with most things concerning Darla, Mother would have been wrong. Darla was far more adaptable than Mother ever would have believed, although she did have a somewhat rocky adjustment period. Mrs. Knowles quickly learned to serve Darla's food on unbreakable melamine plates only.]

My new room was bigger than the one at my old home. The bed was twice the size, with a blue comforter and a mound of fluffy pillows. There were baseball posters on the walls, and the hint of boy the room held excited me in a way I didn't really understand. The excitement reminded me a bit of the Alice book, and I liked it, but it also made me uneasy.

My favorite part of the room was in the corner—a bookshelf full of books. I didn't even care what they were about, I was just pleased to have something to read that was different. Ellie brought over a few of my things from home, but I didn't really care. I wasn't attached to much, and I was content with Mrs. Knowles, but everything was so different. Even though I appreciated the difference, sometimes it was too much for me to remember, and things were out of place, and the schedule was different…

I know I was difficult for Mrs. Knowles in the beginning, but I got better. I got used to life at her house, and as I did, I could feel my old life, maybe even my old self, melting away.

At first it made me feel itchy, but then it felt good.

[Scribe's note: My room at Mrs. Knowles' house used to belong to her younger son, Mitchell. Mitchell had joined the army, had been sent to Vietnam, and his room reflected both the austerity and discipline of his chosen profession. The bedcovers were so tight, I thought even a bullet would have bounced off them rather than punch through. There was no clutter, and what few belongings were in the chest of drawers were folded so exactingly, it looked as though Mitchell had used a ruler.

I felt very comfortable there. Things were predictable, orderly, clean. My own home had devolved into a nightmarish den, dirty and depressing, and Mrs. Knowles's bright, sunny house was a balm to my ruptured soul. I laid my schoolbooks on Mitchell's dust-free desk, which smelled of lemony wood polish, and began to study for my chemistry test. My teacher had assured me that I could be exempt from the examination due to my mother's recent death, but I declined.

If I was going to be accepted into a top-ranked college, and then a top-ranked medical school, I couldn't cut any corners or take any special privileges. Life had shown me, time and time again, that I was not blessed, I was not lucky, I was not special. Everything I achieved would have to be earned, through hard work and unwavering dedication.

With Darla in safe hands, I felt I could, for the first time in my life, focus on myself.

As usual, that turned out to be a mistake.]

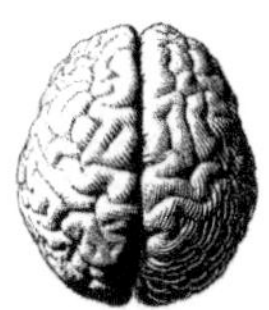

1 9 7 4 - 1 9 7 5

I liked living with Mrs. Knowles. She made pancakes fresh every morning, and she helped me cut mine up. She even tucked a napkin into my collar, which made cleanup much easier. She'd take me on walks around the neighborhood, even when it was cold, and sometimes people would stop her and ask who I was. When she told them, they'd always get this strange look on their faces, like they wanted to cry. Why would they cry for me? I was much better off now than I was before, when I was stuck in the house and Ma was angry with me all the time, even when I was trying to get better on my own.

Eating Mrs. Knowles' cooking, I put on some weight. When I looked in the mirror, I was startled at my reflection. In my mind, I was still a shrimpy eleven-year-old, afraid to leave my room for fear of catching some germ that could make me throw up. Now, I saw a young woman, almost grown, with deep gray eyes, shining brown hair that Mrs. Knowles kept brushed and tidy, and pink cheeks. I thought of my fear, the fear that had led me down this road, that had robbed me of so much, but when I reached for it, it simply wasn't there. [Scribe's note: I've often thought of Darla's absent emetophobia as a phantom limb—as she described, she would reach for her fear, only to find empty space where it had once existed. In truth, that is the same experience she had with many of her mental faculties following the lobotomy. She would reach for normal speech, but it wasn't there. She would reach for proper etiquette, but it wasn't there. She would reach for swallowing functionality, for proper gait biomechanics, for reading ability, for grip strength to hold a pencil—all of it wasn't there, all of it obliterated with the swipe of an ice pick, relegated to the realm of the phantom. Sometimes those things came back. More often, they did not.]

Ellie acted like I used to. She holed herself up in her new room and read books all day, when she wasn't at school. At least she was in the house more now, not always at the library. Even though she didn't come out and talk to me, it was nice to have her close by. [Scribe's note: Without Mother's repulsive presence fouling the atmosphere, I felt safe nestled in my new home. I still spent some afternoons at the library, but I came to enjoy the solitude of Mitchell's room more and more. I tried to maintain the military precision of Mitchell's cleanliness, but I did make the space my own, with my books and my few clothes hanging in the closet.]

Mrs. Knowles tried to talk to me about Ma once or twice, but I think she was upset when I didn't cry. People usually cry when their parents die, don't they? Like with my fear, I tried to reach for sadness, but the tears wouldn't come. Ma hadn't been much of a part of my life since my surgery, so I didn't miss her, and I wasn't bothered by that. Mrs. Knowles was bothered by my lack of strong feelings, I could tell, so she began to steer clear of all topics that touched on Ma or even Pa. Sometimes I wondered if Mrs. Knowles would grow tired of me, or bored of me, or angry at me, and try to get rid of me. Even that thought didn't bother me as much as it probably should have. [Scribe's note: I had this same concern, and it worried me, but I shoved it aside. My studies came first, and besides, I would be eighteen soon enough and out of the house. Surely, when Mrs. Knowles agreed to be our guardian, she had calculated the risks and the effort required to take on the care of someone like Darla. She did not go into this blindly, of that I was sure, and that helped me further quiet my remaining wriggling concerns.]

For Thanksgiving, our first one without Ma, Mrs. Knowles made turkey, and stuffing, and mashed potatoes, and hot rolls, and three different kinds of pie. Her sons couldn't come, so it was just us and Mr. Knowles, who didn't talk very much. I ate so much I felt full to bursting, but I didn't throw up on the table like I did at my twelfth birthday. [Scribe's note: Thanksgiving was an awkward affair, with Mrs. Knowles flitting about, trying to attend to everyone's tiniest need, fretting over the smallest detail. At the time, I assumed she was trying to make the holiday as festive and cheerful for us as possible, so we wouldn't be reminded of our dead parents. Looking back, I think Mrs. Knowles had other reasons, and a different person she was trying to impress.]

Christmas meant another wonderful feast. Mrs. Knowles's boys were still gone. We had our dinner, then the next morning, Mr. and Mrs. Knowles watched Ellie and me open up presents. Ellie got a new set of pens, a hairbrush, and a sweater set, and I got some new books and a soft wool dress. [Scribe's note: Christmas was equally awkward, equally forced. I appreciated Mrs. Knowles's effort, but I'd grown content, before Mother's death, with ignoring the holiday season. There was so much fuss, so much anguish over being happy, or at least cultivating the appearance thereof. I found it tiresome, more than anything, but Darla seemed happy enough.]

There was a commotion not long after Christmas. Right next door, in our old house, there was a family I didn't recognize. David's—well, by then it was mine, I guess—bedroom window looked out over our old driveway. There was a big truck rumbling away, and two big men were bringing box after box into our house. Were Ellie and I moving back in? Was that our stuff in those boxes? I was very confused.

Mrs. Knowles found me sitting on the bed, staring out the window.

"Darla? Are you alright? I've been calling and calling for you, dear," she said, sitting next to me.

I didn't say anything—I didn't know how to form the question I wanted to ask. Instead, I pointed at the big truck.

Mrs. Knowles followed my finger and clucked her tongue. "Oh, don't worry about that, dear."

I made a noise, deep in my throat. It sounded like a grunt. It was my attempt at… what? Frustration? Irritation? I wasn't sure. It was involuntary.

"Darla, you don't live there anymore," Mrs. Knowles said, placing a hand on my shoulder. "You and Ellen live here, with me."

When I didn't move, she continued, "I thought it best to sell the house, dear. Ellen agreed with me. You two won't be needing it anytime soon, and the money can go into a trust fund for you both, to help take care of you. It's for the best."

I didn't completely understand what she was saying, but if Ellie thought it was a good idea, then that was enough for me. When Mrs. Knowles tugged on my arm to bring me downstairs, I didn't resist.

[Scribe's note: Selling the house was a no-brainer. Mother's last will and testament left her and Father's entire estate to me—and me alone. Perhaps she thought that by the time she perished, Darla would be long gone, or maybe she truly hated Darla that much, to erase her so completely. I accepted that I would never know, but I didn't much care. I spoke with Mr. and Mrs. Knowles, expressed my wishes to sell the shitheap swiftly— although not in that same language—and they agreed to help facilitate the sale. I was anxious that the house would sit on the market, gathering dust and breaking down due to neglect, given that two people had died within its walls. When the real estate agent, a smarmy man named Daniels, congratulated Mr. Knowles barely a week later on having the house under contract, and during the holiday season, no less, I nearly cried with relief. The offer was a smidge under the asking price, but I didn't care. Daniels only interacted with Mr. Knowles, but Mr. Knowles deferred to my preferences when I asked him to accept the offer. I later came to understand that our new neighbors were from Kansas, and Daniels had not told them of the house's history. In Daniels's defense, even though it nauseates me to defend that oily stain of a man, the Kansas family had not directly asked if anyone had died in the house, so apparently Daniels felt he was not obligated to tell them. The family's unfamiliarity with the Richmond area saved me, given I don't think a single soul who read the papers in the whole of the city would care to buy the suicide house of Dogwood Lane.]

Later that evening, staring out of my window, I got a better look at the new family. Ellie had told me they were from Kansas, and that they'd bought our old house. She said the money would help us, would make our future easier. Ellie frowned when I shrugged. I didn't much care one way or the other, although I did miss one thing about our old house. At Mrs. Knowles's, I had to go up the stairs to get to my room. At our house, there was only one floor. Stairs had become tricky for me, and I needed help. I was something close to angry, at first, but then I resolved to practice with those stairs, just as I'd practiced with walking and going to the bathroom on my own. It would take time, that was all.

The Kansas family looked like a postcard. The mother was lovely, in a bright pink shift dress and sandals, with shiny blonde hair. The father wore green bell bottom pants and a striped collared shirt, and his mustache was so thick I could barely see his mouth. There was a girl, who looked older even than Ellie, and she was the most beautiful person I'd ever seen. The same shining hair as her mother, with a round face and pink cheeks. As I watched, she threw her head back and laughed. Had I ever laughed like that with Ma or Pa or Ellie? [Scribe's note: No, not even before the surgery.]

The girl was laughing at a boy standing next to her. He was dressed in jeans and a plaid short sleeve shirt. His hair was dark brown, long and swooping to the side. He looked about Ellie's age, and watching him laugh with the girl made my stomach hurt. Even though I lived in David's room now, I hadn't seen an actual boy in… years? I thought again of the Alice book, and the kinds of things she did with boys she liked. I felt like I was hungry, but there wasn't any food I wanted to eat.

[Scribe's note: I wasn't immune to the boy, either. I caught a glimpse of him as I walked back from school. Before he could say anything to me, I hurried back to Mrs. Knowles's door. Years of isolating myself with my books had made having normal social interactions feel like climbing mountains, which I was uninterested in doing, no matter how attractive or magnetic a person might be. At least, that's how I felt at first.]

In the morning, Mrs. Knowles asked me if I'd like to help her make cookies. I'd never made cookies before, but I nodded anyway. It was something different, and part of me wondered if eating a cookie would fill that hunger I'd been feeling ever since I saw the neighbor boy in my old house.

Even though I didn't ask, Mrs. Knowles told me why we were making the cookies. "They're a housewarming present." I blinked at her, and she kept explaining. "For the family next door. It's always a kind gesture to welcome a new family to the neighborhood, especially when they're going to be living right next to us."

I didn't have really any strong feelings about my old house. I didn't really have any strong feelings about much of anything. If Mrs. Knowles wanted to make cookies and give them away, that sounded fine to me.

She started setting out all the ingredients on her kitchen counter. I said the words from the packages aloud. "Flour. Butter. Eggs. Sugar. Vanilla ex—extra—"

"Vanilla extract, dear," Mrs. Knowles said. I felt a flash of anger. I was getting there, after all, I was sounding it out. If she'd just given me another second, I could have gotten it.

She brought out a big bowl and scooped butter into it, then added a big scoop of sugar. She plugged in some sort of mixing machine, then smooshed it all around in the bowl. It was too loud, and I didn't like it one bit. I couldn't hear my own breathing over the commotion.

I didn't realize I was screaming until Mrs. Knowles wrapped her arms around me. "Hush, dear, hush! It's okay!"

I snapped my jaw closed and felt drool fall to the floor between my feet. My throat was scratchy.

Mrs. Knowles rubbed my arms. "Darla, dear, it's okay! It's just the mixer!"

Whether it was the loudness, or my smarting throat, or Mrs. Knowles cutting me off before I could read the words for myself, I don't know. But all of a sudden I was angry, and before I could stop myself, I had untangled myself from Mrs. Knowles and swept my arms across the counter, sending the sack of flour, the box of butter, and the open bag of sugar crashing to the floor.

"Darla!" Mrs. Knowles yelled. She didn't yell at me much, and I felt something like regret.

I stared at her, then looked down at the mess. The flour bag had ripped open, and white powder mixed with the heaps of shiny sugar on the white tiles. I looked back at Mrs. Knowles.

She was frowning. She opened her mouth, then closed it again, like a fish. It made me giggle.

"Please go to your room," Mrs. Knowles said. When I didn't move, she said, louder, "Go to your room now, please."

There was no screaming, no hitting, no insults, but I felt… off. I didn't want to make Mrs. Knowles sad, but how did she not understand why I did the things I did? She was an adult, wasn't she supposed to know more than me?

I went to my room and spent the rest of the morning looking through David's baseball cards, trying to sound out the names. The smell of cookies crept under my door, and my stomach rumbled.

When I came down for lunch, Mrs. Knowles had set a peanut butter sandwich on the table for me, along with a glass of milk.

While I ate, with Mrs. Knowles helping me as needed, she told me why what I did had upset her. "Darla, you can't be destructive in this home," she said. "You made me very sad, dear."

I swallowed a bite of sandwich, trying desperately to keep my mouth closed, and tilted my head. "Why did I make you sad?" It should have been straightforward, but I simply couldn't connect the dots. I'd reacted to a situation that had angered me. Why did that affect Mrs. Knowles? Why was she sad when I was the one who felt so upset?

Mrs. Knowles sighed, and another wave of cookie smell floated into my face. "Dear, when you hurt my things, it hurts me."

That made a bit more sense, but I was still confused. I could understand that hurting people was wrong, but how did that related to hurting a thing? I didn't know if Mrs. Knowles would be able to understand me, so I just said, "Okay."

She smiled. "That's a good girl."

When I was done with my sandwich, she let me have a cookie. "Just one," she said. "The rest are for the Fannins."

"Who?" I asked.

"The Fannins. The new family next door."

I chewed my cookie. When I asked my next question, a clump of chocolatey spit fell onto my lap. "Who is the boy?"

Mrs. Knowles squinted her eyes. "His name is Jeremiah, I believe."

I swallowed. Ah. Now I had a name for the face. Jeremiah Fannin.

[Scribe's note: Darla wasn't the only one who now had a name for a face. On my walk home, before I met Mrs. Knowles in the kitchen, I passed by our old home. There was no car in the driveway, so I stopped for a moment, just to look at it. Had there ever been a time when we'd been happy there? When the future was something to look forward to with hope, rather than something to dread so forcefully the prospect of death was more appealing than living for another moment? My brain was perfectly healthy, but I couldn't recall a single instance of joy in that house, even though I'm sure there must have been at least one, before Darla's descent into her phobia.

"Hey," a voice said, and I nearly dropped my books. A boy—*the* boy— had come up behind me on the sidewalk, his own arms full of books.

"Hello," I said around a lump in my throat, wondering if running away was an option.

He gave me a once-over, and I felt my cheeks grow hot. I was no beauty queen, as the girls at school never failed to remind me, but I knew I wasn't hideous. Still, his scrutiny made the blood fizz in my veins.

"You live around here, right?" he finally said.

I nodded. "Next door," I said, tilting my head towards Mrs. Knowles's house.

"Oh!" he said, grinning. "Neighbors!"

I stayed silent, unsure how to respond.

He added, "We just moved here." He hooked a thumb at our old house.

I cleared my throat, trying to swallow down the lump. "I know," I said, then wanted to kick myself for it. How stupid could I be?

"I'm Jeremiah," he said. "Jeremiah Fannin."

"Ellen," I said, so stunned that I temporarily forgot my own name. Nobody called me Ellen anymore except for Mr. and Mrs. Knowles. To everybody else, and even to myself, I was Ellie. I wanted to correct myself, but Jeremiah was already talking again.

"Do you have a last name, Ellen?"

"Gregory," I squeaked.

"Well, it's nice to meet you, Ellen Gregory."

"You, too," I mumbled. Dear God, would I have to endure years of being called 'Ellen' by this boy?

A thought gripped me, and before he could walk away, I blurted, "I didn't see you at school today."

Jeremiah nodded. "I go to the parish school," he said, shrugging.

"Oh," I said. "I go to Richmond Public."

"I figured," he said. "I would have remembered you."

My heart clenched. I had tried so hard, for so long, to be completely unmemorable. It was a survival mechanism, and most days, it still wasn't enough.

He smiled. "I'll see you around," he said, then walked up the path to his front door.

"Bye," I called after him. I stood there for a moment longer after Jeremiah closed the door, waiting for the lump to dissolve and the heat in my cheeks to fade.

As I finished my short walk to Mrs. Knowles's house—I still couldn't think of it as my home—I tried to parse why Jeremiah made me feel so strange, so uncomfortable.

Finally, it dawned on me, as I opened the door and entered the spacious living room.

Jeremiah had treated me not like a burden, or a freak, or a mother, or an uneasy guest. He had treated me like a person... and it was intoxicating.]

After lessons, Mrs. Knowles sent me back to my room for a nap. I felt like a baby when she said that, but I liked the quiet, so I went without a fuss. Later, when I heard the door open and Ellie come in, I opened my door a crack. If I listened really hard, I could hear Ellie and Mrs. Knowles talking in the kitchen.

[Scribe's note: When I came home from school, Mrs. Knowles told me about Darla's outburst. For a moment, I was terrified that she would rethink her guardianship, decide we were too difficult and would be better off in a foster home. I was determined to keep Mrs. Knowles happy, because if Mrs. Knowles was happy, then she would continue taking care of Darla. If she continued to take care of Darla, then I could take care of me. I assured Mrs. Knowles that Darla had never been violent, and that she shouldn't be concerned about future outbursts. I parroted something I had read in a book about brain injuries, that brains faced with traumatic injuries required significant time to heal, sometimes even years. Mrs. Knowles appeared placated, and reminded me about her aunt who'd been lobotomized, but my hackles were raised. I reminded myself that I couldn't go getting too comfortable with our situation, because, like the flour and sugar, our hopes could be swept to the floor at any moment.]

They were talking about me, about what I'd done. I wanted to be good, to do the right thing, I really did, but right and wrong were murky for me. I tried to remember if I'd always felt this way, but the memories were simply not there.

[Scribe's note: After I allayed Mrs. Knowles's fears about Darla's destructive behavior, she informed me that the three of us—Mr. Knowles was away for work—would be knocking on the Fannins' door that very evening to deliver the housewarming cookies. I was immediately seized with anxiety. How would Darla react to a new person, especially a boy close to her own age? What if she embarrassed me? What if she did something that made Jeremiah think there was something wrong not just with her, but with me, too? The children at school were horrible enough, and the way Jeremiah had treated me felt like an oasis from their cruelty. The thought of Darla snatching that all away with one ungainly movement, one incomprehensible sentence, one slobbery chin, made me want to retch.

"I don't know if Darla should come," I said to Mrs. Knowles.

She pursed her lips. "Why not?"

"She's…" I searched for a reason. "She's not ready yet. I don't know how she'll act around a new person."

Mrs. Knowles frowned. "I think she could benefit from the interaction."

I opened my mouth to protest further, but a wave of shame rose, crested, and then crushed me. What was I doing? I was pushing Darla into a corner, into a shameful box, just as Mother and Father had done for so long. What did I expect? That Darla would now be Mrs. Knowles's shameful secret? That she'd never meet a new person, never have a new experience? Guilt beat like a pulse under my skin. If I ever wanted Darla to get better, truly better, she had to be exposed to typical experiences, to social interaction beyond the confines of Mrs. Knowles's house.

I hung my head, defeated and miserable. "You're right," I said, then I retreated to my room to brush my hair.]

I found Mrs. Knowles and Ellie in the living room. Mrs. Knowles was carrying a blue tray with cookies on it, all covered with shiny cling film. When I reached for one, she shifted away from me.

"These are for the Fannins," she said.

"Oh," I said. I didn't understand why I couldn't have one—there were so many on the tray—but I didn't try again.

"You look lovely," Mrs. Knowles said to Ellie. It was true. Ellie's hair was shiny, pulled up in a bun, and she had some lipstick on. She almost never wore makeup.

"Thank you," Ellie said, pulling at her skirt.

We left the house and walked over to the Fannins'. Ellie looked shaky, and it made me uneasy.

Mrs. Knowles balanced the tray on one arm and rang the doorbell. We could hear the chime, something I remembered so clearly, echoing in the house.

"They're not home," Ellie grumbled, but Mrs. Knowles shushed her.

I was about to try to take a cookie again when the door opened. It was the boy—Jeremiah.

"Oh, hello," he said.

"Hello, dear," Mrs. Knowles said. "Is your father or mother home?"

"Yes, ma'am," Jeremiah said. He called into the house for his parents, and the two adults I'd seen from my window appeared next to him in the doorway.

"Please come in," the woman, his mother, said.

Mrs. Knowles went first, then Ellie pushed me ahead of her. Her hands were sweaty, and I almost stumbled on the doorframe, but Ellie grabbed my shoulder and righted me.

The house looked so different. Our furniture was gone, and the walls had been painted different colors. I must have made a sound, because Ellie squeezed my hand and whispered at me to be quiet.

"We brought you these to welcome you to the neighborhood," Mrs. Knowles said, holding up her tray.

"How thoughtful," Jeremiah's mother said.

"So kind," Jeremiah's father said.

"Oh, and excuse my manners, I haven't even introduced myself. I'm Belinda Knowles, and these are my goddaughters, Darla and Ellen.

They used to live in this house." [Scribe's note: Mrs. Knowles had taken to calling us her goddaughters because, as she explained, 'stepdaughters' was confusing and inaccurate, 'foster daughters' felt stigmatizing, and 'wards' was cold. Also, she felt called to care for us by God, so goddaughter was the most appropriate and least confusing term. I didn't much care.]

"Lovely to meet you," Jeremiah's father said. "I'm Cole, and this is my wife, Sally. Our daughter Debby isn't home right now, but this here is our son, Jeremiah."

"So pleased to meet you, as well," Mrs. Knowles said.

"Hi," I blurted, looking straight at Jeremiah. The strange hunger was back, and I wanted more than anything to reach for a cookie.

"Hi," he said back.

"Nice to see you again," Ellie said.

Jeremiah smiled. "So nice." But he wasn't looking at Ellie. He was still looking at me.

[Scribe's note: It was as though Jeremiah didn't even register my presence. For that single shining moment outside his house, I felt more seen than I had in years. I felt the air was pregnant with possibility, that maybe my existence wasn't the blight on humanity that everybody at school insisted it was. I thought… I thought Jeremiah had felt something, for me. But when I spoke to him, he only had eyes for Darla.

I turned to face my sister, my cheeks on fire. It was only then, contemplating her as Jeremiah might have, that I noticed the changes. Darla's hair was deep brown, lustrous and gleaming—thanks to Mrs. Knowles's ministrations, no doubt. She'd filled out considerably—thanks to Mrs. Knowles's cooking, no doubt. Even though she was two years my junior, her budding bosom was already more ample than mine, and where my forehead and chin were sprinkled with blemishes, Darla's face was clear and glowing, even with the thin sheen of dried drool on her chin.

I couldn't help it. Anger bloomed in my stomach, hot and roiling. I had never thought of Darla as a rival, simply as a person for me to protect. What had there been to be resentful of that would engender feelings of rivalry? I certainly wasn't jealous of Darla's emetophobia, or her lobotomy, or her altered mental capacity, or her diminished physical capabilities.

But now—now I was jealous, and it was the simplest form of jealousy I could imagine. I was jealous of Darla's beauty.]

Mrs. Knowles and Jeremiah's parents talked for a while, then they peeled the cling film off the tray and finally offered us cookies. I took one, being as careful as possible to chew with my mouth closed. Ellie didn't eat a cookie, but she watched me so closely, I thought she might want to take a bite of mine. [Scribe's note: I didn't want a bite. I wanted to make sure Darla was able to swallow without assistance or complication. For God's sake, this was our first meeting with these people. We didn't need them to know everything about Darla. That could come later, if it needed to come at all.]

When we left, Jeremiah walked with me to the door.

"I like your dress," he said.

I looked down. I hadn't given much thought to my clothes. I wasn't sure how to respond, so I just said, "Yes."

He laughed. "I'll see you around," he said.

"Bye," Ellie said.

[Scribe's note: He didn't even hear me. He was too busy mooning over Darla.]

That night, when I went to bed, the strange hunger didn't trouble me. I felt full.

[Scribe's note: That night, when I went to bed late, after nearly an hour spent in the bathroom squeezing my pimples—which only served to cause bleeding and inflammation that necessitated pancake makeup the next day—I felt empty.]

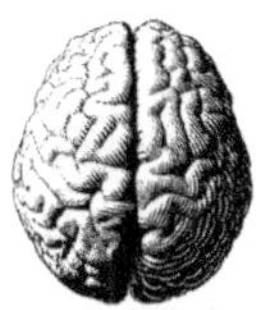

1 9 7 5

One thing I liked about living with Mrs. Knowles was that she took us to church. I think Ma and Pa took Ellie and me before everything got so bad with me, but I don't really remember what it was like. [Scribe's note: Mother and Father did, indeed, drag us to church every Sunday, at least until Darla started refusing to leave the house. Their congregation, a Southern Baptist ministry that, even as a child, I found repulsively aggressive, was like a scratchy wool blanket. Mother made Darla and me dress alike, in crisp dresses and bows, and she and Father would march us into Sunday School, where we'd sit with the other brainwashed-in-training children and listen to someone's grandmother read from a children's Bible. Afterward, we'd eat stale doughnuts in the lobby while Mother and Father shook hands and smiled at the so-called 'friends' they'd spend the entire ride home badmouthing. "Cheryl Gaines acts like a saint, but everyone knows she's sleeping with Gary Snyder." "Macy Tompkins says her chocolate cake is from scratch, but I know for a fact it's from a box." "Gene Fowler spends more money than God, but I heard he's bouncing checks all over town." They spoke in hushed tones, but their voices were completely audible. I suppose they expected their conversations to be over our heads, which might have been the case, but we could both recognize the tone of contempt in their voices. These were ugly discussions, and they both acted like ugly people. The irony that they were compelled to do this immediately after supposedly receiving the word of God was not lost on me.]

Ma had kept me in the house for so long, I'd forgotten what it was like to be around other people. In church, I got to sit right next to Mrs. Knowles and listen in to the adult service. Ellie was on my other side, and I felt…. normal. At first it was hard to stay calm, because everything was so new, and it was overwhelming, but Mrs. Knowles would squeeze my hands if I started being 'not good.' She would tell me all I had to do was sit still and listen. I knew I could do that. I was good at it—it was one of the few things I could do better than most people, even if Mrs. Knowles did have to reach over and close my mouth every now and then, or use a lavender-smelling hankie to wipe the drool from my chin. [Scribe's note: Mrs. Knowles's church may not have been the same as Mother and Father's, but it felt no different. It was Methodist, large, and just as obnoxious. At least she didn't force us to go to Sunday School. During our first service, I struggled to stay awake while the pastor droned on and on about the importance of honoring thy mother and father. The message bored and disgusted me in equal measure, which was no simple feat. What about honoring thy children? What about nurturing thy babies, protecting their fragile bodies, shepherding them safely into the world? What about putting thy children before thyself? The way I saw it, and continue to see it, is that it's all about reciprocity. Parents who honor their children deserve honor and respect in return. Parents who maim, traumatize, and attempt to murder their children deserve pain, anguish, and death in return. I imagine the fire-and-brimstone Old Testament God would agree with me.

As a result of my boredom, I found solace in picking my nails, folding up the day's program into smaller and smaller squares, fiddling with the hem of my dress—anything to make the time pass faster. Mrs. Knowles never said anything during the service, or even on the car ride home, but when Darla retired to her room for an afternoon nap after lunch, she sat me down.

"Ellen, did your mother and father take you girls to church?"

"Yes," I said simply.

"And?"

I stared at her blankly, not interested in continuing the conversation.

Mrs. Knowles sighed. "Ellen, there's a certain way to behave in church. If we don't listen to the pastor's sermon, if we don't fully participate in the service, we won't be able to receive God's wisdom and properly praise His name. In this house, we believe in God, and we worship Him."

She didn't say it outright, but her subtext was clear—*Shape up, or get out. Believe what I believe, or my good Christian charity comes to an end.*

I nodded. "Understood."

Mrs. Knowles smiled and clapped her hands together, as though that was that, and the problem of me and my faith was solved.

"Thank you, Ellen," she said, and I took that as my dismissal from the kitchen.

Every church service thereafter stretched out in front of me, interminable… but then, the very next week, I noticed a familiar face a few rows over from us.

Jeremiah Fannin.]

The service, something about being strong, had just ended, and I walked toward the lobby. Ellie ran ahead, needing to go to the bathroom, and Mrs. Knowles was talking to a friend. My stomach rumbled, and I wanted a doughnut.

I found the box on the table. Chocolate glazed, so delicious. I was about to grab one with my fingers when Jeremiah was suddenly next to me.

"Allow me," he said, and he picked up a napkin. He pulled a doughnut from the box and handed it to me.

"Mmm," I grunted, quickly stuffing a bite into my mouth. I held the napkin close to my face, using my thumb to keep my mouth closed while I chewed.

Jeremiah laughed. "Hungry, huh?"

"Mhmm," I grunted again.

He picked up his own doughnut. I watched him take a bite, much smaller than the one I'd taken, but what was I supposed to do? I was even hungrier now that he was near me, that odd, bone-deep feeling that excited me and made me nervous.

"So," he said. "Do you go to school with your sister?"

I swallowed. What was I supposed to say? How would Mrs. Knowles or Ellie want me to respond? "Mrs. Knowles teaches me," I blurted.

Jeremiah's eyebrows went up. "Oh," he said. "So you don't go to regular school?"

"No," I said, stuffing the rest of the doughnut in my mouth. It didn't taste as good as it did when I'd started eating.

"Huh," he said.

[Scribe's note: When I came out of the bathroom, my heart leapt at the sight of Jeremiah in the lobby, but it crashed to the ground very quickly when I saw he was talking to Darla. He was smiling, his head tilted to one side, his eyes sparkling. I'd observed enough interactions in the hallway at school to know that's how boys looked when they liked a girl.

Darla was staring back at him, the normal vacant expression on her face, her cheeks stuffed like a chipmunk's with doughnut. Even from across the room, I could see a smear of chocolate frosting on her upper lip. I was baffled. Was that really something Jeremiah found attractive?

I began to cross the room, and I picked up the tail end of their conversation. He was asking Darla about school. I couldn't fathom what she might say. Would she tell him about her surgery? About her limitations?

I reached them just as Jeremiah opened his mouth to ask another question.

"She's homeschooled," I cut in, and Jeremiah looked at me for a moment too long, as if coming out of a trance.

"Oh. Hi, Ellen," he said, smiling, but it wasn't as sparkly or high voltage as the one he reserved for Darla.

"Hi," I said. There was a pause, and I could hear Darla chewing her doughnut to pulp. Part of me wanted her jaw to flap open, sending doughnut mush falling to the floor. Would that do it? Would that be enough to show Jeremiah she wasn't the one for him? That she wasn't worth his attention, his infatuation? Even as I cursed myself for thinking this, I opened my own mouth, and ugliness spilled out. "Darla can't go to a proper school on account of her brain damage," I said.

Darla's eyes went from me to Jeremiah, but that placid expression remained. If she was perturbed by what I'd revealed, she didn't show it.

"Brain damage?" Jeremiah repeated, and a small, mean part of me was thrilled to see the light in his eyes dim as he reassessed Darla.

I leaned in close to him. He smelled of fresh cut grass and something oakier, manlier, like leather, underlaid with the unmistakable scent of sweat. "She had a lobotomy a few years ago."

Chills ran down my body. This was the first time I'd ever told anyone outside of the medical profession, voluntarily, about Darla. The most shameful part was that I wasn't doing this for Darla's own good. I was doing this for my own gain at her expense. Dear God, was I becoming my mother?

"What's a lobo—" Jeremiah began, but the arrival of Mrs. Knowles silenced him.

"Hello, Jeremiah!" she said sunnily. "How good to see you."

Jeremiah made pleasant small talk with Mrs. Knowles, and then she was tugging us toward the car. Mr. Knowles would be arriving home shortly, and she had a special lunch prepared for him. We couldn't afford to be late.

As we walked out, I looked back over my shoulder.

Even after all I'd said, Jeremiah's eyes were still locked on Darla.]

I didn't mind Ellie telling Jeremiah about me. I would have told him myself, but I didn't know how to explain it. Now that he knew, I figured things would be easier for me. It was nice of Ellie to step in. I told her thank you once we got back into the car, but I don't think she heard me, because she just looked out the window.

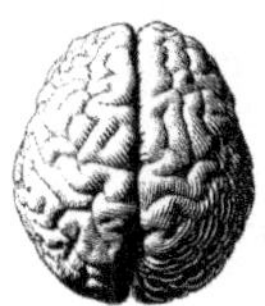

1 9 7 5

Mrs. Knowles wanted me to get more fresh air, so she'd take me outside to the backyard every day, usually in the afternoons. Sometimes she'd sit with me, reading a book, but other times she'd go inside to start dinner, or do chores, or the other things she was always doing. I appreciated Mrs. Knowles, but I wasn't desperate for her company, especially now that I was feeling more in control. My gait had improved to the point where I could walk relatively normally, but I got winded easily. I still had issues with chewing and swallowing and with keeping my mouth closed, but those were getting better, too. I could read, but only in short bursts—my eyes got tired, and if I read for too long, I would get a bad headache that would send me to bed for hours. I still couldn't write, which frustrated me, but Mrs. Knowles was still working with me.

I was in the backyard by myself, staring at an ant on a piece of grass, when someone called over to me.

"Darla? Is that you?"

I couldn't see anyone, and part of me wondered if the voice was in my head, but then the gate in the fence opened and Jeremiah walked into the yard.

"I thought I saw you," he said, smiling at me. Even though I was still full from lunch, my hunger came back, rumbling.

"Hi," I said.

Without invitation, he came over and sat in the grass next to my lawn chair. "It's pretty out here," he said.

I nodded.

We were quiet for awhile, and then he said, "So. How are you doing?"

I thought about it for a moment. "I'm fine," I said.

"Do you like being homeschooled?"

"Yes," I said, because the thought of going to school with Ellie felt impossible now. It would be too much.

"That's good," he said. He paused again, and he started fidgeting with the grass. I wanted to tell him to stop, to not disturb the ant I'd been watching, but then he said, "Look. I did some reading at the library. I found out all about… well, about… your procedure."

I stared at him.

Swallowing loudly, he said, "You know, your… lobotomy." He whispered the word as though it was a shameful secret, which I guess it was.

He looked into my eyes. "I'm so sorry that happened to you," he said, and I thought he might cry, which I found very confusing. Did he not understand that I'd wanted the surgery? That I'd have done anything to rid myself of that fear? Why was the surgery something for him to be sorry for?

Confusion built up within me, and with that came a buzzing anger, like a hive of bees. My face started getting hot, my breathing heavy, and I suddenly wanted to throw myself onto Jeremiah, ripping at him until he was as shredded as Mrs. Knowles's brisket.

Instead, the back door opened and Ellie came out.

[Scribe's note: I was immediately alarmed when I saw them. Darla's face was flushed, her bosom heaving like some Gothic heroine, and Jeremiah was just as red, crouched next to her in the grass. Of course, I assumed something was going on, or had been going on, or was about to be going on.

"Oh, hi, Jeremiah," I said.

"Hey, Ellen," he said, and I tried very hard to ignore the twinge of disappointment I detected in his voice.

"What's happening with you?" I asked.

"Oh, same old," he said. "Lots of studying. Might try out for the baseball team."

"Cool," I said. I couldn't think of a single thing to say after that, but luckily, I didn't have to. From inside the house, Mrs. Knowles called, "Darla, dear! It's time for your bath!"

Relief flooded me. Now Jeremiah could see how infantilized Darla truly was, how much care she required just to function. Being with Darla meant being her caretaker. If that couldn't kill a budding romance, what could?

"Bye," Darla said, rising from her chair. She walked crisply—when did her steps get so even?—past me and into the house.

I took her seat in the chair next to Jeremiah before he had the chance to excuse himself.

"Have a nice talk with my sister?" I asked. Despite the anger I felt, there was also a fierce protective instinct. Darla didn't understand the world of men and women, and anything that happened between her and Jeremiah would be, of course, not completely consensual. How could she consent to something she didn't understand?

"Sure," he said.

I waited for him to say more, to tell me what they'd been talking about, but he didn't. I could feel him readying himself to rise, to walk away, to go back to his house and leave me alone on the patio. The thought of yet another person abandoning me, of exploring who I was, even at the surface level, and finding me unworthy of further connection, made me feel physically ill. There had been something there at the beginning, I knew there had been— maybe I could rekindle it. I didn't have Darla's beauty, but I also didn't have her damaged brain, either.

I began to babble. "You know, I was really worried our house would never sell," I said.

Interest sparked in Jeremiah's eyes. "Why's that?"

I wanted to kick myself. What if the true story scared them off for good?

"Oh," I stammered. "Just, you know… tough market."

Jeremiah wasn't fooled. "Right," he said, smirking. "But what's the real reason?"

"It's nothing," I said.

"Yeah, right. Come on, I can tell you're not telling me the full story." He nudged my knee with his hand, and electricity flew all the way to the top of my head, turning me into putty.

"Okay, okay," I said. "This… is kind of gruesome."

Jeremiah smiled. "I can handle it."

I wasn't sure he could, but the truth was coming out of my mouth before I could stop it. Was this how Darla felt with her drool? "We lived in that house ever since I was born," I started. "And, well… after Darla's surgery, my parents weren't the same. Angry. Mean. Unhappy. And my father, well… he…" I trailed off, trying to calculate the right way to tell this story, how to be tragic enough to bring Jeremiah closer to me without being so horrifying that I scared him away.

"He what?" Jeremiah asked, but I could tell from his frown that he had an idea already what I was getting at.

"He killed himself," I said.

Jeremiah closed his eyes. "I'm so sorry," he said, shoulders slumping.

"Yeah," I said. I wasn't sorry about it, nor was I particularly sad, but he didn't need to know that.

Something occurred to him then, when I didn't continue. "And your mother? I wondered why the two of you live with the Knowleses, but I didn't want to be rude…"

Ah, of course. This time, Jeremiah would not be getting the full truth. "Mother did not take Father's death well, and with the stress of caring for Darla, she… she took her own life, as well."

"God in heaven," Jeremiah breathed, eyes squeezed shut. Was he imagining what he would do in my situation? How desperately sad he would be? "Ellen, that's awful."

"It was hard," I said, lying through my teeth. "But thank goodness, Mrs. Knowles took us in. We don't have any other family."

"Thank God for kind people in the world," he said, and when he opened his eyes, they were full of glistening tears.

"Absolutely," I said. I wanted so badly to kiss him.

"And how did Darla take it?"

My stomach soured. Why bring Darla into this moment between us?

"Oh," I said, taken aback. "To be honest, I don't think she really knew what was happening. The way her brain is now, she has trouble understanding and processing things. It's a blessing, in a way."

"Poor girl," he said. Why not 'poor you?' Why not 'poor girls,' at the very least? Was Darla more worthy of sympathy because her brain was broken? Or was it possible he was seeing something I wasn't—was he seeing Darla differently? As someone more capable, more interesting, certainly more beautiful?

Jeremiah rose from the ground. "I'd better get going," he said. He leaned over and embraced me. Even though the side-hug was awkward, it was so intoxicating, I felt the blood rush to my head. Jesus, was I really that pathetic?

When he released me, I squeaked, "Goodnight."

He smiled, and I melted into goo all over again. "Goodnight, Ellen." But then he had to ruin it all by adding, "And say goodnight to Darla for me, will you?"

I would not, but I nodded anyway.]

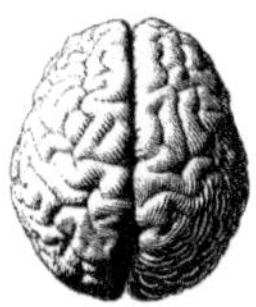

1 9 7 5

The pastor was waving his hands around, and it was making me dizzy.

"God wants us to remain pure and chaste for our eternal partners," he said. I didn't know what he meant. "God wants us to promise ourselves to our husbands, to our wives, and to keep that promise til death do us part." Next to me, Ellie was staring straight ahead, paying attention. She wasn't usually so interested, so I tried harder to make sense of the pastor's words.

"My brothers and sisters, when we feel the need to indulge our sinful urges outside of the bonds of holy matrimony, when the pull of temptation is too strong, we have to remember who is putting those thoughts in our head. It's the Devil, my friends, and we can't let the Devil win."

Could someone really put thoughts in my head that weren't mine? If that could happen, then maybe someone could put the kind of thoughts in my head that would make me better? That would make me able to write again, and to eat normally, and to understand how to behave?

"For those brothers and sisters who have not yet entered the sacred bond of marriage, remember this—God has given you one very special gift, one that you must protect at all costs. That gift is your purity, and you must keep it wrapped up tight until you wed your eternal partner. Your partner is the only proper recipient of that gift, and it is the most significant, meaningful gift you can give. If you throw away your gift on someone who doesn't deserve it, who hasn't committed to you in front of God and your congregation, then what will you have left to give your eternal partner?"

I glanced at Ellie. Her cheeks were bright red, and in her lap, her hands were squeezed into fists. Why was she so upset? Maybe she'd already given whatever that gift was to someone else?

On my other side, Mrs. Knowles was smiling, but her lips were tight, the way she got when I wasn't listening to her. Impatient— that's what it was.

"The joy of intimacy must only be shared within the bonds of an eternal and holy union," the pastor said. "Let us pray."

Everybody around me bowed their heads, so I leaned over, too, but I went too far, sending my forehead into the bench in front of me. There was a loud thunk, and then Mrs. Knowles was pulling me back, whispering into my ear. I don't know what she said; I couldn't hear anything over the pounding in my head. When everybody looked back up, I saw Jeremiah sitting with his family a few rows over. He smiled at me, and my stomach fluttered.

[Scribe's note: I never would have thought that Darla's first exposure to the idea of virginity, or of sex at all, would be at church. What was the pastor thinking, preaching that purity gospel bullshit to an audience that included teenagers and children with their families? Sure, I know he probably wanted to indoctrinate us all as young as possible, but all I felt, sitting there in that dusty pew, was fury. How dare he discuss this here, so openly, so publicly? How dare he fill Darla's head with the kind of confusion I'd been trying so hard to help her avoid? No doubt she would have questions, and she'd inevitably turn to me. If she asked Mrs. Knowles, I could anticipate the response—"Oh, dear, you see, when a man and a woman love each other very much..." But then, of course, she would come to me. I knew it was time to have that talk, probably past due, actually, but I wasn't ready. I thought the more Darla knew about sex and her body, the more dangerous she could be.

Boy, was I wrong.]

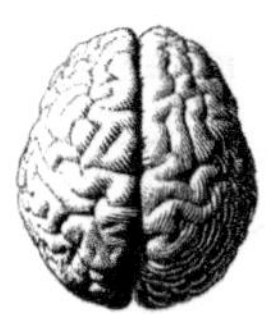

1 9 7 5

"What is my gift?" I asked Mrs. Knowles. Ellie was in her room, and we had just finished lunch. Mrs. Knowles was washing dishes, but she turned off the water when she heard me and came over to the table.

"What do you mean?" she asked, but she wasn't looking at me in my eyes.

"The gift the pastor was talking about," I said.

Mrs. Knowles frowned. "Well…" she paused, staring at the wall behind me. "Let's talk about that when you're a bit older, dear."

"But what is it?"

Mrs. Knowles went back to the sink. "When you're older," she said, and turned the water back on.

I went upstairs to Ellie's room. "What is my gift?" I said. Ellie was at her desk, her nose almost touching a big book.

"Interrupting at the worst times," she said.

"What?"

"Never mind," she said. "What do you want, Darla?"

"The pastor. What was he talking about?"

Ellie sighed. "Do you really want to do this now?"

Confusion filled my head again, and I felt myself growing angry. "Do what?"

"Fine," Ellie said, and pointed at her bed. I sat down.

"When a man and a woman really love each other…" [Scribe's note: I could feel myself falling into the same pattern of speech Mother had used with me, and what Mrs. Knowles would undoubtedly tell Darla when she was ready. I hated myself for it, but what else was I supposed to say? There was a reason those phrases were well-worn to the point of cliché——they served a purpose, exposing children to the concept of sex and marriage without explaining the nuts and bolts.]

I listened to Ellie talk about men and women sleeping in the same bed and how sometimes they could have a baby.

"I want a baby," I said, before I knew what was going to come out of my mouth. I blinked, puzzled. Was what I said really true?

"Huh," Ellie said. "Well, maybe someday. But you're too young now." [Scribe's note: In truth, I thought Darla would always be too young, never quite healthy enough to carry a child. The thought of Darla actually being pregnant, of giving birth and then having to care for an infant, appalled me to my core. It felt so… wrong, as though the clump of cells in her uterus would be taking advantage of her in the worst possible way. I'm sure that sounds evil to you, especially, but I promised to give you the complete and honest truth here, for the first and final time, so you have to accept what I give you.

Then, of course, there was the question of the mechanics of conception— something I thought Darla would never be able to fully understand or consent to. With luck, I figured I could put off the in-depth version of this conversation indefinitely. After all, who would tell Darla anything different? I had come to realize, over the past few months—ever since Mother's death, really—that Darla would be unable to recover completely. As much as I had hoped and pleaded in the beginning for a return to normalcy, I now accepted that such a miracle would never occur. Once I accepted that, I began to believe that just because Darla couldn't recover fully, she couldn't recover in any sort of meaningful way at all. It was a fallacy Mother and

Father had both fallen into, and now, looking back, I can see my mistake as clear as day. I want to yell at my teenage self to open your damned eyes, but what they say about hindsight is true.]

I was quiet. The more I thought about it, the more I was sure I wanted a baby. I didn't know why, but I felt the pull. It went hand in hand with that strange hunger, like they were meant for each other.

"Everything good?" Ellie asked me.

I nodded. I didn't tell Ellie about the strange hunger, and I didn't ask either her or Mrs. Knowles again about my gift.

But I did ask someone else.

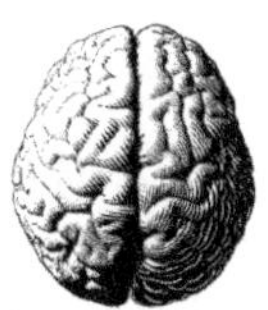

1 9 7 5

Jeremiah had started coming over every afternoon and sitting with me in the backyard before Ellie got home. The days were warmer, but the hours were feeling shorter and shorter, and it started to seem like he'd just sat down when Ellie would pop through the door. [Scribe's note: She's not wrong. Once I realized Jeremiah intended to make his visits with Darla a regular thing, I tried to get home earlier and earlier from school. I stopped lingering in the library, I stopped walking leisurely on the sidewalk. I hightailed it straight home, often arriving back sweaty and thirsty, but that was preferable to permitting Darla so many private moments with the boy I couldn't stop thinking about.]

"Do you believe what the pastor said?" I asked.

He tilted his head. "About what?"

"About my gift."

His cheeks turned red, like Ellie's always did when she got home from school and joined us. "Oh," he said, so softly I could barely hear him.

I stayed quiet, waiting for him to answer my question. Why was everyone so scared to talk to me about this?

I thought he wasn't going to answer me, but then he grabbed my hand, squeezing my fingers. There was pain, but it wasn't unpleasant. "No," he said, his voice shaky. "I don't believe what the pastor said."

"No?" I repeated, and my stomach started to rumble in that strange way.

"No," he said again, still squeezing my hand. "I think... when two people like each other... it's okay to do what feels right."

"Oh," I said, echoing him.

His hand stopped squeezing, then his fingers ran up my arm to my elbow. His other hand rested on my knee.

"Does this feel right?" he asked, and one hand started inching up my leg while the other moved toward my chest.

I felt paralyzed. My mouth was hanging open, and I could feel the spit pooling on my tongue, but I couldn't make myself close it. I wanted to yell at him to stop, but I also started to feel that full feeling that only came from being with Jeremiah. The mix of feelings was so uncomfortable, and I didn't know how to say anything, and then he was leaning in closer to me, his lips just a few spaces away from my open mouth—

The door banged open, and Ellie yelled, "Hey!" She didn't sound angry, but Jeremiah fell back to the grass as though I'd slapped him.

"Ellen," he said, his lips all wiggly.

"What are you two talking about?" she said, sitting down at my feet, next to Jeremiah.

"Nothing," he mumbled.

I finally managed to close my mouth and swallow. Everything was upside down, but that, in itself, was progress, and I smiled.

[Scribe's note: Sure, of course I saw it. Jeremiah crouched over Darla, his hands all over her body, his face getting far too close to hers. I didn't want to scare him off, per se, but I did want him to stop. When I got out there, he looked like a quivering mess of man-jelly, and Darla was grinning like an idiot. Nobody's clothes were rumpled, but they certainly looked like they'd been engaged in something heated, something neither of them needed to— or should— be doing. Don't get me wrong, I'm no prude, but what Jeremiah was doing wasn't right. Can't you see that? Am I the only one?]

"Hi," I said to Ellie.

"Darla, I think it's time for your bath," she said.

I wanted to argue, to stay with Jeremiah longer, but he wasn't looking at me anymore, and things felt different. My stomach went all sour, and I got up and walked inside the house.

[Scribe's note: Part of me wondered if Darla was pleased to be in this situation. Was she, perhaps, a little bit devious? A little bit fast? Her surgery changed her personality, there could be no argument about that, but I was still trying to figure out what those changes were. She was so young when she had the lobotomy—she hadn't even become herself yet. At that time, it remained to be seen what kind of person she would grow into.]

Upstairs, Mrs. Knowles had already run the bath. I got in, and the water was so hot, I could hardly breathe. I didn't mean to, but I started thrashing, and Mrs. Knowles had to yell at me to calm down. She threw a cup of cold water from the sink in my face, and then I felt my body go limp. Water was everywhere in the bathroom—on the tiles, on the wallpapered walls, on the toilet, splattering the mirror. It was even in Mrs. Knowles's hair, and she had a black streak running down her cheek from her eye.

"Darla," she said, squinting at me. "We can't be having outbursts like that."

"We?" I said. Was she talking about how she'd been yelling?

She sighed. "What I mean to say is, dear, you can't be flailing like that in the bath. Look at this room. You've gotten water everywhere."

"Oh," I said. Was it bad to get water places? Even in the bathroom?

Mrs. Knowles leaned forward and grabbed the bar of soap. She rubbed it on my shoulders, working up the bubbles, but she handed it to me to do the rest of my body. It slipped out of my hands and bobbed in the water.

"You're old enough to do this yourself, dear," she said, but her face was all pinched, like she had a stomachache.

"Oh," I said again, and I tried to grab for the soap, but every time I did, my arm fell into the water, making another splash, and sending the bar of soap farther away from me.

Mrs. Knowles stood up. "I'll leave you be," she said. "Call for me when you're ready."

She left the bathroom, but the door stayed open. The water calmed, and I slid down into the now comfortable warmth. The bar of soap floated past my face, but I didn't try to grab it this time.

As I lay there, soaking, a new thought hit me for the first time. *What kind of life is this?*

When I was in our old house, with nothing changing, the sameness felt comfortable. It felt safe. Now, with Mrs. Knowles, with my new room and my new neighbor and my new feelings, I wanted more new things. I wanted to be... what was it, exactly?

Ah, yes. I wanted to be normal. And I was ready to do anything to get there.

[Scribe's note: Jeremiah started fidgeting with the hem of his collared shirt as soon as Darla closed the door behind her. I felt our time shortening, moving past the point of doneness, like an overcooked chicken.

"You know—"

Just then, a commotion from the upstairs bathroom drifted our way. I looked at Jeremiah, and we both listened to the sounds of thumping and yelling.

"Is everything okay?" he asked.

I didn't know, but whatever it was, I was certain Mrs. Knowles could handle it.

"I'm sure," I said. "Darla still needs help bathing, you know."

I intended for the remark to conjure images of an enfeebled, needy girl, but by the look on Jeremiah's face, I could tell I'd miscalculated. He was likely thinking of Darla naked, and of himself helping her, rubbing soap onto her skin.

"I'm so glad you moved in next door," I said, racing to get the salacious image out of his mind. I'd worn makeup that day, and my blemishes were barely visible. Maybe I could get him to see me the way he had that first day, before he'd met Darla.

Jeremiah shook his head, as if pulling himself from a trance. He looked at me, but his eyes were still unfocused. "Yeah, me too," he said.

The conversation was floundering, I could feel it. If I, with my fully functioning brain, couldn't keep things lively, what in the world did he talk to Darla about? Or, I thought, perhaps they didn't do too much talking. The back of my neck grew hot.

"When Darla first had the surgery, she couldn't even use the bathroom on her own," I blabbed, and then I waited for the pang of instant regret. It didn't come.

Jeremiah wrinkled his nose, and satisfaction laid a cooling hand on my neck. "Really?"

"Really," I said, leaning closer to him. "She was pretty much an invalid. I had to help her walk, relearn how to talk, wash her, brush her teeth… well, everything, really. She still needs help, even now." I didn't want to tell him about the progress she'd made, about how she could brush her own teeth now, more or less, about how much better her speech had gotten, about how she could walk on her own, completely unassisted, although not very far.

"Huh," Jeremiah said. "Will she… I mean, do you think she might…"

He looked at me expectantly. "Recover?" I asked.

"Yeah," he said.

Even though I'd spent the past few years wishing for nothing more than Darla's full recovery, even though I'd cried countless times when Darla failed to progress, even though I still wished for her to be able to take care of herself one day, I told Jeremiah the truth.

"No," I said. I didn't want to think about Darla anymore, and whether she would get better. It was time for me to focus on myself, on what I needed and wanted out of life. If Darla couldn't live the way she wanted to, then I would live for her. At least, that's what I told myself.

"Huh," Jeremiah said again, but he didn't sound convinced.

"It's just… it's not easy to get over brain surgery," I said, irritation creeping into my voice. "They scrambled things around in there, and it can't just get fixed with stitches or medicine. Or even time."

"Right," he said.

Before I could say anything else, he slapped his knees and pushed to standing. "I've got to get home for dinner," he said. "See you later, Ellen."

He left me sitting in the lawn chair. I stayed there for a long time, until the light was leaving the sky and Mrs. Knowles finally called me in for my own dinner.]

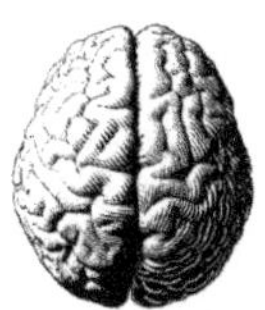

1 9 7 5

Summer came and went, Ellie studied, I sat outside. The weather got colder, Ellie went back to school, and I stopped sitting outside as much. Mrs. Knowles would take me on walks instead, bundling me into her old winter coat and holding my arm as we went around the neighborhood. Sometimes she talked, and I listened, but sometimes we just walked in silence, listening to the leaves crunch under our feet. Every now and then, a neighbor would be out mowing their lawn or getting their mail, and Mrs. Knowles would stop and chat with them. They always said hi to me, and I would say hi back, but I didn't feel like talking. If I was going to get better, I needed to do more listening, more watching. I needed to remember how to be a person that could be around other people not just some of the time, but all of the time.

One afternoon, Jeremiah knocked on the door. Mrs. Knowles answered, and then she called for me.

"Jeremiah has asked if you'd like to take a walk with him," she said.

My stomach rumbled. I'd walk with him anywhere. "Yes," I said.

They both smiled, and then Mrs. Knowles was grabbing my coat.

"Let me," Jeremiah said, and he pulled the sleeves over my arms, then zipped everything up tight. "Comfortable?" he asked.

"Yes," I said again.

"Have her back by four o'clock, dear," Mrs. Knowles called after us as we headed down the sidewalk.

"Yes, ma'am," Jeremiah said.

He was quiet for awhile, and then he started talking. Once he started, it was like he couldn't stop. "I've missed you a lot, Darla," he said. "I know it's too cold to sit in the backyard anymore, and I've really missed talking with you. I mean, I know your sister thinks you can't do much, but I think you can, I really do. When you look at me, it's like you really see me, you know what I mean?" He didn't wait for me to answer. "Nobody really sees me, not my mom, not my dad, definitely not my sister. Not even my teachers or the kids at school. Dad wants me to be an accountant, like him, but I'm terrible at math. I want to be a sculptor, like Michelangelo. Mom is always telling Dad to go easy on me, and then he'll say how can she expect me to grow up to be a man who can provide for his family if they're too soft on me. Then my sister will butt in and call me stupid, which makes both of my parents yell at her, and then she's crying, and then it's all a mess. Everybody looks at us and thinks we have this perfect family. I can tell—everybody at school, at church, in this neighborhood, you all think we have nothing to complain about, but you're all wrong. I know you understand that, Darla. You're the same way—people look at you and think you're one thing, or only able to do a few things, but they're all wrong. Nobody knows what's going on inside you, just like nobody knows what's going on inside me. Nobody except you, I guess."

Jeremiah paused, breathing hard. We hadn't walked very far. Was he really out of breath already? I still felt fine, and I was the one who usually fatigued easily.

He caught his breath and kept going. "What I'm saying, Darla, is that you're the best friend I've got. And..." That heavy breathing again. Was he alright? "And... maybe more than a friend?"

More than a friend? What did that mean?

I stopped walking and turned to look at him. I wished Ellie were there with us. She would have known what he meant, would have known what to do.

Before I could say anything, Jeremiah leaned closer to me, and then his mouth was on my mouth. His hands grabbed my shoulders, pulling me into him. His lips were cold and wet, and they made me think of the leftover salmon Mrs. Knowles gave me for lunch on Saturdays, after the last night's fish dinner. She told me she read in *Ladies' Home Journal* that salmon was really good for you, and so it would help me get stronger, would make my brain work better. I liked it hot, but when it was cold, it always made me feel sick. I ate it anyway.

Jeremiah's lips felt a bit like that. I didn't really like the way they pressed into me, but I stayed there anyway. His hands starting rubbing my back, and then his tongue poked into my mouth. At least his tongue was warm, but it was wetter than his lips, and I could taste the potato chips he'd eaten earlier.

Then it was over. Jeremiah let me go.

"Was that… was that okay?" he asked.

I nodded, and his entire face relaxed.

"I better get you home now," he said. We were quiet the rest of the way back, Jeremiah squeezing my hand like I might run away if he didn't hold on tight enough. When we got to Mrs. Knowles's house, he pressed his mouth to mine again, but this time it was much shorter.

"I'll see you tomorrow," he said. He stayed on the sidewalk until I was inside the house.

"Where have you been?" Ellie asked. She was sitting on the couch, a book in her lap. It was strange seeing her in the living room. I was so used to her holing up in her bedroom, bent over her desk.

"On a walk," I said.

"By yourself?"

"With Jeremiah," I said.

She pressed her mouth into a tiny line, and I wondered if I should do that the next time Jeremiah kissed me. Was that how it was supposed to be?

"Oh," she said.

"He kissed me," I said, wanting to see Ellie's reaction. Could she help me make sense of everything? Could she tell me what to do?

[Scribe's note: I'd known Darla was with Jeremiah. It was the first thing Mrs. Knowles told me when I walked inside and started heading for the back door. Anger flared up in me. I'd thought the colder weather would put an end to their little visits, but clearly, I'd been wrong. I wanted to punch through the sliding glass door. How could Mrs. Knowles be so stupid? How could she let Darla go off on her own with a boy?

Part of me had wanted to run right back out the front door and go find them, but I didn't. Jeremiah had acted so distant, so cold, when I'd run Darla off before, and I couldn't face it again. Instead, I sat on the couch, staring at the front door. I waited, reading and rereading the same sentence in my history textbook until, finally, the door opened, and Darla stomped in.

When she told me about the kiss, I felt a physical pain in my chest, like the wind had been knocked out of me. I was thrown back into *Go Ask Alice*, remembering Anonymous's kiss with her longtime crush, Roger. She'd gone on and on about how significant it was, how beautiful and life-affirming and magical, and, at the time, I'd thought she was being dramatic to the point of histrionic.

I understood it now. I'd been correct before: that brush of the lips held far too much power—both to lift up, and, in my case, to destroy.

Darla was looking at me, waiting.

"What?" I said.

"He kissed me," she said again, and it almost felt like gloating. *He picked me over you. He likes me more than you.*

"Great," I said.

Darla just stood there. She was probably waiting for me to help her get her coat off. I closed my textbook and stood, then I left the room. If she needed her coat off, she could do it herself. Or she could just roast. I didn't much care.]

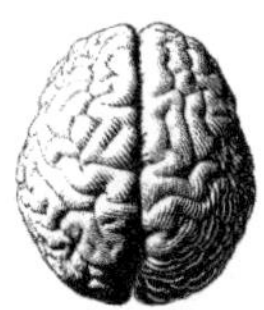

1 9 7 5

[Scribe's note: I caught Jeremiah on the way home from school the next day. He was just about to turn into his house when I tapped him on the shoulder. He jumped, and when he turned to face me, he smiled, but it was the sort of smile you reserve for someone else's small child. It said, *I'm being polite, but I really don't want to talk to you.*

Too bad. We were going to talk.

"Can we take a quick walk?" I asked.

Jeremiah glanced at his house, then back at me. "I really should get home…"

"This will only take a minute," I said.

"Okay," he said, and we continued down the sidewalk. As we passed Mrs. Knowles's, Jeremiah sucked in a breath.

"So," I said, crossing my arms into my chest. "Darla told me what happened yesterday."

I could feel Jeremiah stiffen next to me, could hear the hitch in his step.

"What do you mean?" he said.

Fine. He was going to lie about it, was he? That was okay with me. I leaned into the anger, hoping it would obliterate all of the hurt, the pain, the anguish.

"You kissed my sister," I said.

He cleared his throat. The sound was phlegmy, like he might be getting a cold. He better not have passed that to Darla—that was not something I wanted to deal with, cleaning up her mucus-filled drool and watching snot stream down her upper lip at the dinner table. It had happened before.

"Yeah," he said at last. "I... I did."

"And?" I asked.

"And what?"

"You know she's two years younger than us, right?"

Jeremiah shrugged. "My mom is four years younger than my dad."

His nonchalance enraged me even further. "Did your mom also have part of her brain ripped out?" That wasn't a completely accurate depiction of the lobotomy, but I didn't care.

"Dear God," Jeremiah said. Then, quieter, "No."

"I didn't think so," I said, thinking that was that.

"But there's nothing wrong with Darla," he said.

I couldn't help it—I laughed. "Are you kidding me?" I said. "She's permanently brain damaged, Jeremiah. She can't make decisions for herself. You don't know her!"

Jeremiah seemed unfazed. "I know her well enough."

I snorted. "How could you possible know her well enough?"

"I know her heart," he said self-righteously. "She has a good heart, Ellen."

I didn't give two hoots about that, I'll be honest with you. "That doesn't change anything," I said.

"It changes everything," he said.

The anger inside me was raging, roaring, demanding to escape the confines of my body. This was not how things were supposed to go. Jeremiah was supposed to be my friend. He was supposed to be interested in me. He was supposed to be the shoulder I needed to lean on. How could things have gotten so twisted?

"Darla listens," he said, and something clicked inside me. Of course that's what it was.

I thought about Mother and Father, about how they'd both been sold a bill of goods that was rotten—marry this person and you'll be set for life; have this many children and you'll be accepted; buy this house and you'll live happily ever after. Had Jeremiah absorbed those same sorts of messages about what life was, about what women were like? I could understand it, even if I hated it. In many ways, Darla was the perfect woman, a welcome side effect of her lobotomy. Besides being beautiful, she was, for the most part, docile, obedient, complacent, pleasant. She knew her place. She was quiet, which Jeremiah had probably mistaken for being an avid, rapt listener to whatever spilled out of his mouth, when it wasn't pushed up against hers, that is.

I would never be good enough for him, and there wasn't a damn thing I could do about it (without getting my own lobotomy, of course). In a way, these thoughts almost abated my guilt over Darla's surgery in the first place. Maybe she was better off, if somebody like Jeremiah wanted her so badly.

We'd reached the end of the street, and I turned back around. Jeremiah followed. I walked quicker, but he kept pace with me.

"Ellen?" he said. I didn't want to answer him. I was done. If his expectations of a woman were met by Darla, then I would never satisfy him.

We reached Mrs. Knowles's house.

"You better not hurt her," I said, and then I opened the door.

"I would never do that—"

I slammed the door in his face. When the sound finished echoing, I realized something.

I'd forgiven myself for what happened to Darla. And that felt far better than Jeremiah's clumsy kisses ever could.]

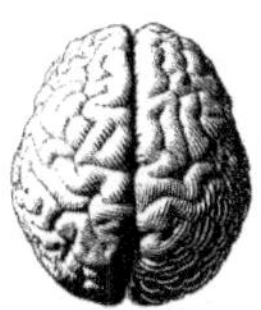

1 9 7 5

"I see you've been spending quite a bit of time with Jeremiah," Mrs. Knowles said as she handed me my plate. She'd made a macaroni casserole the night before, and she'd reheated leftovers for my lunch. It had looked much better the night before, and I told her so.

"Don't be rude, dear," Mrs. Knowles said. "Plenty of children in the world starve. They would love to have food like this."

Was it rude to tell her the truth? I shrugged and started eating, Mrs. Knowles standing near me to help. Would I ever understand the right way to behave? The right way to act? The right way to be?

"Do you like him?" Mrs. Knowles asked.

When I answered "Yes," a glop of casserole fell out of my mouth and onto my lap. It landed in my napkin, but I could still feel the wet warmth of it on my legs.

"Oh, dear," Mrs. Knowles said, but I didn't know if she was talking about the food or how I felt about Jeremiah.

She was quiet a moment, then she said, "Darla, dear, I know we've talked about this before, but you understand how important it is to save yourself, don't you?"

I stopped eating. What was she talking about? Save myself from what?

When I didn't answer, she kept talking. "Pastor Sable talked about our one and only gift as women? Don't you remember?"

I nodded. I didn't understand, but I remembered.

"Well, it's especially important to keep your gift safe now that… that there's a boy," she said.

Was he going to steal something from me?

She kept going. "Don't get me wrong, Darla, dear, Jeremiah Fannin is a lovely boy. Smart, family-oriented, with a strong faith. But even boys like that can give in to temptation. It's our job, as women, to protect ourselves and the boys from that temptation."

I still didn't have much idea of what she was talking about, but I nodded anyway. When she smiled, I figured I'd done the right thing.

But then her eyebrows met in the middle, and she was frowning. "And…" she sighed. "I don't know how to say this, so I'm just going to get it out. With your… condition… it would probably be unwise to engage with boys. At least for right now. Who knows what will happen in the future? But, dear, I'm terrified they're going to take advantage of you."

"Okay," I said, memorizing her words so I could think about them more later.

The smile was back, and she patted me on the shoulder. "Just remember, dear, to hold on tight to your gift. If, one day…" Her eyes got that glittery look, but she was still smiling. She cleared her throat. "If you're ready one day to get married, your husband will want to know you've remained chaste and pure. It's worth saving, Darla."

I tucked that into my mind with the other words, then I picked up my fork and continued eating. The casserole was cold now.

[Scribe's note: I found Mrs. Knowles in the kitchen after dinner, wiping down the counters. She was always doing that—wiping the counters, mopping the floor, vacuuming the rug, scrubbing the baseboards, dusting the windowsills, even when the house was immaculate. I suppose it made her feel useful, that she was in motion, instead of in the sort of middle-aged stasis I've seen on the faces of so many biopsy and cardiovascular patients over the years.

"Mrs. Knowles?" I asked, taking a seat in Darla's usual chair.

She let out an "Eek!" and whipped around, her hand flying to her chest. "My goodness, dear, you startled me!"

"Sorry," I mumbled. I hadn't tried to scare her.

"It's alright," she said, dropping her rag on the counter and turning to face me fully. "What's going on, Ellen?"

This was going to be a difficult conversation, to say the least, and I wanted it to be over as quickly as possible so I could get back to my room to study for my English test the next day. "Jeremiah likes Darla," I said.

"I know," she said, sighing.

"Did you know he kissed her?"

Mrs. Knowles's eyebrows shot up into her thinning dust-brown hair, which was pulled back into a sensible bun. "No, I did not know that."

"Well, he did," I said. "Darla told me so, and I believe her. I even had a talk with Jeremiah myself."

"What did you say to him?" Mrs. Knowles drifted over to the table and took the seat opposite me. She smelled of lemon and vinegar, and underneath that, something meaty.

"I told him I knew what he'd done, and that he better not hurt my sister," I said.

Mrs. Knowles's mouth twisted into a knot. "And?"

"He said he would never hurt her."

She nodded, then sat back in her chair, processing.

"I tried to tell him Darla wasn't mentally capable of a relationship," I went on. "And besides that, she's two years younger than us."

"Mhmm," Mrs. Knowles murmured.

"He didn't care. He said she has a good heart, and that's enough."

Mrs. Knowles scoffed. "Sure," she said. "I've heard that before—'love is enough,' 'love is all you need.' Especially with young people, all of you seem to think love will solve all your problems." She swallowed so loudly

I thought she might be choking. I had the feeling we weren't talking about Darla anymore. "Love is wonderful, of course, but it's not glue. It can't stick two people together forever. It can't put food on the table, or buy school supplies for the children, or mow the lawn when it's supposed to. And it's not permanent, either, Ellen. Don't you forget that."

This sounded nothing like the Mrs. Knowles I knew. I thought of Father, ending his life in our dingy garage, leaving his body for me to find. I thought of Mother, descending into the madness of booze and pills and depression, trying to smother the life out of the daughter she'd had a hand in incapacitating. If anybody needed a lesson about the impermanence of love, it certainly wasn't me.

I didn't tell Mrs. Knowles any of that. "I won't," I said.

I wished I could have ended the conversation there, but I had more I needed to say.

"Mrs. Knowles," I started. "If Jeremiah wants to… take things further with Darla, I don't think she'll be able to stop him. Or want to stop him, for that matter."

"I was concerned about the same thing," she said, wiping her eyes with the hem of her apron, which proclaimed 'World's Best Mom' in bold capital letters. I wondered if she also had a 'World's Best Wife' apron somewhere.

"I think… I know some of the girls at school are on the Pill, and I think we should maybe think about that for Darla?" I said, holding my breath, awaiting her response.

She blanched. "Absolutely not," she said.

"W-what?" I stammered.

"Ellen, dear, the Pill is for loose girls. For ones without a strong faith, a strong family, a strong community. Darla has all of those things now. She can be a nice girl, dear, just like you. You don't want to go on the Pill, do you?"

As with the conversation about my church attendance, I knew there was only one right answer to her question. So, as much as I didn't want to, I gave it. "No," I said softly.

"I didn't think so. Besides," she added, "I already took care of it."

"You did?"

She wouldn't meet my eyes. "I spoke with Darla," she said. "I told her to remember Pastor Sable's sermon, about how, as women, we must save ourselves for marriage, protect our gift."

I wanted to roll my eyes, to call her naive and idiotic, but I didn't. "Right."

"I think I really got through to her," she said, tucking a few stray hairs back into her bun.

"Right," I said again.

"Don't get mouthy with me," she said.

"I'm not," I said. "I'm just… I'm just worried about my sister, is all."

"Well, don't," she said, standing up. There was a smear of red sauce over the 'Mom' part of her apron. "Darla has me now, and I'm going to take care of her," she said.

I wanted so badly to ask her if she'd take care of Darla's accidental baby if it came to that, but I didn't. She'd made her feelings clear, and she was the one in the position of power. Maybe she believed someone like Darla couldn't get pregnant. Hell, maybe she couldn't—I didn't know enough at the time to have any idea.

"Thank you," I said, through gritted teeth. I appreciated Mrs. Knowles, was beyond grateful for her ministrations, the way she stepped up and took us in, but I resented her authority, the way she pushed her will onto us with an iron fist.

Then again, I reminded myself as I retreated back to my room, I would be eighteen soon.

I could be free.]

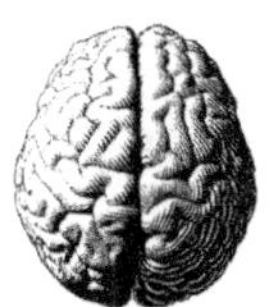

1 9 7 6

Jeremiah held my hand too tight as we walked. When I tried to pull my hand back, he squeezed tighter. "I've got you," he said.

It was still cold, but not so cold that we needed big puffy coats. Jeremiah was so close to me, it was almost hard to walk. I'd gotten much better with moving around, but my balance could still be off sometimes.

The bump in the sidewalk came out of nowhere, and then I was falling forward—but before I could hit the ground, there were two arms around my middle, just under my chest, and then Jeremiah was pulling me back up to standing.

"Whoa, there!" he said. He laughed. "Got to be careful, huh?"

I hated that he laughed at me. I hated that he never let me have my own space. I hated that he squeezed too tight and kissed too long and treated me like I would break if he weren't there to keep all my pieces together.

"I was," I said, finally yanking my hand out of his.

"Hey, Darla," he said. "What's wrong?"

How to tell him how much he was bothering me? How much I wanted to push him away, but at the same time, I wanted him to be closer to me? These feelings were so confusing, and they always ended up just making me angry. I didn't know how to tell Jeremiah all of that, so I said, "Nothing."

I expected him to lean closer, maybe grab my chin, and ask me no, really, what's wrong? That's what Ellie or even Mrs. Knowles would have done. But he didn't.

"So, I think Mr. Crimpton has it out for me," he said. "I mean, it's just eleventh grade math class, but the man acts like every test, every single problem, is life or death. It's like he's taking lessons from my dad in how to torture me."

What was math class like? I wanted to ask. Is it easy to make friends? Do you still have to raise your hand like we did in primary school?

"Seriously, Darla, I think Mr. Crimpton is just waiting for me to fail. He gave Ace Tucker an A on his test, but he gave me a C because I didn't 'show my work,' but I know Ace and I had the same answers! How is that fair?"

We came to the end of the street, and as I started to turn, Jeremiah pulled me closer to him. I knew what was coming—the sweaty smell of his hair, the cheesy taste of his tongue, the cold press of his wet lips. I closed my eyes.

He didn't kiss me. Instead, he said, "Darla, you don't have to be afraid of me."

I opened my eyes. "I'm not," I said. Just annoyed. Just angry. Just confused.

"I want you to know I'm waiting until marriage," he said.

There it was again—the waiting. The marriage. Why did he care? Only women had gifts we had to protect. Right?

"Okay," I said.

"I'm not going to force you into anything," he said.

And then he pushed his lips onto mine, slipped his tongue into my mouth, and made me taste what he'd had for lunch that day. From what I could tell, Mrs. Fannin was a terrible cook.

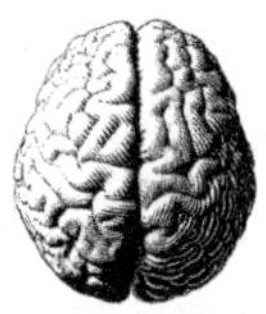

1 9 7 6 - 1 9 7 7

Summer came and it got hotter and Jeremiah and I sat in the backyard again. He was always touching me. A foot wiggling on mine, a finger rubbing the back of my hand, a hip bone nudging into my stomach. Did all boys do this? Were girls supposed to like this?

The week before Jeremiah went back to school for his last year, he took my face in his sweaty hands and said, "Darla, this is real, okay?"

Even though we were under an umbrella in the backyard, it was too hot, and too humid, and I wanted his hands off of my face. "What?" I said, trying to shake his fingers off.

He held me harder. "You and me, Darla. Us. Together. It's real, and I don't want you to think I'm going to leave you, even when I go to college next year."

I didn't know exactly what he was talking about. He was always speaking in riddles, and sometimes it gave me a headache. Most of the time, I just nodded and let him think I understood. That seemed to make him happy, which would make him let go of me for a little while.

"Okay," I said, nodding. He finally pulled his hands away, leaving wet patches on my cheeks.

[Scribe's note: I spent my summer taking extra classes at the community college. It was just a short bus ride away, and those classes would look good on my college applications. I had pulled myself up from academic despair over the course of my high school career, and I wasn't going to trip at the finish line. I didn't want to go to just any school. I wanted to go to the best. I wanted a life completely different from the one I'd been living, which meant I needed to work harder, be smarter, and outlast everyone else around me. With Mrs. Knowles taking care of Darla, I felt comfortable focusing on my studies instead of on my sister. I rarely saw her that summer, with the exception of a single glimpse through the back window of her and Jeremiah on the lawn, cuddling. At first, the sight made me dry heave. As the summer waned, I felt nothing. Mrs. Knowles had told me she'd taken care of the potential pregnancy problem, and I didn't have the mental bandwidth to worry about it anymore. Let Darla have her connection with Jeremiah. I figured it would be the only one she'd ever have in her life.]

Then Jeremiah started back to school, and instead of him coming over before lunch and sometimes after lunch, too, he just came over for awhile before dinner. That suited me just fine. With Mrs. Knowles, I was getting even better at reading, and I could chew chicken without my mouth falling open and spilling food on my lap. I still couldn't hold a pencil well enough to write, but Mrs. Knowles walked with me around the neighborhood, and most of the time, I could go the entire walk without needing to stop and catch my breath. Without Jeremiah talking to me all the time, I could hear some of my own thoughts. I felt like I was starting to wake up again after being asleep for far too long.

[Scribe's note: My senior year began with Carla Romano stuffing dead fish into my locker, then spreading the rumor that my locker smelled the same as my... well. I'm sure you can figure it out. The janitor helped me clean and disinfect everything, but the smell never completely went away. I stopped storing my textbooks in my locker, and instead started carrying everything I needed in my book bag. Every day, I came home stooped, my shoulders and lower back aching so much I had to use a heating pad to relieve the pain enough that I could get some sleep. Those high school assholes were cruel, but I turned my attention to my studies and found solace, as I always had. I had something Carla Romano and Gina Fletcher and Trudy Winthrop and all those other girls and their sniveling, oafish boyfriends didn't have: intelligence. Work ethic. Drive. Ambition.

My senior year passed in much the same way my summer had—I put my nose down, worked hard, applied to five of the very best colleges I could find, along with one safety (life had taught me nothing if not the need for a backup plan), and waited. I even prayed a bit, just to see if it worked or if Mrs. Knowles and Pastor Sable were full of shit. I think you can guess how that turned out.

When I felt worried, or stressed more than usual, or anxious, I just worked harder. Studied longer. Read more. At night, when I closed my eyes, I counted variables in calculus equations instead of sheep.

Eventually, all of my hard work paid off.]

Ellie never came home early anymore. [Scribe's note: I had no interest in seeing the nauseating spectacle of Darla and Jeremiah's young love any more than I absolutely had to.] So, when she came home one day before Jeremiah, even, Mrs. Knowles said, "Ellen! You're home early!"

Ellie said "Hi," to us both, really quick, then she went into the living room. She had that heavy book bag on, but her hands were full of long pieces of paper.

"Ellen, dear? Is that the mail?" Mrs. Knowles asked, following Ellie from the kitchen.

"Yes!" Ellie said, and I got up and followed, too.

Ellie was sitting on the couch when I caught up, and Mrs. Knowles was standing over her.

"Dear, is that…?" she asked.

"Yes!" Ellie said again. I didn't know what they were talking about, but if Ellie was excited, I was, too.

Ellie grabbed one of the pieces of paper—I realized it was an envelope—and ripped it very slowly on one side. She pulled out a piece of paper and stared at it. She smiled, and then she said, "I got in!"

Mrs. Knowles squealed. "To where, dear? To where?"

"To UVA." Ellie said, and Mrs. Knowles started breathing really hard.

"Incredible, dear!" she said.

"It's just a safety," Ellie said.

"Still, dear, that's quite an accomplishment! Open the rest, open the rest!"

I'd heard Jeremiah talk about colleges, but he hadn't gotten any letters yet. I wondered if his would come in the mail today, too. I was sure I'd hear about it if they did.

Ellie opened another envelope. Her smile broke and melted. She was quiet for awhile before she said, "It's a no from Yale."

"That's okay, dear, really," Mrs. Knowles said. "Keep going."

Ellie ripped open a third, a fourth, and a fifth envelope. "No from Brown." "No from Cornell." "No from Columbia."

Her eyes were looking all glittery, and I knew what that meant. She held one more envelope in her hand, and she looked more terrified than I'd ever seen her.

"Go on," Mrs. Knowles whispered.

Ellie's hands were shaking, and she almost ripped the envelope right down the middle.

"Do you want me to do it?" Mrs. Knowles asked.

"No," Ellie said, swallowing. "I can do this."

She got a fingernail at the edge of the envelope and ripped it open gently. She inched out the piece of paper inside so steadily, I wondered if something was wrong with my brain and I was seeing things in slow motion.

Finally, when the paper was out, Ellie took her time unfolding it. My palms were sweaty, and Mrs. Knowles's hands were fisted together at her chest.

Ellie read the paper. The look on her face was like nothing I'd ever seen before, even when Ma and Pa died. She looked like the entire world was falling to pieces around her.

"Dear—" Mrs. Knowles said, but she didn't get to finish, because Ellie threw the paper on the ground and ran out of the room. Mrs. Knowles started after her. I stayed and picked up the paper.

"To Ellen Gregory, after careful consid— consid— consideration of your app—appli—application, I regret to inform you that we are unable to offer you ad—admish—admission to Harvard University's class of 1981…"

I couldn't pronounce all of the words, but I figured Ellie didn't get in to that school. Why was she so sad, though? She got in somewhere else.

I dropped the paper on the coffee table with the other letters and went back to the kitchen to finish my glass of milk.

[Scribe's note: Darla was right. I felt worse about the Harvard rejection than the deaths of my own parents. What else could I have done? I'd worked so hard, eschewed friendships, extracurriculars, dating, clubs, hobbies, even family… and what did I have to show for it?

"There's still UVA, dear," Mrs. Knowles said, entering my room, where I'd fled.

I didn't want her comfort. I didn't deserve it.

Mrs. Knowles started rubbing my back, and part of me wanted to tell her to fuck off, but another part of me desperately craved that physical touch, the comforting warmth of a mother figure. My own mother had abandoned her role years before, and I hadn't realized how much I'd needed somebody to bear witness to my vulnerability without rejecting me.

"Ellen?" Mrs. Knowles said, and now she sounded scared.

"What?" I said through snot and tears, my voice thick.

"Well, dear… do you know if…"

She was beating around some sort of bush, and I was not in the mood.

"What?" I snapped.

"Are they offering you a scholarship, dear?"

I'd only read the first line of the letter, the part where they congratulated me on my acceptance. I hadn't read the rest, so a scholarship wasn't completely out of the question.

"I don't know," I said flatly.

"It's just… and I hate to bring it up at a time like this, but we need to face the harsh realities of the world. How will you pay for this, dear?"

The illusion of motherhood vanished immediately, as though someone had flipped on a light switch in a dark room, sending all the shadows scurrying away to the cobwebby corners. She didn't say 'How will *we* pay for this,' she said 'How will *you* pay for this.' It was a stark reminder that I was not, nor would I ever be, her biological child. As a result, she felt no financial responsibility for me. She just needed me to reach eighteen, and then Darla would be her only burden.

"I'll figure it out," I mumbled, trying to hold back a fresh wave of tears. I felt out of control, powerless, and I hated it.

"Alright," she said, removing her hand from my back. Had the room always felt so cold?

Mercifully, she didn't say anything else, just left the room and allowed me to be alone, to grieve the loss of five potential futures that died with each new slit of an envelope.

The University of Virginia was barely an hour away from Richmond. Would I really feel like I was escaping, or would it feel like an extension of the home I was so eager to leave?

And what if I didn't go at all? What if I rejected those rejections, and said no to college altogether. What then? My only remaining option would be to stay in Richmond, near Darla. I'd get a useless job with no opportunity for advancement, I'd probably shack up with some worthless idiot just for the company, have a few bratty kids… Jesus, I'd have to buy in to the whole lie Mother and Father had been sold, about how papering over your anguish with what society expects from you—marriage, children, the house, the fence, the dog—would make you better, worthy. Happy.

No. I knew how that story ended, and I refused to let that story rule my life. Otherwise, I'd end up like Father and Mother—dead in a dingy garage, huffing noxious fumes, or covered in my own pill-speckled vomit, stinking of booze, cigarettes, and shame.

I sat up straight on my bed and wiped my face on the hem of my blouse. It was time to face up to the hard truths. I was so close to getting out of there; I couldn't fall to pieces yet—or maybe ever.

So, I thought, I'm headed to UVA in a few months. What I didn't want to tell Mrs. Knowles was that even if I didn't have a scholarship, I had a decent nest egg from the sale of our old house. It would be enough, and if it wasn't, I'd work to pay for it myself. A useless job wouldn't be useless if it helped me obliterate the version of my life where I became my mother.

That's how I decided to make the best of things, just as I'd done with everything else in my sick, sad life.]

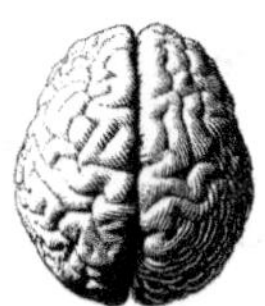

1 9 7 7

"My mom told me Ellen got into UVA," Jeremiah said while we were walking, holding my hand too tight.

"Okay," I said.

Jeremiah squeezed my fingers. "Well? Is it true?"

"Yes," I said, trying to pull my hand away. He squeezed harder, keeping me in place by his side.

He grumbled something, but I didn't hear him.

"Darla? Did you hear me?" he asked.

"What?" I said.

We neared the end of the block and turned around. He tugged me harder than usual.

"I said UVA isn't that great of a school," he said.

I didn't know what to say to that, so I stayed quiet.

"I mean, good for Ellen and all that, but a big state school like that can't offer the same level of individual attention that a smaller school can," he said.

"Okay," I said.

"I mean, Jansmore College may not have all those pretty buildings, but the education is solid. And there's no Greek life to distract people from studying."

"Okay," I said again.

"Seriously, Darla, I'm better off than someone like Ellen, honestly. Just wait. You'll see."

"Okay," I said for the third time. I felt like a rag doll with a string you pull to repeat the same word over and over.

When we got to Mrs. Knowles's house, Jeremiah yanked me closer for the kiss I'd come to dread. All wet lips, sweaty hair, hot stinking breath. When it was over, Jeremiah squeezed both of my hands again, pushing my bones together. "I'm going places," he said. "Just you wait, Darla. Jansmore is just the beginning of the rest of our lives."

I didn't know how Jansmore would in any way affect my life, but I was tired and didn't want to talk anymore. He hugged me and finally left me alone.

[Scribe's note: It doesn't surprise me in the least that Jeremiah Fannin was jealous of me. Jesus Christ, Jansmore? That school had—and probably still has—a nearly 100% acceptance rate. They're practically begging people to attend. I can't think of one single person who has made anything worthwhile of themselves who graduated from Jansmore. Can you? Why don't you stop and go Google it. I doubt you'll find anything.

At the time, I didn't know much about Jeremiah's college plans, and I didn't much care, either. He was, and I can say this now with zero remorse, a limpdick piece of shit. But, at least he was a limpdick piece of shit who kept my sister company so I didn't have to.]

It was getting hotter again, and Ellie and Jeremiah graduated, but not from the same school. Their graduations were on the same day, and Mrs. Knowles took me to see Ellie walk across a big stage. Everybody was clapping, so I started doing it, too, but Mrs. Knowles put a hand on my shoulder and told me to stop. [Scribe's note: It was sweet of Darla to clap for me, but the issue was that she didn't stop clapping. Even during the name announcements that had nothing to do with me. It was embarrassing, and I'm glad Mrs. Knowles put a stop to it.]

Afterward, we found Ellie in the gym, where there were tables with cake and soda.

"Ellen, dear, I'm so proud of you," Mrs. Knowles said, grabbing Ellie in a hug. I didn't think Ellie liked it.

"Thank you," she said. "And thanks for coming. And... for bringing Darla."

"We wouldn't miss it for the world. Right, Darla?"

I smiled.

Mrs. Knowles kept talking to Ellie, and I kept looking over at that cake. It was cut into little squares and each square had its own plate, with a fork. Other people were taking plates, so I went over there and took one, too. I don't know if it was all the excitement, or all the people, or all the newness, but I couldn't make myself focus on eating the way I'd been practicing. Bits of chewed cake kept falling out of my mouth, but it was so good, and I didn't want to stop.

[Scribe's note: I was pleased that Mrs. Knowles brought Darla, I really was, but I was also anxious. Darla hadn't been in a situation like that before, with so many people, and, frankly, so many expectations. Church was different—you just had to sit, and the congregation was much smaller than my graduating class of four hundred and five. I spent the entire ceremony digging my nails into my palms, girding myself for the inevitable scene Darla would cause. My only solace was that after that day, I never had to set foot in that horrid school again, never had to face those brutish kids with their taunts and jeers and dirty pranks.

I was so relieved when the ceremony was over and we all met in the gym. I thought the hard part was over, but then Darla wandered away while Mrs. Knowles was blabbing on about the significance of that day and how my parents would have been so proud of me (yeah, right). By the time we noticed Darla wasn't with us anymore, we started hearing the laughter from the table with the cake.

There was no kidding myself. I knew exactly who everybody was laughing at. I ran to the table and found Darla standing in front of the punch bowl, a plate of cake in her hands, globs of spitty frosting dribbling down her chin. There were smears of blue on her cheeks, even on her nose, and her dress was ruined, smudged with chocolate crumbs and more of that heinous, ultramarine frosting. Carla Romano was whispering to Gina Fletcher, but it was the sort of stage whisper everyone within earshot could hear. They were both pointing at Darla and laughing.

"Take a look at that spaz," Carla said. "I think she needs a bib!"

Gina laughed, and then Trudy Winthrop joined them. "Guess Smelly Ellie's sister is just as dorky as her!"

More laughter.

I grabbed Darla by the arm. "What are you doing?" I said into her ear.

"I don't know," Darla said, mouth full of cake. More of it dribbled out and fell onto her paper plate with a wet smack. I could hear Gina Fletcher heehawing like a donkey.

"Come with me," I said, pulling her back toward Mrs. Knowles.

"Oh, dear," Mrs. Knowles said when she caught sight of Darla. "Let's get you cleaned up."

Together, we brought Darla to the bathroom and wiped her down as best we could. The dress would need special laundering, and her teeth were stained blue, but there wasn't much more we could do.

"These things happen," Mrs. Knowles said as we exited the bathroom. "Ellen, dear, would you like to go back to your party?"

I would have rather swallowed a whole bottle of Valium like Mother than walk back into that gym. "No, thank you. I'd like to go home now, please."

Mrs. Knowles sighed. "Don't you want to say goodbye to your friends?"

I almost laughed at her lack of awareness. Had she not realized over the past few years that I had no use for friends?

"No, I'm alright," I said. "Let's go."

When we got back to Mrs. Knowles's house, I went straight to my room. I stuffed my graduation cap and gown into the back of my closet, then spent the rest of the afternoon filling out the paperwork for UVA enrollment.

After dinner, Mrs. Knowles presented me with a cherry pie. I wasn't hungry, but I didn't want to make her feel bad, so I took a few bites of my slice. It was overly sweet and the crust was undercooked, which surprised me. Normally, Mrs. Knowles's baking was nothing short of excellent.

Darla didn't care. She ate her piece so fast she nearly choked. At least the food all stayed inside of her mouth that time.]

"I looked for you at graduation, but I didn't see you," Jeremiah said to me the next day. We were in the backyard, and his foot was touching mine.

"I was with Mrs. Knowles," I said.

"Were you near the back?" he asked.

"I was in the middle," I said.

"I would have seen you, then," he said. "You would have been close to where my parents and sister were sitting."

"No, I wasn't with them," I said.

He was getting angry. He jabbed my foot with his big toe. "Then where were you, Darla?"

"At Ellie's school," I said.

He hissed. He sounded like the neighbor's cat. "I should have known," he said.

I pulled my feet closer to me.

"Darla, when you love someone, you're supposed to support them," he said.

"Okay," I said. I had. I'd been there for Ellie.

He stared at me. "Darla? Are you hearing me?"

"Yes," I said. Sometimes he could be so confusing, I wanted to scream.

"I'm saying I love you, Darla," he said.

"Okay," I said.

He growled. "Aren't you going to say it back?"

"I love you," I said. Was this how relationships went? One person said one thing, then you had to say the same thing back? Did it matter if it was true or not?

He smiled. "Good," he said. "But seriously, Darla… I mean, I knew I was going to have to teach you a bunch of stuff, but some of these things you should really figure out on your own. You went to Ellie's graduation, but you didn't go to mine?"

"It was the same day," I said.

It was like he didn't hear me. "So you'll support your sister, but not the man you love. Okay, got it. Great."

The smile was gone, and I was getting tired again.

"I want to take a nap," I said.

Jeremiah threw up his hands. "I don't understand you, Darla. We're together, like together together, and you're not supporting me? You're not listening anymore?"

My eyes felt dry and heavy. Instead of answering him, I stood up. "I'm going inside," I said.

Jeremiah stood up, too. "Good grief, Darla," he said. "I see how it is."

He huffed and then turned around and left the backyard. I was glad he could understand me now, could see how things were. He didn't always have to make things so complicated.

[Scribe's note: The more I learn about Jeremiah Fannin, the less I like him, even now, and I didn't like him much back then (at least not since he chose Darla over me—but you know what, thank the baby Jesus I do not believe in). What a sniveling prick. I was thrilled he'd be going off to college, even if it was only Jansmore, which barely qualified as a place of higher education. It was two and a half hours away, far enough that Jeremiah wouldn't be constantly hanging around Darla anymore. With any luck, he'd find a new girl to moon over. I think his repressed desire to be a sculptor seeped into his relationship. He wanted more than anything to have a girl who was a lump of undefined clay, someone he could mold into the perfect wife. Clearly, Darla had shown too much uncontrolled shape for him.

Good for her.]

Jeremiah came back the next day and told me he was going away for awhile.

"Okay," I said.

He squinted at me, like he was having trouble seeing. "I'm sure you'll miss me," he said. "I'll miss you."

I didn't think I would miss him. He made me tired, and then he got mad when I wanted to go sleep. That strange hunger I'd felt when I first saw him had been gone for awhile. Now, every time I saw him, I felt too full, like I was going to be sick, like how I felt the time I ate four slices of Mrs. Knowles's pineapple upside down cake in one sitting, or the time, during my twelfth birthday, when I ate too much and threw up on the table.

When the quiet went on for too long, he got that mean, pinchy look on his face again and said, "Who knows? Maybe I'll find somebody else while I'm gone." Then he got up and left, and I was finally able to take a nap.

[Scribe's note: I found out from Mrs. Knowles that Jeremiah's parents were sending him to a remedial summer school on the other side of the state. Apparently, even Jansmore had its standards. One of the conditions of his acceptance was that he receive passing grades in algebra and in American history, which required summer classes. When Mrs. Knowles told me, in that hushed whisper she used when she was talking about other people, I laughed. She scolded me, as was the good Christian thing to do when someone laughed at another person's misfortune, but I didn't care. I also seriously doubted Jeremiah would find another girl out there—Mrs. Knowles also confided that the summer school he would be attending was boys only, so that everyone would have an easier time focusing on their studies.

Although, I must say, if Jeremiah had come back with a new love from that particular institution, I wouldn't have been completely surprised.]

The summer was nice. Ellie was around more, even though she was usually in her room reading books. She wasn't in high school anymore, and she hadn't started college yet, but she still had her nose deep into those textbooks.

"Why are you reading that?" I asked her one afternoon.

She didn't look up at me. "I have to stay sharp," she said. "I don't want to lose my study habits right before I have to buckle down. That would be foolish."

"Oh," I said. "What are you studying?"

She bit her fingernail, chewed it, then spit something out onto her carpet. "Biology," she said.

"Why?"

She sighed, like Mrs. Knowles did when I 'regressed,' as she called it. "Because I'm going to be a doctor."

My heart started beating faster, and my head started to pound. "Are you going to…"

She looked up then, saw me, and closed her eyes. "Darla, I'm so sorry," she said. It was like she could read my mind. "I'm not going to be like Dr. Hupman. I'm going to be better than him. I'm going to be the kind of doctor you should have had."

We hadn't ever really talked about the surgery; it was just a fact of my life, of my personality. Something like sadness washed over me, but it felt more like a thin blanket than a wool overcoat. I could feel it, barely, but it didn't penetrate, didn't envelop like it probably should have. "Okay," I said, my voice squeaky.

Ellie put her book down on the bed and came over to where I was standing near her desk. Her eyes were glittery again. "Darla, I'm so sorry about what happened to you," she said. "I want to be a doctor so I can make sure nobody has to go through that again."

She hugged me, real quick, then went back to her bed. The glitter was gone from her eyes, like she'd taken all her sadness and zipped it away where it couldn't hurt her. Was that better than not really feeling it at all, like me?

[Scribe's note: Guilt crushed me in that moment, steamrolled me into a flat pancake. How could I ever forgive myself for what I hadn't done? I hadn't stopped the operation. I hadn't fought for Darla before it was too late. I hadn't intervened when it could still make a difference.

In that moment, when she looked at me, fear in her eyes, I broke. My acceptance of her situation, and the peace I'd found, disintegrated. My emotions got the better of me, and I'm ashamed for that. I never wanted Darla to see my weakness, only my strength. I had to be strong enough for the both of us.]

I left Ellie's room and we didn't talk much again for the rest of the summer. We'd pass by each other in the hall, on the way to the bathroom, talk a bit at dinner, but it wasn't much. It wasn't meaningful. But I understood—Ellie had other things to think about, now.

The day before she left for UVA, I got a piece of nice paper from Mrs. Knowles's stationery set. I folded it in half so it looked like a card you got at the store. Her fancy pens were almost too heavy in my hands, and I had to fight to hold onto them.

It wasn't perfect, but I wrote a few letters. 'M,' 'I,' 'S,' 'S,' 'Y,' 'O,' 'U.' Then I signed my name.

[Scribe's note: I still have the note Darla wrote me, although 'note' is a strong word. Don't get me wrong, she tried her best, but it was still barely legible. It made me sad, not the sentiment of it, but her persistent inability to do something she should be able to do—write. As with everything, I squeezed the sadness deep inside of me until it was a hard stone of anger, which was far easier for me to tolerate.

When she handed me the card after my last dinner of meatloaf and mashed potatoes, Mrs. Knowles made a big fuss about how far Darla had come. She had, it was true, but in a way, she hadn't come far at all. She couldn't live on her own. She wouldn't be able to hold down a job. She wasn't getting a legitimate education, and I mean that as no slight to Mrs. Knowles's homeschooling.

Not for the first time, as I looked at the card again, I wondered what

Darla would have been like today if she'd never had the surgery. Would she have burrowed deeper and deeper into her phobia, until we found her dead one day in her dirty nest, like a child's hamster? Or would she have grown out of it, eventually rejoining the society we were raised in, becoming the sort of young woman our parents could have bragged about at the neighborhood barbecues?

The questions were a waste of time, because there was no way to ever glean the answers, and I wasn't keen on torturing myself with fanciful imaginings of different versions of Darla. Just like I couldn't restart my life and make different choices, there was no reset button for Darla's brain.

Pushing everything out of my mind, I thanked Darla for the card and praised her almost as effusively as Mrs. Knowles. But, as with most things, the bad thoughts never stayed buried deep enough. The past is far from past, and the operation would never cease to haunt us.

The next morning, I left the house, closing the door silently behind me, not wanting to wake up Mrs. Knowles or Darla. I dragged my suitcase to the corner, and when the bus came, I got on and left Richmond behind for the next eight years.]

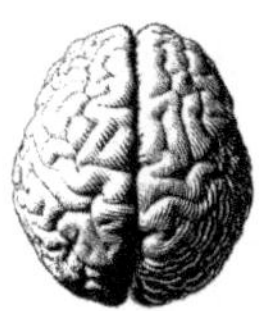

1 9 7 7

Jeremiah came home the day after Ellie left for college.

"Is Ellen gone now?" he asked me. It was hot, and we were in the backyard again. My stomach hurt, and I wanted to be alone.

"Yes," I said.

"UVA must start early," he said. "Jansmore values quality over quantity, Darla. I've got another week before I leave."

"Okay," I said. My stomach clenched. I knew that sort of feeling would have scared me once, long ago, when I was somebody else. Now, where there had been fear, there was only the pain. There were no thoughts around the pain beyond wanting to get through it. That was normal, right?

"What should we do with our last week, Darla?" Jeremiah was rubbing my arm with his sweaty fingers, leaving little sticky trails, like a snail.

"I don't know," I said, already wishing the week was over and Jeremiah was gone.

"I want to take you somewhere," he said. "Like out to dinner. Something nice. When was the last time you went out to dinner?"

I couldn't remember ever going out to dinner, although I was sure it must have happened at some point in my life. Mrs. Knowles always cooked, and Ellie was too busy to go to restaurants. I shrugged.

"It's settled, then," he said. "I'm taking you to——"

A groan fell out of my mouth. The pain was pulsing, too much.

"Darla, please," he said. "You haven't even heard my plan yet."

Then, suddenly—a release. There was a gush down below. When I looked, I saw a pinprick of red in my lap, growing steadily.

Jeremiah followed my eyes, looked down, too. He went pale, then squinted like he did when he was upset with me. "Oh," he said. "Um, I better—I'm getting Mrs. Knowles." Before I could say anything he was inside the house, yelling.

What was happening to me?

Mrs. Knowles rushed out and grabbed me by the shoulders. "Oh, dear," she said. "I figured it was about time for this." She shouted to Jeremiah over her shoulder. He was standing on the patio, still pale as a sheet. "Jeremiah, dear," she said. "Why don't you head on home. I'll take care of this."

He ran through the house and out the front door without saying goodbye. Whatever was happening with me must have been really bad.

"It's alright, dear," Mrs. Knowles said, patting my back. "Let's get you inside and cleaned up."

She helped me change, and that's when I saw that it was blood coming out of me. I knew I should be worried, I *wanted* to be worried, but I felt too detached. I couldn't understand any of it. It didn't seem real.

"Now, dear," Mrs. Knowles said as she fetched a thick piece of cotton from the bathroom. "You're lucky, they just came out with this new kind. It's sticky on the bottom, so all you have to do is press it into your panties."

"Why?" I asked at last.

Mrs. Knowles didn't get as pale as Jeremiah, but she did purse her lips into a thin white line. "Sometimes I forget you have no one else to tell you this," she said softly, but I heard every word. "We ladies have our one precious gift. You remember Pastor Sable talking about that?"

I nodded.

"Good. Well this blood is the other side of that gift—the curse. The blood means you could have a baby now, that your body is capable. Don't get confused, though, dear, that doesn't mean you are ready just because you are capable. Protect your gift above all else. If the blood doesn't come every month, well…" She stopped, stared off somewhere behind me.

"What?" I said, grabbing for the wad of cotton in her hand.

She pulled it back, out of my reach. "Don't worry about that for now. Just know that every month, this will happen, but it shouldn't be a surprise like it was today. Your stomach will probably hurt, and you might feel a bit out of sorts, then the blood will come. Be prepared, and use this to keep from making a mess." She shook the cotton pad. "When one gets… full, change it for another one."

How was I supposed to know when it was full? And I had to do this every month? How would I remember?

"What happens then?" I asked.

Mrs. Knowles pursed her lips. "What do you mean?"

"What happens after the blood comes?"

"Well, you'll bleed for a few days, then it will stop. Then, the next month, it will come back."

"But why?" I said.

Mrs. Knowles sighed. "That's just how women are made, Darla. You're getting old enough now that I thought maybe it wouldn't come for you at all, but here it is."

She handed me the pad, then left me in the bathroom. "Take care of yourself," she said.

I don't know why she thought I could do that. It had never been my job before.

[Scribe's note: I learned later, in medical school, that brain trauma can affect the onset of menarche. Traumatic brain injuries can cause hormone disruption and imbalance, which can lead to missed menstrual cycles, irregular cycles, or cycles that are absent altogether. To be honest, I'd forgotten about Darla's burgeoning puberty after my conversation with Mrs. Knowles about Pastor Sable's purity sermon, when she told me she'd taken care of things. I figured she'd take care of the menstruation conversation when it came time to do so, too. I was right, I can see that now, but I also wish I'd been there to explain things better for Darla. Mrs. Knowles only scratched the surface, and without enough knowledge and understanding, Darla was even more vulnerable.]

Putting the pad into my underwear was hard, but I did it. When I came back downstairs, Mrs. Knowles said, "Everything shipshape?" I nodded, then went back out to the yard. Jeremiah did not rejoin me, which was just fine. The stomachache was back, but it wasn't as bad now, and I even fell asleep in the shade.

Jeremiah didn't take me to dinner. When he came over the next day, he said, "It's not the right time. What we've got here is just fine. I'd rather be here with you than in a stuffy restaurant anyway."

I shrugged. It didn't matter to me.

[Scribe's note: I'm fairly certain Jeremiah got cold feet. No man is comfortable around menstruation, except for the rare male doctor, and seeing Darla's blood come for the first time soured him on her, I think. If that wasn't it, then I assume either Mrs. Fannin or Mrs. Knowles heard about his plans and discouraged him. Jeremiah was wearing rose-colored glasses when it came to Darla, in many ways, and he wasn't capable of handling her in a new environment, where she could be unpredictable. That's the optimistic explanation, at least. The pessimistic version is that Jeremiah or Mrs. Fannin thought being seen in public with Darla, especially in a nice restaurant, would be shameful. Unfortunately, after her display at my graduation, I can't really blame them, even though I condemn their mean-spirited thoughts. Yes, I understand my own hypocrisy, thank you, but I'm her sister. It's different when you're family. You understand that, don't you?]

The week went by quickly, I got used to the blood, and even got better about putting the pad in. By the end of the week, my blood stopped coming and my stomach didn't hurt anymore. It was also time to say goodbye to Jeremiah.

He came over in the morning, just after I'd finished breakfast.

"Well, this is it," he said. He handed me a clump of flowers. They looked like the same ones Mrs. Knowles grew near her mailbox. "I'm going to miss you so much, Darla."

I took the flowers. There was a black ant crawling in the middle of one of the orange blossoms.

He leaned into me, squeezing me into a hug, crushing the flowers between us. Then he started crying, so hard I thought he was going to start coughing. "How can I just leave you, Darla? What will you do without me? Will you be okay? Who will you talk to? Who will keep you company?"

He was far more worried than I was.

"I don't know," I said, but nothing about that scared me.

He pushed me back, holding me by my shoulders. His eyes were red, and his breath smelled like old eggs. "I love how strong you're being," he said, then pressed his wet lips to mine. I realized he didn't just smell of eggs, he also tasted of eggs. I was relieved he'd never invited me over for his mother's cooking.

Then the kiss was over and I heard a horn honking outside.

"That's my dad," he said. "I have to go."

"Okay," I said, wanting more than anything to wipe my mouth off of my face.

"I'll write to you," he said. "And phone calls whenever I can." He opened the front door. "I love you, Darla," he said.

The car honked again.

"I'm coming, dad!" he yelled over his shoulder.

The honk came again, and Jeremiah ran outside. When I went to close the door behind him, I saw him getting into the front seat next to

Mr. Fannin. Jeremiah saw me looking and blew me a kiss.

A second later, the smell of eggs hit me again.

Then he was gone.

Mrs. Knowles came into the living room. "Was Jeremiah here?" she asked.

I turned around.

"Darla, are those my lilies?"

[Scribe's note: In my professional medical opinion, Jeremiah was projecting all of his fears for himself onto Darla, using her as a blank canvas just as he'd used her over the previous few years. He was the one who was terrified of making friends, of losing someone to talk *at* (not talk to, never talk *to*), of being rudderless without Darla's placid, unchanging presence.

Jeremiah left at the right time, both for Darla's sake and his own. She didn't need him, didn't want him, that much is now clear, but knowing what I know now, he saved himself. Darla wasn't a mean person, but she wasn't the meek, kindhearted, featureless soul Jeremiah thought she was, either. She was like a fluffy little dog that looks sweet, but will snap at you with no hesitation. Jeremiah left before he could get bit.]

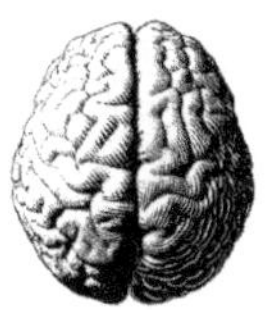

1 9 7 7

Phone calls were expensive, according to Mrs. Knowles, so Jeremiah wrote me letters. Most of them went the same way: he'd tell me he missed me, he'd talk about his classes, he'd talk about his new friends, and then he'd say how excited he was to see me the next time he came home. I got a new letter at least twice a week.

At first, anyway.

Even though Mrs. Knowles had been working with me, my writing still wasn't something anybody could really read. I tried to answer Jeremiah's letters, but when I asked Mrs. Knowles to post a letter for me, she looked at it and shook her head.

"Darla, dear," she said, "I'm so sorry, but I don't think Jeremiah is going to be able to read this. Do you want to tell me what you want to say, and I'll write it for you?"

You'll probably think it's foolish, but I said no very fast. Mrs. Knowles was kind, and she'd taken such great care of me, but it was getting harder for her to see that I was actually getting better. She'd been part of even my most private moments—bathing, toileting, even menstruating. Now that I was a woman, according to her, I felt like I wanted more real privacy. The kind no one else knows about.

All that meant I didn't want Mrs. Knowles inside my head, too. I didn't want her to know what I was saying to Jeremiah. What if she didn't like it? What if it surprised her?

"Oh," she said when I told her no, thank you. "Alright, dear. Just let me know if you change your mind."

That wasn't the only reason, though. I thought if I couldn't write Jeremiah back, but at least I'd tried, then he shouldn't be angry with me. He knew my limitations… but with each unanswered letter he sent, he got a little bit angrier.

Darla, why aren't you writing back? Darla, don't you miss me, too? Darla, I love you, you know that, right? Darla, can't you say something? Darla, this is getting ridiculous! Darla, I'm going to stop writing to you. Darla, I'm serious. Darla!

Then a week went by without a letter, then another. It had been a couple of months, and Thanksgiving was coming up. Mrs. Knowles had already told me Ellie wouldn't be coming back for the holidays, since gas was so expensive, whatever that meant. She didn't know what Jeremiah would be doing.

It had been three weeks since his last letter when he knocked on the door.

I opened it and just stared at him. I couldn't help it. Luckily, I remembered to close my mouth. He was so…. different. His face was the same, but plumper. He'd grown a beard that looked like Mrs. Knowles's threadbare spare blanket. His eyes were red, and his flannel shirt looked like it would pop a button. Had his hair always been so thin on the top? I couldn't remember.

"Hi, Darla," he said.

"Hi," I said.

"Can I come in?"

Mrs. Knowles was preparing lunch in the kitchen, and I didn't want to bother her.

"I want to walk," I said, pulling on my jacket. It wasn't yet cold, but the air was brisk and bright.

We started down the sidewalk. He didn't take my hand like he usually did, so I stuffed both of mine in my warm pockets.

"So," he said. "How have you been?"

I shrugged. "Fine," I said. I'd learned from Mrs. Knowles a while ago that this was generally a good thing to say, regardless of how you were really feeling. In my case, I was actually fine. Better than that, in fact, ever since Jeremiah left. No more sweaty squeezing hands, no more wet wormy lips, no more bad breath or too-tight hugs.

"Good," he said. "Did you get my letters?"

"Yes," I said.

"Damnit, Darla, why didn't you write me back, then? I figured they either got lost in the mail, or you'd moved and didn't tell me, or something was seriously wrong!"

"But I'm fine," I said.

He grumbled. "That's not the point," he said. "You didn't respond to me. Do you know how that makes me feel?"

"Fine?" I said. I knew it wasn't the right answer, but I didn't know what else to say.

"For God's sakes!" he cried, stopping me in the middle of the sidewalk with his fingers around my arm. "Really, Darla? You know I love you, I write to you all the time, and you think hearing absolutely nothing from you makes me feel just fine?"

I shrugged. "I don't know." Another standard answer. I was starting to understand how convenient it could be to hide behind peoples' expectations of me. Nobody thought I understood what was going on. A lot of the time, they were right. But, more and more, they were wrong.

Jeremiah closed his red eyes and breathed out a big cloud of meaty air. "I didn't want to have to tell you this," he said.

"Okay," I said.

He opened his eyes, squinted at me. "I met someone," he said.

"Okay," I said again.

"A girl," he said.

"Okay," I said, yet again.

He let go of my arm, pushing me away, almost knocking me down to the sidewalk. "That's it, Darla! If you don't even care about that, nothing will make you care. I'm done!"

He didn't wait for me to say something—not that I would have. Without another word, he turned and ran back to his house. I started walking to Mrs. Knowles's. I heard the Fannins' door slam a little while later.

My mouth curled into a smile as I walked back. I wasn't the kind of happy you see on TV shows—I didn't know if I would ever be able to feel anything like that—but I was pleased. Most of all, because I wouldn't have to taste Mrs. Fannin's idea of a Thanksgiving meal on Jeremiah's tongue later. It was over.

[Scribe's note: Jeremiah, Jeremiah. I didn't know exactly how it ended, but now I do, and I'm glad for it. Although, what a little bitch way to go about it, really. I figure Jeremiah was either lying (most likely) or he'd managed to find some girl even more broken than Darla to latch onto, leech that he was.]

Ellie didn't come home for Thanksgiving, but she did write to us. She said she was really liking college and all of her classes, and that she'd found a job to help pay for school. She'd get overtime pay if she worked over the holiday, so it made sense for her to stay—plus, gas was still so expensive. I was fine with that. Mrs. Knowles wasn't.

"I don't understand how your sister can be alone on campus on Thanksgiving when she could come here and be with family," she said while we ate turkey. Mr. Knowles was home, but he was so quiet it was almost like he wasn't there. I wondered if he thought about me the same way.

"It's okay," I said. "She's working."

"Still," Mrs. Knowles said, jabbing her spoon into a pile of mashed potatoes. She was wearing bright red lipstick, different for her, and it left waxy-looking rings around the top of her spoon. "This is a family holiday. And after all I've done for that girl…"

"Belinda, please," Mr. Knowles said. "She's not wrong. Gas prices are highway robbery right now." It was one of the few times I heard him speak, and I was surprised again by how high-pitched his voice was. Even though it was squeaky, Mrs. Knowles scrunched down a bit in her chair, like a balloon with a hole in it. She didn't mention Ellie again.

[Scribe's note: I wasn't completely truthful about my rationale for staying on campus. Yes, it was true that gas was expensive, and that I would get overtime pay for working the holiday, but those weren't the real reasons. In reality, I'd been invited to join my biology professor's Thanksgiving at his home in Charlottesville. He'd invited a few select students to join him and his family. Most of them lived far enough away that it was too impractical and expensive for them to go home, anyway. I certainly could have gone back to Richmond, but the thought of sitting through another turkey dinner with Darla shoving spoonful after spoonful into her already full mouth, Mrs. Knowles trying to make tedious conversation, and Mr. Knowles sitting like an angry, lumpy toad at the head of the table made me want to jump off of a very tall building. Stronger than my desire to avoid that display, however, was my instinct that having a strong ally in my biology professor could be a crucial advantage for me. My current job was nothing, an assistant at the library, but I wanted to level up to research. My professor's laboratory studied neurological connections in the brain through mouse models, and I desperately wanted to be a part of that. Face time with the professor would get me closer to that goal, which would, ultimately, get me into the best medical school. All in service of earning me a full adult life that was diametrically opposite from my childhood.

So, while Darla and Mrs. Knowles sat silently, chewing their food, with Mr. Knowles lording over it all, I was seated at a long table in Professor Gantry's Georgian Revival mansion, the only female student, in fact. There weren't many ladies in the pre-medical program, which I'm sure doesn't surprise you, given the times. The competition amongst us could be fierce, and I'd begun to attend to my appearance fastidiously. Always remember this—we women must be beyond criticism and above reproach if we want to succeed in what is still a man's world. You can't give them any ammunition they can use to shoot you down.

At Professor Gantry's, we were eating the kind of catered Thanksgiving meal I could only have dreamt of. Don't get me wrong, Mrs. Knowles was a lovely cook, but it was home cooking. Professor Gantry's Thanksgiving was elevated cuisine, and I savored every bite. The Professor himself was seated next to me, and I used the opportunity to ask him every question about biology, his laboratory work, and neurological research that I could think of. By the time the hired help brought out an assortment of pies, I believed I had sufficiently impressed Professor Gantry.

So, no. I don't regret staying away from Richmond. Does that make me a bad sister?

It didn't matter. I had all but disavowed that life.]

A few weeks later, when Mrs. Knowles was decorating the house for Christmas like she did every year, we got another letter from Ellie. She said she'd switched jobs, and was now working in a laboratory, whatever that was. The job was harder than her old one, and she was working with animals, so she'd have to stay on campus over Christmas to tend to them. I always wanted a pet. Ellie was right to stay and take care of the animals.

"She can't do this to us again," Mrs. Knowles said. She stopped hanging a stocking over the mantel and stared at the couch, where I was sitting, reading a book about butterflies. "Darla, don't you miss your sister?"

I shrugged. "The animals need her," I said.

"That's just an excuse, I'm sure," Mrs. Knowles said. She threw the stocking she'd been holding onto the floor. The toe of it read 'Ellen.' She stomped out of the room and into the kitchen.

A moment later, I called to her, "Can we get a pet?"

"Absolutely not!"

[Scribe's note: To be fair, my letter wasn't completely accurate. After Thanksgiving, Professor Gantry had agreed to hire me as a research intern, which was a big deal, because I would be the youngest student in the laboratory, and one of only two women. The pay wasn't quite as high as my library assistant job, but I didn't care. I would make do, even if it meant skipping meals, which would only help my waistline, anyway.

My duties in the Gantry laboratory were minimal, mostly involving observing the more senior members of the lab perform experiments, writing hypotheses, and caring for the mice. I asked plenty of questions, and I wrote down all the answers in my lab notebook.

A graduate student, Benjamin, was tasked with feeding and attending to the mice over Christmas. I had volunteered to help him.

All that is to say that while I wasn't technically needed in the Gantry laboratory over the winter holidays, there was nowhere else I wanted to be. Plus, Mrs. Knowles couldn't touch me. I was paying for school with my own money, and there was no way she was going to throw Darla out on the street just because I didn't come back for the holidays. Now that I was in the world of UVA, I was fully immersed. I didn't want to pierce that protective shell and venture back into a life I couldn't bear, even if only for a few days.]

For Christmas, Mrs. Knowles gave me a new sweater set. It was pink and blue striped, and very pretty, almost as pretty as the red silk blouse she wore. She'd unbuttoned it to just above her breasts. For Mr. Knowles, she got a box of cigars. Ellie's stocking wasn't hanging on the mantel, but her two boys' stockings were, even though they weren't there, either.

Mr. Knowles left the house right after Christmas dinner. I helped Mrs. Knowles clean up, and the whole time, she had that glittery look in her eyes.

[Scribe's note: I'd suspected for a while that Mr. Knowles felt rather trapped in his marriage, that Mrs. Knowles was not exactly his cup of tea, if you understand my meaning. I think their quiet toxicity pushed their boys away, and perhaps Mrs. Knowles felt she had a second chance to make the perfect family with Darla and me.

This all underscored the importance of picking the right partner. Unfortunately, I learned that lesson too late.]

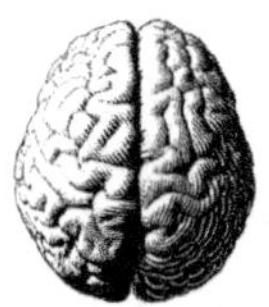

1 9 7 8

Winter went by. My chewing and swallowing got better, and I could walk farther without getting too winded. I could read whole chapters of books on my own, and when Mrs. Knowles gave me an arithmetic test, she told me I passed.

Writing was still hard, though. Numbers were okay, but letters of the alphabet were tough. I could see the characters in my brain, but I couldn't make my hand write them onto paper. If we'd had a computer back then, my whole life would have been different, I think.

[Scribe's note: I think so, too. If Darla had taken up typing classes early, she probably could have developed the dexterity needed to type her thoughts. As it was, by the time she saw her first computer and keyboard, she didn't have the energy to learn. I know what you're thinking—*Why couldn't she use dictation software once it became available?* Don't you think I thought the same thing? As soon as I could, I equipped her with the best technology I could afford. And you know what? She didn't like it. She said talking out loud to herself made her feel like a crazy person.

The irony, right? It just about kills you.]

In the spring, Mrs. Knowles told me we were going to visit Ellie.

"UVA isn't so far away that Mr. Knowles will complain about the gas. Besides, it will do you good to get out, see something different," she said.

Different made me feel anxious, but the thought of seeing Ellie again made me feel less like I might float away.

Mrs. Knowles packed an overnight bag for me. I went to sit in the backseat of her car, but she told me to come to the front, like an adult. It felt strange, but I did it anyway.

"We'll only be on the road an hour or so, dear, but I don't want to feel like your chauffeur," she said as I buckled myself.

I didn't know what a chauffeur was. "Okay," I said.

Mrs. Knowles turned up the radio loud to a Christian station. A man who sounded like Pastor Sable was talking about the virgins that waited for a groom, but then some of their lights went out, and then they couldn't go eat at his wedding dinner.

When the story was over, Mrs. Knowles said, "You best remember that, Darla."

When I didn't say anything, because what was there to say, she poked me with her finger. "I want to raise you to be a good Christian," she said. "That means you have to be prepared. You have to say your prayers. And you have to stay chaste until marriage."

"Okay," I said. This close, Mrs. Knowles smelled like powder and the sort of dried flowers that have gone sour. I hadn't noticed it before.

[Scribe's note: Darla might not have been able to see it, but I knew what was happening. Mrs. Knowles was getting old, and Mrs. Knowles was getting ignored by her husband. Of course she was trying to cover all of that up with some new scent. By the sound of it, she had misfired with the perfume and ended up in geriatric territory.]

We parked on the street near the campus, and Mrs. Knowles helped me out of the car. "Alright, Ellen's schedule says she'll be getting out of chemistry class in about ten minutes. We can wait for her outside the classroom. She's going to be so excited to see us, dear!"

Mrs. Knowles gripped my hand almost as tightly as Jeremiah used to and pulled me along the brick sidewalk. "She doesn't know?" I asked.

"Hmm, dear?" Mrs. Knowles said, craning her neck to look at the big grassy field and all the pretty little buildings around it.

"Does Ellie know we're coming?"

Mrs. Knowles didn't stop walking. "No," she said. "It's a surprise."

I didn't think Ellie would like that, but I let myself be dragged along. Everything was happening too fast, and the buildings were too close together, and there were too many people. My chest felt all fluttery.

"This should be it," Mrs. Knowles said when we reached a big brick building with lots of windows. "Come along, dear. We don't want to miss her."

Inside, the building smelled like alcohol and something burned, like overcooked toast. Our footsteps were loud in the hallway. My toe hit the back of Mrs. Knowles's foot, and I stumbled.

"Careful!" she said, more harshly than usual. "You need to be on your best behavior, Darla."

What was that supposed to mean? The only place I'd been even kind of like this building was Ellie's graduation, and I didn't think that had gone the way she wanted.

She stopped in front of a set of double doors, and I nearly ran into her. A moment later, the doors opened, and girls and boys Ellie's age came rushing out into the hall. I flattened myself against the wall like one of Mrs. Knowles's pancakes, trying not to get crushed. My heart raced, and I desperately wanted to be back outside, where there was at least a little more space.

"There she is!" Mrs. Knowles cried, and then she was yanking me into the crowd by my wrist.

"Ellen! Ellen, over here!" Mrs. Knowles waved and rocked on her heels. "Ellen!"

Then I saw her. My sister was standing on the opposite side of the hallway, talking to an older boy with dark brown hair and blue eyes. He had a short beard and round glasses. Ellie looked different—she stood up straighter, her skin was clearer, and she had on the sort of outfit the girls in the neighborhood back in Richmond had started wearing—jeans with big flared bottoms and a flowy shirt.

"Ellen!" Mrs. Knowles shouted again, and that's when Ellie looked over at us. Her face got really pale, and her eyebrows shot up to the top of her forehead. Her mouth fell open, and I wondered if someone else would have to close it for her.

"Oh," she said, very softly. "Oh."

[Scribe's note: Mrs. Knowles's surprise intrusion into my life at UVA was, in a word, unwelcome. Make no mistake, I was indebted to the woman for keeping us out of foster care, and for continuing to care for Darla somewhat indefinitely. She'd helped us when there was no one else for us to lean on... but that didn't give her the right to disturb me whenever she wanted. I thought she would have taken the hint when I didn't come back for Thanksgiving or Christmas, but apparently that wasn't the case. Even worse, she was dragging Darla behind her, who looked like a deer caught in the headlights. What was Mrs. Knowles thinking, bringing Darla into a wildly new environment, and one with so much chaos as a college campus?

Darla was more fleshed out than she'd been when I left. There was a cherubic roundness to her cheeks, and her gray eyes were deep and soulful, like they were beaming the deep tragedy of her life outward. Mrs. Knowles still had her dressed like a little Christian Barbie, but it didn't matter. On Darla, everything looked beautiful. I'm not too petty to admit she was radiant, but I knew her. Even though she looked like a picture-perfect teenager, she invariably ended up slipping, revealing herself, like she was wearing a mask that was too loose. Mrs. Knowles had her trained, but not for every situation. Darla would regress, would slip and show herself, I was sure of it—I just didn't know how, or when. With these thoughts came the shame, the guilt, the feelings I wanted to obliterate. The only coping mechanism I'd found that even came close to working was distance—and Mrs. Knowles had just taken that away.

I wasn't the only one who noticed Darla's beauty. Benjamin, standing next to me, caught sight of Darla and couldn't seem to pull his gaze away. The thought of Benjamin leaving me the way Jeremiah had made me feel sick to my stomach.

Mrs. Knowles and Darla finally fought their way through the crowd and stopped in front of us. "Ellen!" she said, looking me up and down. "It's so good to see you, dear! What has it been? Eight months? Ten?"

Her mouth was smiling, but there was a pinch of rage at the corners of her lips. What she was really saying was, *How dare you not come home? How dare you force us to drive all the way here and hunt you down just to see you?*

"It's been awhile," I said, still shellshocked. My protective college bubble had been burst, and I felt like I was deflating the longer I looked at these two people who felt like remnants of the old skin I wanted so desperately to shed.

Mrs. Knowles turned to Benjamin. "And who is your friend, Ellen? Aren't you going to introduce us?"

Benjamin peeled his eyes away from Darla. "Oh, uh, hello, ma'am. I'm Benjamin Bertucci."

"He works with me in the laboratory," I said.

Mrs. Knowles glared at me, then turned her smile back on full blast and looked at Benjamin. "It's nice to meet you, Benjamin. I'm Belinda Knowles, and this is Ellen's sister, Darla."

Benjamin grabbed Darla's hand and shook it. "Nice to meet you, Darla," he said. I thought I might throw up.

"Yes," Darla said, and I was grateful there was no food around. Darla would have a harder time making a scene in here, I hoped.

"Shall we have lunch?" Mrs. Knowles asked. "Benjamin, would you like to join us?"

Dear God, please no. I'd rather have died. "Actually, Mrs. Knowles, Benjamin and I were just about to head back to the lab. We're running an experiment this afternoon that—"

"Ellen," Mrs. Knowles said, a growly warning in her voice I'd never heard before. "Your sister and I drove all this way to see you, and with gas prices this high, I think the least you can do is go to lunch with us."

My legs started to quake—rage, embarrassment, shame, guilt, sadness all swirling inside of me like a toxic tornado.

"You go ahead with your family," Benjamin cut in. "I'll take care of the experiment for this afternoon. We can talk tomorrow."

"Are you sure you won't join us?" Mrs. Knowles said.

Jesus Christ, I could see him hesitate. His eyes were still glued to Darla, and I thought, for a brief moment, he was going to say yes, what the hell, I'll join you, and then that would have been it. He'd have been lost to me.

"No, thank you, ma'am," he said. "I really have to get those experiments up and running."

"Alright," she said. "Well, it was lovely to meet you."

"And both of you, as well," he said, speaking only to Darla, whose face had remained completely expressionless throughout the entire painful conversation.

"Ellen, shall we?" Mrs. Knowles said, and then, against my will, she was escorting me away from Benjamin, away from my lab and the life I'd built for myself, and back into the past.]

Ellie's friend made that strange hunger rumble in my belly again, the way Jeremiah used to. It made me feel less anxious. I wanted him to eat lunch with us, but I understood that he was busy.

Mrs. Knowles talked the whole way to the cafeteria, about the neighbors, about how well I was doing, about how we spent Thanksgiving and Christmas. Ellie still looked pale.

Inside, the cafeteria was full of people like Ellie, with those flared jeans and flower-shaped tops, and boys like Benjamin. Mrs. Knowles pulled us through the line and ordered for all of us. We followed her to a table by a window.

The food was tasty, and I started eating while Mrs. Knowles and

Ellie talked, their heads close together. I was pleased they were getting along, because Mrs. Knowles hadn't sounded all that happy.

[Scribe's note: Leaning over a plate of fried chicken, Mrs. Knowles wasn't filling me in on Darla's rapid progress—or lack thereof—or congratulating me on a successful school career thus far. No, she was laying into me about my absences during the holidays, which had apparently caused a much bigger stir than I had anticipated. I wasn't even really part of the family, so why did it matter if I was there? I was sure Darla didn't care.

"Do you understand how much that upset your sister?" she whispered at me, not wanting Darla to hear. She needn't have bothered. Darla was chin-deep in a bowl of chili, which seemed a terrible choice for her on Mrs. Knowles's part. It was almost as though she wanted to cause an incident, to punish me publicly for what she saw as my failure—but what I knew was my escape.

"I'm sorry," I lied. "I couldn't get away."

"Nonsense," Mrs. Knowles hissed. "All the other students were safe and warm and happy with their families. I cannot imagine the school would make you stay here. I just cannot fathom it. We would have sent you gas money!"

"Well—"

"Do you understand what I mean, Ellen? If the school didn't make you stay here, and you didn't even ask for gas money, then you're lying to us. And if you're lying, then that means you're covering something up. What is it, Ellen? What are you hiding?"

I was taken aback. I hadn't seen this paranoid, nasty side of Mrs. Knowles before. Like the water in a heated kettle, the ire sloshing inside of her had reached a boiling point, and she was shrieking loud enough for the whole world to hear. At the time, I couldn't understand where it was coming from, but now, with the benefit of hindsight and what I ultimately learned about Mr. Knowles, I can trace a direct line between her husband's infidelity and her ridiculous paranoia. It was simple transference—she couldn't be angry at him, so she took her feelings out on me.

I could handle it.

"I'm not hiding anything," I said.

"Do you still have your gift?" she said.

"What gift?"

"Your gift! Your special woman's gift! The gift you only get one time, and once you give it away, it's gone!"

I bit my lip, trying not to laugh. She was worried about my virginity? "I'm still a virgin," I said. "Not that it's any of your business."

She gasped. "Ellen! I am trying to keep you safe! That's all I've ever wanted to do!" Tears sparkled in her eyes.

"I'm sorry, I'm sorry," I said. "I know. I'm sorry."

She sucked in the start of a runny nose. "Does that mean you'll be home for Easter?" she said.

Easter? I didn't get any official time off for Easter. Even if I did, I wouldn't want to spend my time freezing in the dark during a sunrise Easter service on the church lawn. Last year, my toes got so cold I thought I'd gotten frostbite.

"I don't know if I can," I said, trying to be gentle.

Mrs. Knowles exploded, causing the students seated around us to turn and stare. "Seriously, Ellen? Seriously? After all I've done for you? After all I still do for Darla? You can't even grace us with your presence a few times a year?"

With that, she shot up from the table, nearly upending her basket of fried chicken, which was still untouched. Darla gasped, which caused her to aspirate chili, which led to her choking. After a moment, she dislodged a chunk of ground beef, which went sailing over our table and splatted against the window. Darla heaved breath after breath, the bottom half of her face entirely brown with sauce. Some of it had dripped down onto her blouse, making her look like she'd been slurping out of a mud puddle.

"Darla, we're leaving," Mrs. Knowles said. She didn't even bother to clean Darla up; she grabbed her by the elbow and dragged her toward the exit, the eyes of dozens of diners following them.

The moment the door slammed, the entire restaurant turned to look at me.

Next to me, a boy I recognized from a first semester English class tapped me on the shoulder. He pointed to the basket of chicken, my pristine plate with a club sandwich, and Darla's half-finished bowl of chili. "Are you going to eat that?"

"No," I said. "It's all yours."

"Right on!" he said. The volume in the restaurant returned to normal, everybody turning back to their lunches, their conversations, their lives that were far less tragic than mine.

By the time I got back out onto the sidewalk, Darla and Mrs. Knowles were long gone.]

My throat hurt from the chili I'd coughed up. The rest of it was drying on my face and starting to hurt, but Mrs. Knowles didn't stop. She walked faster than I thought she could, and she just kept pulling me, not even slowing down when I stumbled. When we got back to the car, she pushed me into the backseat.

She slid behind the wheel. "Might as well act like a chauffeur," she said, but I didn't think she was talking to me. "I'm worthless, after all. Completely worthless."

My hand found my overnight bag. "Where are we sleeping?" I asked.

"We're going home now," Mrs. Knowles said. "This was a mistake."

A black seed buried itself inside of me. Had I done something wrong again? Was this like Ellie's graduation?

I didn't know, and I spent the rest of the drive back to Richmond trying to figure it out.

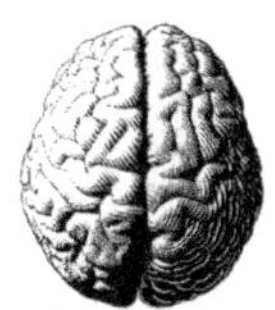

1 9 7 8 - 1 9 8 1

After we got back from visiting Ellie, Mrs. Knowles was different. She still worked with me, trying to get me to learn more math, get better at reading, that sort of thing, but she didn't cheer when I did something new for the first time, like she used to do. She still cooked for me, too, and the food was still good, but she didn't smile while she ate with me, and she didn't reach over to close my mouth when I forgot to—although that barely happened at all anymore.

Mrs. Knowles started to get thinner, and one time I went to the backyard, and I found her sitting in my usual chair, smoking a cigarette. It reminded me of Ma, but how she was at the end—scary, angry, far away.

Another day, while we were eating our lunch of leftover spaghetti casserole, I said, "Are you okay?"

She dropped her fork onto her plate, said, "Don't talk with your mouth full, dear," and then she started laughing. She laughed so hard tears started coming out of her eyes.

Had my question been funny? I didn't think so, but since she was still laughing, I joined in, too.

Without any warning, she stood up, dropped her uneaten plate of casserole in the sink, and ran out of the kitchen.

If Ellie had been home, I would have asked her what was going on, but I had no way to talk to her now. Mrs. Knowles said phone calls were too expensive, and I still couldn't write well enough to communicate with her. So, I finished my casserole, put my plate in the sink, and went to my room to read a book. From downstairs, I could hear Mrs. Knowles starting up her shower. It didn't turn back off for a very long time.

[Scribe's note: Goddamnit, I do wish Darla had found a way to tell me about Mrs. Knowles. Or, more realistically, I wish I had bothered to cough up the cash and call once in a while, to speak to my sister and understand her situation. But after their visit to UVA, I wanted absolutely nothing to do with Mrs. Knowles, which meant I also had nothing to do with my sister. In case you're wondering, yes, I do regret my total and complete removal from their lives, especially given what came next. If I'd known, I could have prevented it, could have changed the entire course of all of our lives. Yours, too.]

Spring turned to summer, then fall, then another winter without Ellie at our Thanksgiving and Christmas tables. Even Mr. Knowles was barely there—he and Mrs. Knowles didn't even speak to each other. Then spring again, and summer, and fall, and winter. Then again. And again and again and again and again, over and over, the same thing.

And then something different happened.

[Scribe's note: To her credit, Mrs. Knowles did leave me alone in those ensuing years. Not so much as a phone call or a Christmas card. I felt free— like I could completely start over, and Darla and Mrs. Knowles were a part of my old life, one I didn't have to live anymore if I didn't want to. I think you can guess what I wanted.

In Professor Gantry's laboratory, Benjamin and I became good friends. I trained with him diligently, until he trusted me to run experiments on my own, without his supervision. I excelled in my classes, earning a report card sporting only A's at the end of my freshman year. All of my time was tangled up in the laboratory and my classes. I barely made time to eat or get out in the fresh air, which left me quite thin and pale by the start of summer. Luckily, at least, my acne had cleared up, and the scars left by my squeezing fingers were barely visible. I continued to put effort into my appearance, which I had quickly come to understand was extremely important as a woman in a male-dominated field. The men did not want us there, do you understand? If we were going to squeeze our way in, we had to not only be smarter than them, but we had to be easy on the eyes, too. It wasn't fair—it's still not—but that's how things are.

You might think me cruel, but I'm going to tell you the truth. Only once between her visit to UVA and the start of summer did I think of Darla. It happened in my biology class. Professor Davidson was at the blackboard, pointing at a diagram of a human brain with his long wooden rod.

"The frontal lobe is located here, in the anterior portion of the brain. How many of you have ever decided what you want for dinner?"

All of our hands tentatively went up.

"How many of you have answered one of my questions in class?"

The hands stayed up.

"How many of you have felt bad for someone else?"

Still, the hands.

Professor Davidson smiled. "For all of that, you have your frontal lobes to thank. The frontal lobe is involved in a litany of what we call your 'executive functions,' things like organizing and making decisions. It also plays a role in your speech, your emotions and feelings, your understanding of and adherence to rules, even your memory. In laboratories all across the country, researchers are working to understand the frontal lobe, and the brain in general, in even greater detail. Much of what we know comes from Brenda Milner and her colleagues in Montreal, if you're interested in further researching the topic on your own time."

I filed the name 'Brenda Milner' away for future use. A powerful woman in the sciences would earn my attention any day.

We all lowered our hands, except for one student. Professor Davidson pointed at him. "Yes?"

"Professor, how do researchers study the brain to figure out how parts of it function? Wouldn't you have to have a live subject for that?"

Professor Davidson nodded. "Absolutely. A cadaver brain can give us clues about physical structure, but not much about function."

The student raised his hand again, and the Professor called on him. "Isn't it unethical to experiment on living people?"

"That's a good question, and one I hope you all never lose sight of as budding scientists. The ethics of our profession are extremely important. There are ethical ways to research living subjects, including humans. In the case of much of this brain research, scientists study patients who have experienced brain trauma. One of the most impactful case studies of the frontal lobe involved a man named Phineas Gage. Nearly a century and a quarter ago, a thick iron tamping rod was rammed through Mr. Gage's skull as he was working as a railroad foreman. The rod entered through his left cheek, pierced his brain matter, then exited his skull. Miraculously, Mr. Gage was able to walk and to speak, and he even remained conscious as he sought medical attention.

However, despite having survived the horrific accident, Mr. Gage did not have a happy ending. Those who knew him reported that, following the accident, the young man's personality changed, and he became a surly alcoholic, completely different from the man he had been before his traumatic brain injury.

Mr. Gage's case had a profound impact on the study of the brain early on, and helped us understand that the frontal lobe is linked to an individual's personality."

The students around me were silent, rapt.

Professor Davidson continued, "What we can take from cases like Mr. Gage's is that by gathering information about a patient's behavior before the trauma, observing the patient's behavior after the trauma, then using imaging techniques to assess that trauma, we can build a picture, however blurry, of how the damaged portion of the brain functioned."

My fingers were gripping my pencil so tightly I thought it might snap in half.

Then, Professor Davidson finished with what felt like the twist of a knife in my guts. "Many patients who have helped further our understanding of the frontal lobe were actually subjected to lobotomies, which, thank God, are no longer performed."

The same student raised his hand again, was acknowledged, and asked, "What's a lobotomy?"

It took all of my strength to stay in that room while Professor Davidson explained, in broad strokes, the history, rationale, protocol, and aftereffects of the lobotomy. Most of it I had already heard before, whether I'd researched it myself or gathered it from others.

"The lobotomy has been discredited, and rightly so," Professor Davidson said. "It is an imprecise, barbaric, and, in my opinion, criminal procedure."

Barbaric. Criminal. Fresh waves of shame, guilt, and sorrow rolled over me, so heavy I was surprised I wasn't flattened under their weight.

"You okay?" a girl next to me nudged my hand and whispered. "You're white as a sheet."

I glanced over. This girl and I had never spoken before, but she had a kind face and big green eyes. She smelled of mint. "I'm fine," I said.

She nodded, smiled, and looked back to Professor Davidson.

When the lecture was finally over, I ran to the bathroom and vomited bright yellow bile into the dirty toilet bowl.

After that, I worked even harder to push thoughts of Darla further down into my memories, where they would stay locked up tight.]

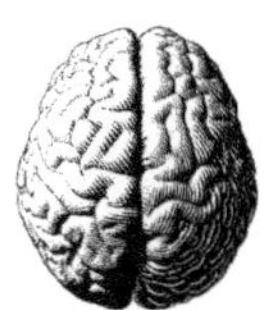

1 9 7 8 - 1 9 8 1

My chest continued to grow. Mrs. Knowles bought me new brassieres. I read a book about a girl named Carrie. She was even more wild than Anonymous in the Alice book. I liked it so much I read the book four times before Mrs. Knowles realized it wasn't about a nice teenager going to her high school prom and took it away.

[Scribe's note: I suppose I should tell you more about Benjamin now. It's probably not hard for you to guess what happened. After all, you're smart—somewhat, anyway.

We worked hours upon hours together, sometimes late into the night, if an experiment demanded it. Professor Gantry was pushing us to produce results for his next published paper, and even though I, as an undergraduate, could let Benjamin shoulder the burden of the research, I didn't want to.

The night we completed our last set of experiments and wrote up our results for Professor Gantry, Benjamin turned to face me. We were sitting side by side at the lab bench. He didn't say anything, he just took my face in both of his hands, pulled me closer, and kissed me.

Benjamin was the first boy to show me any attention since that brief flicker with Jeremiah Fannin, and we both know how that turned out. I was young, I was foolish and stupid and green, and I let Benjamin have all the pieces of myself I didn't absolutely need. If I'd been talking to Mrs. Knowles,

I would have loved to tell her how I'd thrown away my woman's gift, just to hear the shock and disapproval in her voice. Over the next three years, we studied together. We worked together. I even earned a spot as a co-author on one of Professor Gantry's papers, which was practically unheard of for an undergraduate, especially a female undergraduate. Before my junior year, I moved into Benjamin's studio apartment, and we walked to campus together every day. If Professor Gantry noticed our relationship, he didn't say anything about it. Why would he? Benjamin and I were a powerful team. We'd given Professor Gantry result after result, facilitating his elevation into the top science publications.

Benjamin earned his PhD two months before I graduated summa cum laude. I had already received medical school acceptances from Harvard, Yale, Columbia, Cornell, and, as a backup, UVA. I was just waiting for Benjamin. He had applied for post-doctoral research positions at those same five schools.

I think you can guess which school I had my eye on.]

I knew Ellie was going to medical school. Some of her acceptance letters had come to Mrs. Knowles's house. I opened them when she wasn't home and read them all. I wondered if I'd get to go to Ellie's UVA graduation, but I figured probably not.

Before Mrs. Knowles came into the living room, I hid all the letters under the couch. I can't tell you how, but I knew the letters would only make Mrs. Knowles angry, and when she was angry, the food she cooked wasn't as tasty.

[Scribe's note: I'm glad Darla hid the letters from Mrs. Knowles. She would only have had further reason to be angry with me, because clearly, I was going to venture even farther away, and her already severely minimal hold over me would diminish even more.

On my graduation day, I half-expected Mrs. Knowles to be perched in the audience, clutching Darla's arm, just to spite me. But when I looked out over the crowd, my diploma in my hand and the navy blue gown sticking to my sweaty legs, the only person I saw was Benjamin, sitting near the front, smiling and clapping.

He took me out to dinner that night at a fancy Charlottesville restaurant. We ate steak and baked potatoes, and Benjamin even ordered us a massive slice of chocolate cake for dessert.

That moment is bittersweet for me, because it's the last time I remember feeling truly happy.

When we got home from dinner, Benjamin rushed to his mailbox.

"Ellen! It's here!" he said, running to sit at our tiny kitchen table.

My stomach did a flip, and I regretted stuffing myself so fully.

Benjamin slid a finger through the top of the envelope and pulled out the crisp sheet.

Have you ever seen a person crumple from within? First, their mouth twists into a tight frown, then their nostrils flare, then their eyes go flat and expressionless, as though the very force animating them has been vacuumed out of their body.

"It's a no," Benjamin finally said, tossing the letter onto the table. I grabbed it, quickly reading Harvard's rejection.

Now how about this—have you ever felt your own self crumple from within? I had worked so hard—*so hard*—to earn my spot at Harvard's Medical School. But what was I supposed to do? I couldn't leave Benjamin. He was, at that point, as integral to me as my DNA. More shamefully... I was afraid. I was afraid of losing the one person who had ever felt really, truly close to me. Over the years we'd been together, I'd convinced myself I could survive anything with Benjamin. The flip side of that coin was devastating: without him, I could survive nothing. Or so I thought.

I hugged him. "It's okay," I said. "There will be others."

And there were. The next day, Cornell rejected him. The day after, Yale and Columbia both said no.

He cried when he got his acceptance to UVA, whether out of relief or disbelief, I wasn't sure. I cried, too—but mine were tears of rage. Of bewilderment. Of how-could-I-have-worked-so-hard-only-to-stay-in-the-same-place.

Benjamin knew about my own acceptances. He knew about my dreams. But there was nothing else to do. The pull to feel whole and complete with Benjamin was stronger than the tug of my aspirations. I told myself this wasn't the end, I could still accomplish what I desired—just at a different time.

"I guess we'll be renewing this lease in the fall!" he said, and for God's sake, I think he was genuinely happy. His goals weren't as lofty as mine, and he didn't think twice about staying in Charlottesville, of living the past three years over again.

"I guess so," I said, and we hugged, and we made love, and then, while he snored in the dark, I mourned.

I submitted my paperwork for the University of Virginia School of Medicine the next day.]

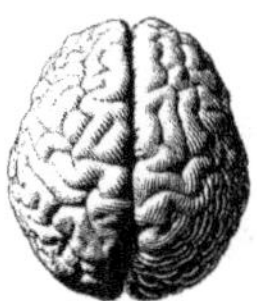

1 9 8 1 - 1 9 8 5

I got lost in the grocery store while I was with Mrs. Knowles—or, Mrs. Knowles lost track of me, I guess. They had to call over the store speakers to find me. I don't know why they made such a big fuss about it—I was only looking at cereal boxes, trying to decide which one might taste the best. I wasn't ready to leave, so I ignored the big loud voice. When Mrs. Knowles spotted me, she click-clacked on her heels all the way to where I was standing.

"Darla, don't you ever scare me like that again!" she yelled.

We left without buying any cereal, and I didn't speak to her for the rest of the day.

[Scribe's note: I received a scholarship to UVA's medical school, but it didn't pay for my books or my rent. Professor Gantry offered me my old position in his laboratory, but the thought of going back there made me feel like my forward momentum had died, so I said no, and I begged him to tell Benjamin, if he asked, that there wasn't any room in the lab for me now that I'd graduated.

Instead, I found a position in Doctor Cooley's lab, studying the effects of different hormones on cancerous tumors in murine models. I enjoyed the work, especially dissecting the sacrificed animals. Actually seeing, with my own eyes, the physical effects of the cancers on those mice was illuminating. The acts of slicing, of separating and suturing and probing, felt holier than church.

I suppose it's no surprise I found surgery to be my calling. As thrilled as I was by these micro-autopsies, I was equally disgusted by the classes I took that dealt with medications. It had been nearly ten years, but I still remembered how the Thorazine dulled all of my senses, then left me spasming on the floor like a madwoman. Then, of course, there was the Valium that had killed poor Mother.

No, I would not be a pill dispenser for devious junkies. You could fake pain, but you couldn't fake a tumor, or a hernia, or a broken bone.

As a surgeon, I'd also be able to fix people directly—remove that tumor, repair that herniated tissue, mend that bone. Did I wish I could have been the one to go into Darla's brain and physically fix her before that butcher Hupman got to her? Of course I did—but who knows if even that would have helped her.

I saw less of Benjamin on a daily basis, but we still spent hours together in the evenings, strolling the campus and talking about our respective research. Benjamin was continuing the projects he'd been working on before he got his PhD, and, frankly, I found them profoundly uninteresting. There was nothing new there, nothing exciting, not like what I was doing. But when I tried to tell him about my own research, about what it was teaching me about myself and who I wanted to be, he invariably shut me down, either with a sloppy kiss—sometimes with alcohol on his breath—or with the kind of shoulder caress I used to find romantic, but now felt patronizing.

But damn it all, I still loved him. After I graduated medical school, I figured we would get married, buy a house, thrive in our careers... and, before you ask, no. I did not see children in that picture, and since Benjamin never mentioned babies, I figured we were on the same page.

Isn't life funny, sometimes?]

Mrs. Knowles was angry a lot. She yelled at me if I left the water running in the bathroom, which I only did a few times. She yelled at me if there were crumbs on the floor after I ate. She yelled at me if I left the back door open when I went outside. She yelled at me if I couldn't remember how to do a math problem she'd taught me before. She yelled at me so much that I started doing those things on purpose. Sometimes, I even wanted to hit her, not because I was upset, really, but just to see what it would feel like.

I never cried, because her yelling was silly, and it couldn't touch me where I actually lived, inside my serene pond. Nothing could, so I kept doing what I wanted to do, and I let her keep yelling.

And then, one day, she went to the grocery store. She didn't take me with her anymore.

She didn't come home.

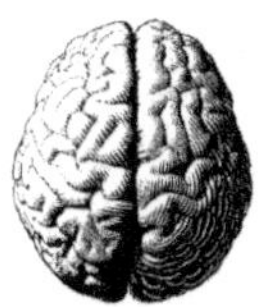

1 9 8 5

[Scribe's note: It happened in February, three months before I would graduate with my MD. Why couldn't she have waited just a little bit longer?

The official cause of death was massive blood loss due to head trauma sustained in an automobile accident. The woman had driven her sedan straight into a light pole, which had embedded itself into her forehead when she catapulted through the windshield. She hadn't been wearing her seat belt.

The death was ruled an accident, even though the police officer I spoke with had his suspicions that it was a suicide.

Of course it was.

Darla was, by that point, a legal adult. There would be no foster care for her, and Mr. Knowles was so completely out of the picture—there were whispers of another man, I found out later—that there was zero possibility of leaving Darla in that household.

Mrs. Knowles's funeral took place the first day of my general surgery clinical rotation. I ignored the black dress in my and Benjamin's shared sliver of closet and donned my scrubs. When the surgery was over—an appendectomy—I borrowed Professor Gantry's car and drove all the way to Richmond. Darla was alone in the Knowles house when I got there, sitting in the dark on the living room couch.

"Hi, Ellie," she said when I walked in, like she'd been expecting me.

"Hi, Darla," I said. I was shocked by her appearance. She looked so... normal. Hair neatly combed, black dress free of wrinkles, kitten heels polished to a shine. She was even wearing a touch of makeup, which only enhanced her beauty.

And then she sneezed, failing to cover her mouth and letting snot drip down the front of her dress.

"Let's go," I said, uninterested in searching the house for signs of Mr. Knowles.

We packed up her clothes, her toiletries, and some of her books, and we were back on the road to Charlottesville within a half hour.

When we walked into the apartment, Benjamin was sitting at the little table. He hopped up, hair still wet from the shower, and smiled so wide I thought his face might break in half.

"Darla!" he said. "It's so good to see you!" It had been nearly eight years, yet Benjamin acted as though he and Darla were old pals. My throat felt tight. As Benjamin took in Darla's appearance—the snot on her dress had dried and flaked off—I felt acutely aware of my own body. My hair was neatly combed, my scrubs had remained spotless, but I knew there were dark circles under my eyes, and my bosom didn't strain at the seams of my clothing like Darla's did.

Dear God, what had I done bringing Darla here?

"She'll sleep on the couch," I said, pointing to our tiny loveseat.

"Nonsense," Benjamin said, slinging an arm around Darla's shoulders. "Take the bed. You and Ellen can sleep together. I'll take the couch."

"But, Ben—" I said.

"Nope," he said, his attempt at gallantry so cartoonish I wanted to laugh. "What sort of gentleman would I be if I let a lady sleep on a couch when there's a perfectly good bed right there?"

"We're going to need a bigger apartment," I grumbled, but Benjamin was too preoccupied staring at Darla to hear me.]

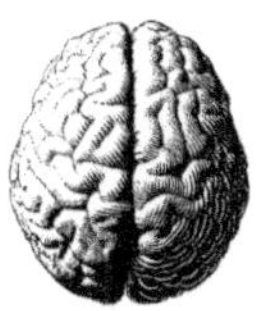

1 9 8 5

I didn't like how small the apartment was, and it smelled different than Mrs. Knowles's house, and I didn't have my own space, and my fists started clenching. But then Benjamin put his arm around me, and he told me I could sleep in the bed, and I felt better.

Hungrier.

The bed was comfortable, and I curled up around Ellie and fell asleep fast, just like when we were children. [Scribe's note: Darla's body heat was so intense and so inescapable, I barely got any sleep.]

Ellie left early the next morning. When I got up to use the bathroom, Benjamin was still asleep on the couch. He looked silly, with his feet hanging off the end. When I laughed, his eyes popped open.

"Good morning," he said, smiling.

"Hi," I said, then, remembering I really had to use the bathroom, I left.

When I came back into the room, Benjamin was at the counter, making coffee.

It had been a very long time since I'd woken up somewhere that wasn't my room at Mrs. Knowles's. Was there bread? Was there a toaster? Did they have jelly?

I didn't know where to start, and my confusion soured into anger, and then I was throwing open cabinets, digging around for something to eat.

"Whoa, whoa," Benjamin said, putting a hand on my wrist. "What are you looking for? I can help."

I sat down in the middle of the floor, feeling limp. "I'm hungry," I said.

"Of course you are," he said. "What would you like?"

"Breakfast," I said.

He laughed. "Right."

He didn't ask me another question, just started pulling things out of the refrigerator. He helped me move to the small table, and a few minutes later, he put a plate in front of me. It had brownish scrambled eggs and a shriveled-looking sausage on it. It was all wrong.

"No," I said, then I pushed the plate off the table. It fell to the floor, but it didn't break. Instead, those oddly colored eggs and the sad sausage splattered against the black-and-white linoleum.

"Darla," Benjamin said, but he didn't sound like Mrs. Knowles used to when she was unhappy with me. He bent down to pick up the plate, then swept up the food with a broom. "You don't like eggs?"

"Breakfast is bread and jelly," I said.

"Well, we don't have any bread, or any jelly, but I can pick some up at the store later, okay?"

I nodded.

"We have bananas, and there's some milk in the fridge," he said. "I have to go to the lab now, but I can come back around lunchtime with something else for you, okay?"

I nodded.

"Clearly I'm not the best at guessing what you like, so can you just tell me this time would you'd eat for lunch?"

I thought for a moment. "Chili," I said. [Scribe's note: No, okay? I hadn't fully thought through what taking care of Darla would look like given my current living situation. At that point, I was solely focused on applying for residency positions. I had to finish what I'd started. I couldn't drop everything and make sure Darla had bread when she needed it, or that she had something to entertain her while I was working. Looking back, I can see my mistakes very clearly. Whereas I had assumed Darla would function more as our house cat, roaming as she pleased and generally taking care of her own needs, Benjamin treated her as an affectionate, if surly, dog who required more attention than his own girlfriend.

In other words, I know what you're going to say. I should have seen it coming.]

Ellie didn't cook, but when she tried, she was no Mrs. Knowles. Her food was so plain, so boring. Canned peas and plain noodles. Runny eggs. Campbell's soup and crackers. I missed Mrs. Knowles's spaghetti casserole, her meatloaf, her mashed potatoes and cherry pie.

Benjamin fed me most of the time. He'd try to get me whatever I asked for, which was much better than what Ellie made for herself. He cooked sometimes, too, and it was always silly to see a man in the kitchen.

Even if he only brought or made food for me, he'd usually sit with me at the little table. It was so small our knees touched. He'd talk to me about his work, about his family, about Ellie. He talked a lot about her.

That strange hunger was back, and it was stronger than it had been around Jeremiah. Sometimes, I'd finish the food he'd brought me, only to still feel hungry. I think he felt it, too.

"You're very beautiful, you know that," he said one day, after I finished eating a turkey sandwich. Somehow, I'd managed to keep myself clean.

I nodded.

"You're so… different from Ellen," he said. "Yes, she's beautiful, too, and driven, and ambitious, and so goddamn smart…"

He put his hand on my knee under the table. I felt warm all over.

"But sometimes… sometimes, Darla, she's *too* smart. Do you know what I mean? It's like she always knows exactly what to do, and how it should be done, centuries before anybody else catches up with her. Including me."

He looked at me and frowned. I frowned back.

"You get it," he said. "I can see that."

His hand moved farther up my leg.

"Don't get me wrong, Ellen is amazing. But sometimes I just want her to let me be the man, let me be the smart one. I know she got into fucking Harvard Medical School and that she stayed here for me. I know that. But she doesn't have to bring it up every time we get into even the tiniest little argument. It's not fair."

I nodded.

"And I know she's looking at residency positions all over the country. She's probably not going to stay here after graduation, and I'm not ready to leave here yet. So… so what's really the point, you know what I mean?"

I did not. I nodded anyway.

And then his lips were on mine, and they were warm and dry and tasted like peppermint, nothing like Jeremiah. His hand squeezed my leg, but not too tight, and I felt dizzy with that hunger. His other hand started rubbing my other knee, and then he was lifting me out of my chair, bringing me to the bed, and I didn't know what to do, but I didn't want it to stop.

He pulled my shirt over my head and groaned, like he was in pain. He started putting his lips all over my neck, going farther down.

And then the door opened.

[Scribe's note: That motherfucking piece of shit asshole. Darla had been living with us for one goddamn week, and the scumbag was already pouncing on her. I came home early that day to change into a fresh pair of scrubs (my other pair was covered in blood after assisting during a valve surgery), and the first thing I heard was Benjamin's groan. I knew that groan, of course I did. It wasn't meant for anyone else but me.

At first, I thought he was simply pleasuring himself—don't be a prude, you know this is a thing men do—but then I remembered Darla, and how she hadn't left our apartment since she'd arrived.

I rounded the corner past the bathroom and saw them on the bed. Darla's ample chest was exposed, and Benjamin was on top of her.

I screamed.

Benjamin leapt off the bed, sputtering. "It's not what it looks like! Ellen, listen to me!"

Darla still lay on the bed, her annoyingly voluptuous breasts splayed out, her expression placid, dreamy.

"How dare you?" I screamed.

Benjamin's cheeks were scarlet, his brow looked fevered. "Ellen, baby, please! Don't be like this!"

"Don't be like what, Benjamin? I come home to find you taking advantage of my brain damaged sister. What exactly do you expect me to be like? Huh?"

Yes, I felt bad about calling Darla 'brain damaged,' but how could Benjamin not see the wrongness of what he'd been doing? Then again, Jeremiah hadn't seen it, either, but it had never gotten this far…

Something inside of me broke, and I winced. "Get out," I growled. "Get out now, and I don't ever want to see you again."

"Ellen, please," he whispered, but the fight had gone out of him. "I love you."

I waved a hand at Darla, still half naked on the bed. "Funny way of showing it," I said.

His eyes went from teary to angry. "I do love you!" he hissed. "But how am I supposed to love someone who treats me like I'm inferior?"

"What are you talking about?" I said.

"We both know you got into Harvard, okay? I know you're the smarter one, the harder worker, the *better* one of us. I know it, because you never let me fucking forget it."

And there it was, out in the open.

"Are you punishing me?" I asked. "Is this how you want to hurt me, just because of what I've worked so hard my entire life to earn?"

Benjamin grabbed his backpack from the couch, crossed to the dresser—not without snagging another glance at Darla's breasts—and started stuffing clothes into it. "Yeah, right," he grumbled. "Maybe women don't belong on campus."

That didn't even warrant a response. I'd never seen this side of Benjamin before—biting, cruel, misogynistic, illogical. Was this the effect Darla had on him, or had this always been hiding just beneath the surface?

At that moment, as I watched him, I couldn't remember if he was my father, or if he was Jeremiah, or if he was Benjamin... and then the moment passed, and I fought to regain control of myself and my memory.

He finished packing his bag. With one more longing glance at Darla, he pushed past me and left the apartment.

"Get dressed," I told Darla, and then I locked myself in the bathroom, took a long shower, changed into clean scrubs, and went back to the hospital, feeling like half of a person.]

I pulled my shirt back on, but I didn't get up. My body pulsed, and I wanted Benjamin to come back. Why had she sent him away? [Scribe's note: And this is the crux of the problem. Darla would never understand boundaries. She would never understand her effect on men, or the consequences of what she—and they—did. She didn't think about how it would hurt me.

I was through with men. I was through with the ache of profound emptiness that ripped me apart after I lost yet another man to my sister, who had nothing but beauty to offer. I was through handling men's fragile egos with kid gloves. I was through letting a man's choices and limitations dictate my life.

So I considered that part of myself—the sexual part that longed for companionship—dead.

After changing the locks on the apartment, I spent the remaining months of medical school keeping Darla alive, applying for residencies, and assisting with surgeries. On the day of my graduation, I locked Darla in the apartment with a loaf of bread and a jar of peanut butter. With my fellow graduates, I took the Hippocratic Oath. I received my doctoral hood. I listened to the speeches drone on and on, and I didn't search the crowd for any familiar faces.

When the ceremony was over, I returned to the apartment. Darla was asleep on the bed, her face covered in peanut butter, which she'd managed to smear all over the pillows.

I should have felt elated, but all I felt was bone-deep exhaustion. I lay down next to Darla, breathing deep of her peanut butter smell, and I fell asleep.

When I woke up, Darla was sitting on the couch, watching me. The peanut butter was dry and crumbling off of her cheeks.

The bed creaked as I stood up. It came with the apartment, and I wasn't sad to leave it behind. It reminded me too much of Benjamin, of the happy nights we'd spent here for so many years.

I pulled my suitcase from under the bed and started packing.

"Where are we going?" Darla asked.

"We're moving to Boston," I said.

"Okay," Darla said.

She watched me in silence as I shoved as many of my things as I could into the suitcase. The letter about my residency had come the day before, and I was already dreaming of a new life.

This time, no man would stop me. In one month, I would be one of Harvard's newest residents, and I would be bringing Darla with me.]

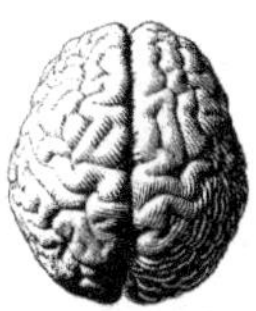

1 9 8 5 - 2 0 0 4

Boston was cold and windy, even in the summer. At least I had my own room in Ellie's new apartment. It made moving easier, because I could have my own space, like I'd had at Mrs. Knowles's. I didn't care that the room was small. Ellie said she was happy we were going to Boston, but she frowned all the time.

The day after we got our telephone set up, it started ringing so loudly it gave me a headache and made me angry. Ellie answered it, and her frown got even deeper, like the corners of her mouth might just slide down her neck. I went into my room and sat on my new bed, but I could still hear what she said. [Scribe's note: Of course I was frowning. I wasn't simply angry—I was furious. I was incandescent with rage. I'm sure you can guess who was on the phone.

"Ellen, just listen to me," Benjamin said as soon as I picked up.

"How did you get this number?" I said, tempted to shove the phone back into its cradle.

"It doesn't matter. Please, I just want to talk," he said.

"I'm going to hang up right fucking now unless you tell me how you got this number," I said.

He sounded sheepish. "I called the hospital administrator. I told her I was your cousin, and that your aunt died, but I didn't have your new number because you'd just moved, and I needed to get in touch with you right away."

I choked out an unhappy laugh. "Of course you did," I said.

"Ellen, I'm really sorry about everything that happened," he said.

"Oh, you mean how you tried to force yourself on my invalid sister?"

He was quiet a moment, then he said, "It wasn't like that."

"Sure it wasn't," I said.

"It wasn't!" he said, more loudly. "And she's not an invalid, Ellen. She can do a lot more than you think. She can *be* a lot more than you think."

"Right. I'm going to take the opinion of some sex pervert who has known Darla for a few weeks over the evidence of my entire life."

"Ellen," he said, and there was a note of warning in his voice that he'd occasionally used when we were fighting, back before Darla came to live with us. I always hated that tone.

"What? What are you going to do? Huh?" I was being combative, but I didn't care.

"Come on, Ellen," he said, sounding defeated.

"What do you want, Benjamin? Why are you calling me?"

"I wanted to say I'm sorry," he said.

"Okay," I said. I wasn't going to tell him I accepted his apology—because I didn't. He was dead to me.

He didn't say anything, and for a moment, I thought I heard soft crying.

"Is there anything else?" I asked.

"It's just—" he snorted back tears.

"Just what?"

"I... I love her, Ellen. I know you don't want to hear it, but I do. Please. Please just let me talk to her."

"Go fuck yourself," I said, my fingers gripping the plastic telephone so tight, I thought it would crack.

"No need to be nasty, Ellen," he said.

"Right, I'm sorry. I meant to say go fuck yourself, please."

"It's not right," he said. "What you're doing."

"What are you talking about?" My voice was flat, a dead thing in my throat. I'm sure you're wondering why I didn't just hang up the phone, let Benjamin grovel to himself, but the truth is—I missed him. I hate writing that, I absolutely abhor that weakness in myself, the vulnerability. But you have to understand, he was an integral part of my world for nearly eight years, and I thought he would be a necessary part of my future for the rest of my life. To have that ripped away so suddenly, and so painfully… it hurt. It still hurts, when I think about it, even after everything that happened. My brain knew the love was dead, but my heart hadn't gotten the message, and hearing his voice made me ache, as though I'd eaten too much candy, but I couldn't keep myself from unwrapping another piece.

"It's not right how you keep her penned up inside like an animal. You never even give her a chance to live her own life, to do what she wants to do."

"Benjamin, she isn't capable," I said, my voice rising. "She will never live on her own, okay? She is never going to get better!"

I screamed this last sentence, and then I was sobbing, and I was so angry that I was sobbing, and the last thing I wanted was to give Benjamin the satisfaction of knowing he'd pierced my shell, so I finally did hang up.]

I heard Ellie yell that I was never going to get better. I grabbed my pillow off of my bed and threw it at the door, but it didn't make a very loud sound. My face felt hot. I wanted to throw something else—because Ellie was wrong. She was wrong!

[Scribe's note: My hand pulsed when I released my grip on the phone. I buried my head in my hands and let the tears come, all the tears I'd never shed before, all the tears I'd kept penned up inside, as Benjamin had claimed I'd done with Darla.

Was he right? Had I become no better than Mother, shoving Darla away into a dark corner, hiding her as my dirty little secret, never expecting her to move past her trauma? I used to be her champion, to push for her to have new experiences, new interactions, new skills. But I just didn't have it in me anymore.

I sobbed harder. I only stopped when the phone rang again.

I ignored it.

It ceased, then took up its rattling shriek again, and again, and again.

This was before cell phones, before you could silence your ringer with a flick of a switch or block someone's number from ever darkening your screen again.

At last, just to make it stop, I picked up again.

"Jesus Christ, Ellen!" Benjamin yelled. "Why are you doing this?"

I forced my voice to sound steady. "I should have gone to Harvard four years ago," I said. "Back when I had the chance the first time. Instead, I made the mistake of hanging around with a zero like you. Your reach school is my fucking safety. I'm done with you, Benjamin."

I hung up the phone for the second time that day, then I unplugged it from the wall.]

When I came out of my room, Ellie's frown was deeper than I'd ever seen it, but she wasn't crying anymore, and I wasn't as angry anymore.

"I'm ordering pizza," she said.

"Okay," I said.

As I ate my pepperoni that night across the table from Ellie, I tried harder than I ever had before to chew with my mouth closed, to swallow before taking another bite, to wipe my mouth with my napkin if any sauce dripped. More than anyone, I wanted Ellie to see what I could do.

[Scribe's note: I didn't even notice. I was too busy pressing napkins into my pizza to absorb the grease and thinking about Benjamin, about how his disgusting assignation with Darla was a good thing, because if he hadn't done it, I might never have ended up at Harvard.]

Ellie started her job at the hospital. She was gone a lot, which meant I was inside the apartment on my own. A lot. She showed me how to lock the door from the inside, and she told me to never go outside on my own. [Scribe's note: What could I do? I couldn't babysit her, I didn't think she'd respond well to a stranger, and I couldn't have her wandering around downtown Boston on her own. My options were limited, and I did the best I could.]

She brought me books from the library, but she didn't have time to read them to me like she used to. I was okay with that—I could read them on my own now, and if I didn't know a word, I looked it up in the little dictionary I kept next to my bed.

I missed my outdoor walks and spending time in the sun. Mrs. Knowles's backyard hadn't been big, but it had been grassy and clean, and it always smelled like flowers. Ellie's apartment smelled like old food and antiseptic.

I had nobody to talk to except for Ellie, and by the time she came home, she was usually so tired she collapsed in her room right after dinner.

I was lonely. I missed Mrs. Knowles. Even Jeremiah. And Benjamin, too.

Ellie had just left for the hospital when I plugged the phone back in for the first time. I sat next to it all day, waiting for it to ring. When I heard Ellie's key in the lock, I pulled the plug and went to sit on the couch with my book.

I did the same thing the next day, and the next, and the day after that.

And then, one day, it rang.

I picked it up. The phone was cool in my hands, and heavier than I expected. I couldn't remember the last time I'd talked on a phone. Nobody had ever called me.

"Hello?" I said.

There was a gasp on the other end. "Darla? Is that you?"

"I'm Darla," I said.

"Oh, my God! Darla! I can't believe it!"

He didn't say his name, but he didn't have to. I knew it was Benjamin.

"Hi," I said.

"Darla, I can't tell you how much I've missed you," he said.

I didn't know what to say, so I stayed quiet. It was so nice to hear someone else's voice.

"Is Ellie there?" he asked.

"No," I said.

"Good," he said. I could hear him breathing. And then he started talking. He told me about what it had been like for him after Ellie threw him out. About his new apartment, and what he was working on, and somebody who worked with him who he didn't like. I wasn't upset that he didn't ask about me. I had nothing to tell.

"God, I missed you," he said. "Listen, Darla, I have to go now, but I want to talk to you again. Can I talk to you again?"

"Yes," I said. When I'd first picked up the phone, the sun had been peeping through the window. Now it was high overhead. Time had passed, and I was glad of it.

"When can I call?" he said.

"Ellie works most days," I said. "I plug in the phone when she's gone."

He grunted. "Jesus," he said. "Okay, I'll call during the day whenever I can get away. Is that alright?"

"Yes," I said.

"Darla?" he said.

"Yes?" I repeated.

"I love you," he said. For a moment, I couldn't remember if I was talking to Jeremiah or Benjamin, but then I realized it didn't matter, because either way, I knew the right answer.

"I love you, too," I said.

[Scribe's note: When I got home that day, Darla seemed brighter, a bit sunnier, like she'd had a particularly good day. I was too tired to ask her about it. Now I wish I had. I don't think she would have lied to me, and then I could have nipped everything in the bud. That would have been far better, I think. I'm sure you don't agree. Or maybe you do?]

It got even colder in Boston. I only know that because I could see snow outside of our windows. When I touched the glass, my hand felt frozen.

My days were all the same. I woke up, usually after Ellie had already left for the hospital. I made my bread and jelly, and I practiced eating it like Ellie was there. I walked around the apartment to keep my strength up. I read whatever book Ellie had brought me from the library. She usually picked something good. I liked mysteries, and stories where the girls were the ones doing the solving, or the rescuing, or the winning.

I ate lunch. I wasn't too hungry, so I usually just had an orange or a banana. Then I plugged in the telephone.

In the afternoons, Benjamin called.

It didn't happen every day, but either way, I'd spend the time after lunch until Ellie got home sitting at the table, next to the telephone. Whether he called or not, I always unplugged the phone when I heard Ellie's key in the lock.

He told me about his days at work, his friends, how he was thinking of getting a dog, how much he missed me.

I told him nothing, because he didn't ask.

[Scribe's note: Benjamin was using Darla as some kind of free therapy, as a release valve to take some of the pressure off his fragile male ego. She couldn't see that, I know. But it makes me angry. He used her, and he promised her nothing in return.

I know what you're thinking. *If he loved Darla so much, why didn't you just let him have her?*

You want to know why? Because he was a fake. He didn't really want Darla; he wanted the idea of her. He didn't want a wife who couldn't hold a pencil, a wife who would never be able to drive a car, a wife who couldn't be trusted to go out to dinner or meet his friends without making a spectacle of herself. He wanted a woman who existed solely in his mind, someone he could pour himself out to, who asked nothing in return. He wanted a sex doll, and I'd be damned if I let him turn Darla into something so cheap and tawdry.]

Benjamin told me one day that he wanted to come see me.

"I don't know," I said. That hunger fired up in my belly again. Would it be like the last time I saw him? What would Ellie do if she found out?

Would we have to move again?

"I'll be quick," he said. "Ellen won't ever find out."

"I don't know," I said again.

"Come on, baby—" There was something rustling in the background, and I heard a woman's voice. Then Benjamin said, "Oh, it's just someone from work. They had a question about the autoclave." His voice was all muffled, like he was talking through a scarf.

There was more rustling, and then I could hear him better again. "Sorry about that," he said. "Actually, I don't think I can come up this month. But I want to see you."

"Okay," I said, and the hunger died in my belly. I wasn't too sad to see it go. It was uncomfortable.

[Scribe's note: I can't believe I didn't know about this at the time. If only Darla had told me. The bastard wanted to have his sophisticated, well-bred girlfriend down in Virginia, but he was too selfish to let Darla go. He was too pathetic to let the real girlfriend see all of him. He reserved the pinkest, fleshiest parts of himself for Darla, because he knew she would never say a word, would never reject him. I'm glad I remained celibate for so many years after Benjamin.]

Benjamin kept calling, but the calls didn't happen as often. Sometimes, there was that rustling in the background again, and then he'd have to go. He kept talking about his friend Nancy, and how she drove him crazy, but she was a good girl so he didn't want to lose her. I listened, as always. Benjamin had stopped feeling like a real person to me, and started seeming more like a radio program I listened to. As the days went on, then weeks, then months, then years, and the calls kept coming, I could barely remember what Benjamin looked like, what that strange hunger had felt like in the pit of my belly.

[Scribe's note: I'm going to speed things along now. You don't need to know about the nearly twenty years we spent in that apartment in Boston, about the minutiae of our daily lives. Darla's didn't change much, but she didn't ask for it to change, understand? I completed my residency, then a fellowship in neurosurgery at Harvard. I was hired as an associate professor at Harvard Medical School, and I began my career as a full-time surgeon at Massachusetts General Hospital. My life got busier. I'd come home each night, or sometimes each morning if I'd been on the night shift, to find Darla. I always peeked into her room to see if she was sleeping. If it was morning, she'd sometimes be at the table, eating her bread and jelly.

As long as I kept her supplied with interesting library books and portion-controlled amounts of bread, fruit, and pasta, she was content. She didn't cause me trouble. On my rare day off, we would watch movies together and eat popcorn. We didn't talk much.

And no, before you ask—the comparison to a household pet did not escape me then, nor does it escape me now. She was like a prickly cat, always there, a semi-comforting presence, but not a creature that wanted to be petted.

How quickly twenty years can pass when nothing important changes.]

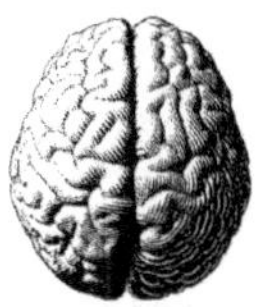

2 0 0 4

Then, something changed.

Ellie came home one day, earlier than usual, and I had to rush to unplug the phone. Ellie had her own phone by then, a little silver rectangle with tiny buttons, and I hadn't seen her use the big plastic telephone in a long time.

When she opened the door, she wasn't alone. She walked in, pulling another person behind her—a small man, with brownish hair and watery blue eyes. He was pale and slim, and when he smiled at me, his teeth were uneven, but they were white.

"Darla," Ellie said, looking between me and the man. "I have someone I'd like you to meet."

I stood up from the couch with a bit of struggle. Ellie had replaced it with something plusher the previous year, and I still wasn't used to how much I sunk into the cushions.

"This is Howard," Ellie said, waving to the man to come farther into the room. "Howard, this is my sister, Darla." Ellie smiled, but it didn't look real.

"Hi," I said.

"Hello, Darla," the man—Howard—said. "I've heard so much about you."

"Okay," I said.

There was silence, and then Ellie said, "Come, Howard, sit here. I'll get some coffee on."

Howard sat at our small kitchen table and stared at me. He didn't look at me the way Jeremiah or Benjamin had, with a glint in their eyes. Howard looked at me like he was watching the television, waiting for something to happen. I didn't like it.

I picked up my book from the coffee table and went back to my reading.

"Darla, it's rude to ignore our guest," Ellie said, bringing a mug to Howard. He slurped at it loudly. If Mrs. Knowles had been there, she would have snapped at him, I was sure of it.

I put my book back down and looked up at Howard and Ellie. They were both people, and I thought they were about the same age, but otherwise, they looked like two halves of different sandwiches. The same person would not want to eat both.

"Howard is a medical supply salesman," Ellie said, still with that fake smile stretching her lips.

"Okay," I said.

Ellie leaned closer to Howard and said something I couldn't hear.

"What are you reading?" Howard asked, pointing at my book.

I lifted it and showed him the cover.

"Ah," he said. "Harry Potter and the Philosopher's Stone. I've heard that's a good one."

"Yes," I said.

Howard slurped from his mug again.

"Darla," Ellie said. "I wanted you to meet Howard because... well, because we're dating."

"Okay," I said.

Ellie squinted at me. "Howard is my—my boyfriend," Ellie said, but she stuttered, like she was having trouble getting her words out.

Howard smiled next to her, but his didn't look real, either.

"Okay," I said again.

Ellie leaned closer to Howard once more and whispered something. Howard tilted his cup up and slurped the last of his coffee. When he put the mug down and smiled again, his teeth were brown. I wondered how Ellie could stand to kiss him. I thought about reaching out and pinching his cheek, to give him some more color, and to see if it would make him stop smiling.

"It was lovely to meet you," Howard said, and then, without waiting for me to say anything, they both stood up.

"Darla, I'll be home later," Ellie said. "There's pasta in the fridge. From Maggiano's."

I smiled then, and mine was real, because Maggiano's was my favorite.

"Okay," I said.

Then they left, and I ate my dinner. I spilled some red sauce on the Harry Potter book, but I could still see the words through the stain, so I figured it was okay.

I was in bed by the time Ellie came home.

[Scribe's note: Howard was no Benjamin, okay? I know that. You know that. Everybody in the world could see that, if you put the two of them side by side. But Howard was straightforward, and Howard was steadfast, and, to be honest with you, Howard was the most unassuming wisp of a man. You want to know something else? Something I've never told anyone before? Howard couldn't even maintain an erection. He was impotent, which explained why he was forty-five and had never been married. For most women, clearly, that had been a dealbreaker. For me, it was a dealmaker. I was no longer interested in the physical side of love. I'd had my fill. But companionship? The sort that can have an intelligent conversation? That was something I did yearn for.

I met Howard at the hospital. I don't know what it was about me that made him bolder than he usually was, but we struck up a conversation, and then, before I knew it, he had asked me to dinner, his voice trembling, and I had agreed. No, I didn't find him handsome. But I did find him nonthreatening.

On our fourth date—although Howard was unromantic to the point of being utterly platonic, so 'date' is a loose term—I told him about Darla. He gasped in all the right places; he reached across the table and held my hand in his clammy, cold palm; he molded his face into an expression of concern and grief. I'm not saying he didn't feel all of those things, because I believe he did, but I was—and still am, as you know—very skeptical of peoples' intentions. The men in my life did not have a good track record when it came to Darla.

We continued our courtship for several more months. I would have been content to keep things that way—nice dinners, decent enough conversation, perhaps a chaste kiss at the end of the night. Howard never asked to come to my apartment, and he never invited me to his.

Until the day he did. Howard didn't drink much, but on one particular date at a new Italian restaurant, he had one too many glasses of red wine. Through purple teeth, he asked me if I was ready to take the next step.

Think whatever you want about me, but I was lonely. It had been so long, and I knew Howard would never hurt me, so I said yes.

His apartment was devoid of any personality, but his bed was comfortable enough. I was no spring chicken, but I'd kept my figure and always maintained a pleasing appearance, and Howard sounded reasonably excited when I removed my brassiere.

He flicked off the light, climbed on top of me, and... I waited. And waited. And waited.

After far too long a time, Howard rolled off of me and began to cry softly.

"I'm sorry," he said.

"For what?" I asked, but I knew. Of course I knew.

"I... I can't be with you. In that way," he finally choked out.

Instead of being angry, or disappointed, or anguished, I was relieved. I was so relieved, in fact, that I started laughing.

"Just leave!" Howard said, with more venom than I'd ever heard from him.

"I'm not laughing at you!" I said. "I'm not. I promise. I'm laughing because…" How to explain it? "I'm laughing because I'm not… particularly interested in intercourse. I'm laughing because I'm relieved."

Howard turned to face me. In the dim light coming through the blinds, I could see the tears still streaming down his face. "Really?" he said, his voice tiny.

"Really," I said. I grabbed his face and kissed him, inhaling his wine-and-garlic breath, and then I stood to refasten my brassiere.

"I love you!" Howard said, desperately, as though this might be the end.

I surprised myself. "I love you, too," I said. I didn't know if I meant it, but I knew he needed to hear it. "I'll see you next week."

I took a taxi back to my apartment. Whatever Howard and I were, it was something I wasn't ready to end. Howard was one of the first men I'd ever truly known who didn't want a woman who was a blank canvas. He was blank enough himself, and he was looking for someone to bring some color to his life. That was something I could live with.

So, we resumed our courtship the following week, but Howard never again asked me back to his apartment.

Several more months passed by like this, until I figured it was time to introduce Howard to Darla. If he was going to fail now, I wanted to see it with my own eyes.

But you already know how this story ends, don't you? Howard didn't fail.]

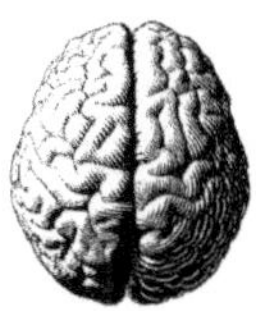

2 0 0 4

The next time a man came into our apartment, it wasn't Howard.

Benjamin called me one afternoon. It had been a long time.

"Darla," he said. "It's so good to hear your voice."

I hadn't said anything yet. "Yes," I answered. My stomach cramped. My blood would come soon.

"Listen," he said, and he sounded like Ellie did when she drank too much coffee. "I'll be up at Harvard in two weeks, presenting a paper at a conference."

"Okay," I said, gritting my teeth against the pain. It had never gotten easier.

"I… I'd like to see you."

I was quiet. I knew Ellie wouldn't like it.

"Nancy won't be with me. We're… we're taking a break. She's unreasonable, Darla. Now that the kids are teenagers and don't need her as much, she wants to spend more time with me, but what am I supposed to say? She's had three children, Darla, *three*, and it's taken a toll on her body. Things aren't where they used to be. Meanwhile, I'm over here, running every day, saying no to dessert, trying to keep myself attractive, and she still expects me to want her like that? It doesn't make sense. And then she has the gall to get angry with me when I tell her I'm not interested, like I'm the bad guy."

"Oh," I said.

"Anyway," Benjamin said. "I know it's been a long time, but I really want to see you. Please say okay? Please?"

What would Ellie say? Ellie would be furious, I knew that, but Ellie would get over it. She always did. I wanted something different. I wanted something more.

"Okay," I said.

"Yes!" Benjamin cried. "I'll see you in two weeks."

He asked for my address and I gave it, and then he hung up.

[Scribe's note: Darla is correct. I would have been furious if I'd known, and I would have put a stop to it. Even knowing what became of everything, I still would have stopped it.]

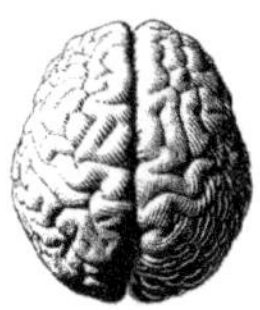

2 0 0 4

Benjamin telephoned on a Monday to tell me he'd be coming over the next afternoon. My stomach fluttered. I'd nearly forgotten what that felt like.

[Scribe's note: A few years earlier, I'd had a patient who needed a double bypass. The woman was older, maybe twenty years my senior. During our consultation, the woman stared straight ahead, as though she couldn't see me. She did not flinch during the physical exam, or when one of the nurses took her blood. Her expression never changed. She looked like she was dreaming with her eyes open.

I picked up her chart, scanning her medical history. Her daughter, sitting in a chair in the corner, said, "Momma had a brain surgery when she was thirty-one."

My stomach clenched. "What kind of brain surgery?" I asked.

The daughter's voice went down an octave, even though the three of us were the only ones in the room. "A lobotomy," she whispered.

Nausea tickled the back of my throat, but I shoved it down. "Oh," I said. "I see."

"She hasn't been the same since," the daughter said. "I was seven years old when she got it. She was pretty worried all the time before the surgery. Daddy said she had a neurosis and needed help. But when she came back, she was really different. She was like this." She waved at her mother.

"I see," I said again. "Does she live with you?"

"Oh, no," the daughter replied. "She lives in a nursing home now. I tried to keep her with me for awhile, but I have little ones, and I couldn't take care of her. When Daddy was still alive, we had more help, but he's been gone ten years now."

"So your mother requires full-time care?" I asked, my throat aching.

"Yes," the daughter said, looking down at her hands in her lap. "She's still alive, but she's not really in there anymore. I know that."

I looked down at the chart again. I was supposed to perform a double bypass—a major heart surgery—on this woman who was, even to her daughter, little more than a shell. Why? What would be the use?

"I still visit her every week," the daughter said. "Nobody really knows what that doctor did to her. I keep hoping one day, she'll wake up."

Ah. Now I understood.

"I'll take good care of your mother," I said.

Her mother survived the surgery. I don't know how much longer she lived after that, but, for her sake, I wished it wasn't long. I'd never before understood just how good Darla had had it. The lobotomy was unpredictable, ridiculous, and barbaric, and yet it hadn't made a complete vegetable of Darla. Should I have been grateful for that? How could a person be grateful for something that still carried the weight of so much tragedy? But were there degrees of tragedy?

Or, maybe, tragedy was one hulking monolith that would crush you, regardless of its size.]

My newest piece of clothing was a red blouse Ellie had bought me for my birthday five years before. I didn't need many clothes; I never went anywhere. My skin was so white I looked like a glass of milk.

My stomach flipped as I buttoned my blouse and pulled on my black skirt with the stretchy waistband. I sat on the couch and waited for the knock.

When it came, I unlocked the door and saw a man standing there. He had loads of gray hair, round glasses, and a bit of a scruffy beard. He was tall, but not as lean as he used to be. It took me a moment to recognize him.

His eyes slid all over me, up and down. "Darla," he said. "You look exactly the same. My God."

I stepped aside to let him in, but he crushed me in a huge hug first, then pulled me into the apartment before shutting the door.

He let me go and took a few steps back. "I can't believe it's really you," he said.

"It's me," I said.

"You look so… you look so good, Darla. I can't believe it."

My cheeks burned. Was it that surprising that I had gotten better? That I looked like me?

"Well," he said. "Um, should we… should we take a seat?"

I walked over to the couch and sat down, sinking into it. Benjamin took off his jacket and sat at the other end, but then he scooted closer. He put his hand on my bare knee.

"How have you been?" he asked.

"Fine," I said, after a moment.

"Good, good," he said. "I just… I can't believe it. I really can't. After all these years, and you still look so beautiful… I mean… If you can keep your body, why can't Nancy, you know?"

How could somebody lose their body? Of course I kept my body. As I did whenever we were on the phone, I stayed quiet and let him talk, let the words spray down over me like a hot shower.

"I'm not a bad husband, Darla, I'm really not. But when a man marries a woman, there are promises that are made. Certain expectations go into it. She promised to be a loving wife, but how is that supposed to happen when she doesn't stay looking like somebody I want to love?" He shook his head. "God, I must sound so ridiculous to you."

I blinked.

He ran a hand through his thick hair. It smelled like dust and the lavender soap Ellie liked to use. "I don't want you to think I'm a bad person."

I blinked again. Something tickled my eye, making me shake my head.

"Good," he said. His hand moved farther up my leg, under my skirt. "Should we... should we pick up where we left off?"

[Scribe's note: I considered leaving out the next part, because who needs to hear that? But Darla insisted I put everything in.]

Benjamin picked me up and carried me into the bedroom. It was Ellie's, but I didn't get a chance to say anything. His mouth was on my mouth, and he tasted like peppermint and cigarette smoke. He undid the buttons on my blouse, pulled it off, then unhooked my brassiere. He gasped, said "Dear Jesus, you're pristine," and then pulled off my skirt and panties.

I thought about Mrs. Knowles the entire time, about the woman's gift she cared so much about. There was a little bit of pain, but Benjamin seemed to love every single moment, so I didn't stop him. I felt like I was floating over us, looking down, watching myself. I was smiling, mostly because Benjamin was smiling. His hands were everywhere, his lips were everywhere, and then, not long after, he shook, and it was over.

He rolled off of me, his sweaty hair on Ellie's pillow. "That was incredible," he said, one hand squeezing my breast.

I lay there, and I finally stopped feeling like I was floating. I'd never been to a petting zoo, but I'd read about them in my books, and I think that's what the air smelled like.

"I haven't been with Nancy like that in... Jesus... fifteen years, maybe?" he said. "Christ, Darla, what have I been waiting for all this time?"

My legs felt sticky, and his hands felt rough on my skin.

"Darla?" he said.

I turned to face him. He'd taken off his glasses, and his eyelids were heavy. "Yes?" I said.

"I love you. I always have. You know that, don't you?"

I knew the right answer. "Yes," I said.

He smiled, and then he fell asleep.

[Scribe's note: I hadn't had time to go to the grocery store the day before, and I knew Darla would be out of cheese and bread for sandwiches, so I picked up a few things between surgeries and dashed back to the apartment to drop them off before I had to go back to the hospital.

I knew something was wrong as soon as I opened the door. It wasn't locked, which was never a good sign, and the first thing I saw was a man's jacket on the couch.

The backs of my legs tingled. *Dear God, not again.*

The déjà vu was so intense I thought I might be dreaming—but no. My bedroom door was open, and I could hear snoring coming from inside.

I dropped the bag of food on the floor. Something—maybe the glass jar of jelly—shattered. I didn't care.

"Darla?" I called out. "Darla?"

The snoring stopped, and then there was a frantic rustling. I thought I heard a man's voice whisper, "Shit!"

In an instant, I was standing at my bedroom door, already knowing what I would find.

Darla lay on the bed, completely naked, looking like a goddamned Botticelli painting. Benjamin—I knew it was him, immediately, even though it had been decades—was standing at the side of the bed, fumbling with his pants. His glasses were askew on his nose, so fogged I didn't think he could see.

Rage is a funny thing. Sometimes it feels like thick channels of ice in your veins; other times, it feels like a bubbling pit of lava, waiting to devour everybody in its path and cook them down to nothing but ashes. This rage felt more like a hurricane-force wind, whipping through my body, pushing me forward, knocking down everything in front of me, conflating the past with the present.

"What the fuck are you doing here?" I yelled, and was I twenty-seven again, or was I forty-six?

Benjamin met my eyes, but his glasses were still fogged. "Jeez, um, hey Ellen, I was just—"

"I can see what you were 'just' doing, asshole," I spat. "How dare you? How fucking dare you?" I was screaming, but I couldn't have lowered my voice even if I wanted to. The rage was controlling me, spinning me in destructive circles, hellbent on pulling Benjamin apart at the seams.

"It's not what you think!" Benjamin cried, and it was so cliché I wanted to laugh, but I couldn't. The rage would have turned it into another scream.

"Oh really?" I said. "Because I think you just came here, raped my sister, and now you're trying to get out before I call the goddamned police on you, huh?"

Benjamin's blue eyes went wide, and he started to blubber. "Ellen, please, come on, it wasn't like that, please—"

"She can't fucking consent, you pervert!" I yelled, and the room started to look like our apartment in Charlottesville, and then it rippled, and I was back in Boston, in the life I'd built on my own. "You took advantage of her, just like you wanted to do before. How did you even know where we lived? How are you even here right now?"

His face burned, turning a deep scarlet. "She wanted it, okay? We talked about it!"

"Oh, yeah, sure," I snarled. "Did you just come in and say, 'This is happening,' and she said 'Okay?' She says 'okay' to everything! Don't you get that?"

"We've been talking!" Benjamin whimpered, finally pulling his zipper all the way up. He grabbed his shirt from the floor. "We've been talking on the phone!"

I finally turned to Darla. She'd been silent the whole time, that dreamy look plastered on her face, the same one from twenty years ago. Had any time really passed at all, or was I living in an alternate reality?

"Darla? Darla!" I said, snapping my fingers. "Did you talk on the phone to Benjamin?" I asked.

Her eyes came into focus. There was something in them I didn't recognize. Something... cold. I took a step back. "Yes," she said simply.

"See? See? I told you!" Benjamin said. "We've been talking on the phone for a long time!"

"How long?" I hissed.

"Years!" he said. "Since you left!" But wasn't I still in Charlottesville? No, no—this was Boston, this was Boston.

"What?"

"You weren't answering my calls, Ellen! So I just kept calling, okay? And then someone answered, and it was Darla, and we just sort of... kept talking."

I looked back at Darla. Her eyes sparkled. She'd made no attempts to cover herself. "You've been talking to Benjamin for years? Behind my back?"

Darla smiled. It wasn't a nice smile. "I had nobody else to talk to," she said.

The entire room froze, or at least that's how it felt. My rage died down, but I wasn't sure if we were in the eye of the storm, or the hurricane had fully passed. Either way, with the retreat of the stress, I could think clearly again. Darla wasn't wrong, after all. I'd spent most of my time buried in work. When I was home, Darla had felt more like my pet.

Damn it all. I realized then that I'd stopped seeing her as a person years ago, that I'd only seen her as a constant animal presence that would never change. She was alive, sure, but she wasn't living.

I was no better than my burning-in-hell mother, after all.

"Christ," I said, regaining my voice. I turned to Benjamin, who was now fully dressed. "Get the hell out of here," I said, but there was no venom left. The raging storm was gone.

"I'll call you," he said to Darla.

"Oh no, you won't," I said. "I'm throwing that telephone into the fucking garbage. If I ever so much as hear your name again, I will call the police and tell them what you've done. And if that doesn't scare you enough, I'll call your goddamn wife, Benjamin. Yep, that's right, I know you're married, you fucker. And you have three kids, for God's sake! What are you doing?" I still read the UVA alumni publications.

Benjamin looked as though I'd slapped him. I wish I had.

"It's not what you think," he said limply, but even I could tell he didn't believe himself.

"Get out," I said.

He grabbed his jacket from the couch and scuttled away. When the door closed behind him, I rushed to lock it.

"Do you think I'll still get into Heaven?" Darla said. I jumped; she was standing right behind me. She'd pulled her underwear back on and buttoned her blouse.

"What?" I said, my voice hoarse.

"Remember what Pastor Sable said? About a woman's gift?"

It took me a minute, but then I made the connection.

And then I laughed. I couldn't help it—the question was so absurd, so juvenile, so innocent, after everything we'd gone through. Eventually, Darla laughed too, but there was no mirth on her face, no understanding.

When I stopped at last, I said, "Sure, Darla. You can still get into Heaven." She surely deserved it more than I did, even if it was all a farce.]

Before Ellie left to go back to the hospital, she cut the telephone's cord with a pair of scissors, then threw the whole thing in the trash.

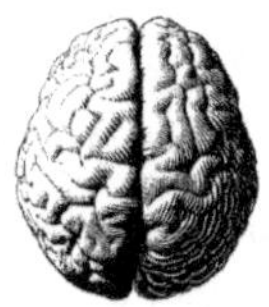

2 0 0 4 - 2 0 0 5

My life didn't change, even though I felt different. My head started hurting. When I woke up in the morning, my stomach cramped like it did before my blood came, and then I'd have to throw up. I felt angrier, and I cried a lot. I thought maybe I was getting sick, but I didn't want to tell Ellie. I knew she would be unhappy. She dealt with sick people all day at work, she didn't want to deal with sick people at home.

It wasn't hard to hide how I felt. Even after Benjamin, Ellie didn't spend much time with me. I thought maybe things would have changed, but they didn't.

[Scribe's note: I was one of the most in-demand surgeons at Massachusetts General, and my schedule had been booked months in advance. I also had classes to teach, and several medical interns to shepherd here and there. I couldn't stop to spend more time with Darla. I could barely stop long enough to attend to my own physical needs—haircuts, mammograms, Pap smears, you understand. I still saw Howard every week. I even told him about Benjamin, and what he'd done. Howard was aghast, and insisted I should have taken Darla to the hospital for a rape kit, but I shut it down. What good would that have done, besides traumatize Darla and put her at risk for acting out? She never did well in new environments. And it wasn't like we were going to actually prosecute Benjamin. A jury wasn't likely to believe a credible woman, much less a woman with the brain function of a child who would say she'd consented to the intercourse. Before you think I was being cruel, go do some research of your own. I wasn't being evil or heartless. I was being pragmatic.

I explained all of that to Howard, and he eventually quieted down and accepted my course of action, as I expected him to. Whether or not he agreed with me, he was scared of me, and that was what I needed.

So, no. I didn't notice what was happening with Darla. If I had, I would have taken care of it.]

I started feeling better after a few months, but I slept a lot more. I didn't mind; with no telephone in the house, there was no reason for me to stay awake in the afternoons anymore. My stomach rumbled more, but the foods I used to like made me feel sick.

One night, Ellie came home with a plastic takeout bag.

"I have Maggiano's," she said. "I thought we could have dinner together?" [Scribe's note: You can't tell me I didn't try, okay? I did try, but no matter how much I gave Darla, it would never be enough.]

When I stood up from the couch to come to the table, Ellen looked at me like she'd never seen me before.

"Want some… pasta?" she said slowly, still staring at me.

Pasta didn't sound very good, but I nodded anyway. My eyes hurt like I was going to cry again.

I sat down across from her. My stomach pressed against the table. When had that started to happen?

"Darla?" she said. "Darla, what…"

When she didn't move, I took the plastic container out of the bag myself. There were no forks in the bag, so I started scooping it up with my hands. It didn't taste good, but I ate it fast so it would be over and my stomach would stop rumbling.

[Scribe's note: I didn't realize until that moment how much I had missed. You're probably thinking I'm stupid for being so ignorant, but as I've told you,

I had an extremely busy schedule. If I had taken more time off to be with Darla, people would have died. I am not exaggerating. I do not feel bad about my decision, but I do have regrets.

By the time we had that dinner, it was obvious. Darla was starting to show, and it was so grotesque that all semblance of appetite left me immediately. I could feel my grasp on reality starting to quake, but I forced it to settle, taking as many calming breaths as I could muster. This was no time to fall apart.

I counted backwards. Darla was well into her second trimester.

How had I not noticed? How?

An even more disturbing question haunted me, and, to be honest, still haunts me to this day: Would the baby be like Darla was before the surgery—a neurotic, skittish, self-destructive creature?]

When the pasta was gone, I felt so tired. I stood up, and my belly flipped the pasta container over.

"Christ," Ellie said.

[Scribe's note: I made the first OB/GYN appointment for her the next day at a clinic near the apartment that was not affiliated with Harvard or Massachusetts General in any way. The last thing I needed was for word to get out that Dr. Ellen Gregory not only had a brain damaged sister, but she had a pregnant, forty-five-year old pregnant sister. I had tenure, but gossiping tongues can do so much damage.

At the appointment, which I had to reschedule a surgery to attend, a technician smeared jelly on Darla's belly and performed the ultrasound. Darla squirmed and tried to bat away the technician's hand, and I had to hold her arms down. We discovered you were a girl. You were healthy. Darla was healthy. I did not tell the doctor about Darla's lobotomy. There was no need, and I didn't want their judgmental stares, their whispering.

Before you start asking too many questions, let me be clear. Benjamin is the one who impregnated Darla, that much you have grasped, surely. You're smart, I suppose. If you want to know who he is, I've given you enough information to figure it out for yourself, but I will not speak of this any more.

Remember this above all else: Benjamin is married, or at least he was. He has a real family. He will not want to meet you.]

Ellie told me I was going to have a baby. When I asked her where it was, she shook her head. She pointed at my belly, which was much bigger than it used to be.

"There is a baby," she said. "In there."

I looked down at myself. "How?" I said. I felt confused, and angry, and calm all at the same time, and I didn't like the cold goo on my stomach.

Ellie frowned. "It doesn't matter," she said. "All you need to know is that you're going to have a baby. But don't worry. Once it's over, you won't even realize anything happened. It's going to be okay."

I didn't know what she was talking about, but I felt happy all of a sudden. Really happy, something I didn't know I could feel. I'd always wanted a baby.

[Scribe's note: I told Howard at dinner the next day.

"How did this happen?" Howard asked, which was a stupid question, because he knew exactly how it must have happened.

"I never suspected…" I said. "For God's sake, we're old! Even if I'd noticed that Darla missed her period, I would have thought menopause was more likely than a pregnancy!" Howard flinched at the mention of menstruation, as all men do. I'd undergone the change myself a few years earlier, which suited me just fine.

"What are you going to do?" he said.

"Well, it's too late for an abortion," I said. "Jesus. I suppose I'll put the baby up for adoption."

Howard grabbed my hand, nearly knocking over my water glass. "No," he said. His eyes were sparkling, and he looked more excited than I'd ever seen, more excited even than when he saw my breasts for the first and only time. "Don't do that."

"Why not?" I said, trying to pull my hand away. He held on tight.

"Ellen," he said. "I know… I know I'm not who you probably thought you'd end up with, but I love you. I love you so much, and I've always wanted a family. I never thought... I never thought I could have one." Tears filled his eyes, threatening to spill over. I looked around, hoping no one was watching this display. "This is my last chance."

"Okay?" I said.

"We could... I could help raise the baby, Ellen," he said, so softly I wasn't sure I'd heard him. "I know I could do it. I... I need to do it."

"What?" I said. "You want this baby?"

"Yes!" he cried, far too loudly, earning a few looks of disapproval from the diners near us. "Yes, Ellen! I do! And before you say we can't do it, or it'll be too hard, just listen, please? Just listen. I was going to wait to do this, but now it feels like the right time."

Before I could stop him, Howard was getting down onto the dirty floor, bending painfully on one knee. The diners who'd glared at us just seconds before started grinning. I wanted to knock the teeth out of each and every one.

Howard pulled a small blue velvet box from his pocket. "Ellen Gregory," he said, his voice shaking like a teenager's. "Will you marry me?"

He popped the box open, revealing a modest princess-cut solitaire, no bigger than one carat. Practical. Timeless. Very... very me, I had to admit.

The diners around us all held their breaths, waiting for my answer.

I stared into Howard's wet blue eyes. I never wanted him, not really, and I never wanted children. I never wanted Darla to live with me forever. I never wanted Benjamin back in my life.

But I had wanted to make it to Harvard, and I had wanted to be a doctor, and I had wanted to be successful.

Maybe that was enough.

"Okay," I said, and the diners cheered. Howard smiled wide enough to show his gold-capped molar. He made his way haltingly back to his chair, and a few seconds later, a waiter presented us with a plate of chocolate-chip cannolis, impaled with sparkling candles.

"Congratulations to the happy couple!" he said, and there were more cheers, and then the ring was on my finger and I was an engaged woman. I would never be utterly alone, which was some comfort.

We were married at the courthouse the following week. There were no guests. I wore a pink dress I'd bought years before for a Harvard gala, the last of its kind I'd attended. Howard was in an ill-fitting suit. There was no photographer, no cake, no reception. After the ceremony, we had dinner at an Indian restaurant, and then Howard went back to his apartment, and I went back to mine. I took Howard's surname, happy to shed the weight of the Gregory lineage, which had brought me nothing but anguish.]

"We're moving," Ellie said one morning. She was still in her pajamas, sitting at the table when I got up.

My ankles felt heavy, and walking was hard. I sat down slowly across from her.

"Where?" I said. A new ring sparkled on her finger. I pointed at it.

"Howard and I are now married," she said. She wasn't smiling. "We're going to move to a bigger place. A house."

I squealed. A house? With a backyard? Would I be able to go outside again? Maybe walk around a neighborhood like I had with Mrs. Knowles? Anxiety and excitement churned in my stomach, and I could feel my cheeks getting hot.

"It's going to be okay, Darla. But things are going to be… different," Ellie said. "Howard is going to take care of your baby."

All I could think about was green grass, and the sun on my face, and dirt under my feet. I leaned over and grabbed Ellie. She yelled, but then she calmed down as I squeezed her.

[Scribe's note: Howard quit his job. We didn't really need the money, not with my income. I earned four times as much as he did.

He found us a modest three-bedroom brick house in the Boston suburbs, thirty minutes from Harvard. My commute would be longer, but honestly—I relished the thought. A longer commute meant less time spent at home.

Darla was thirty weeks pregnant when we made the move. I found her a new doctor closer to the house so that Howard could take her. I'd stopped caring what the OB/GYN or the nurses thought. Let them think Howard was Darla's husband. I knew he wouldn't—and couldn't—lose himself in the role, even if he'd wanted to act on any urges he might have felt.

It was six o'clock in the evening, a week after we'd moved in. Boxes were still piled in the living room, but Howard had made good work of most of it. Darla was sitting in the grass in the backyard. The air was warm for April. She looked content, dreamy, like she did the times I'd found her with Benjamin, but I didn't forget she could still be that angry dog with sharp teeth if she wanted to be.

She looked up at me in my deck chair. "I still want to write a diary," she said.

"Still?" I asked, sipping an herbal tea. Howard was inside, cleaning up after dinner. He'd been on a health kick, insisting Darla needed the best nutrition for her baby. I didn't care much about that, but I appreciated the steak salad. I'd never realized how good of a cook Howard could be.

"The Alice book," Darla said. "I want to write something like that."

I snorted. "You remember that?"

"Yes," Darla said simply. Then, "Please, Ellie? Will you help me?"

Call it guilt, call it a shred of sibling loyalty, call it penance—call it whatever you want, but I said yes.

The book you're reading now is the result. I spent the next few weeks with Darla whenever I had a few pieces of spare time. She'd talk, and I'd write, cleaning things up as I went, injecting my perspective as needed when Darla couldn't remember things correctly. Sometimes she looked forlorn, sometimes she recounted the most horrific memories with an unbelievable placidity, and sometimes she got angry. Her pregnancy hormones made her feisty and fitful.

"I want my baby to know me," she said when I asked her why this diary, why now.

It was so fatalistic, I wondered if she knew something I didn't.]

I liked talking to Ellie. We hadn't really talked in so long, and I think she was surprised at me, at what I remembered, at what I could say. [Scribe's note: I was. I truly was, and with that surprise came the old shame.]

My life hasn't been all that happy, I know that. But I didn't suffer too much, and I know there are so many other people who have.

I've lived all my life in closed rooms. It's been very small. If I can give my story to you, my life won't feel so small anymore. Nobody probably cares enough to listen to my story, but I hope that you will. One day, when you're old enough to understand things, and wise enough to let your anger go. I want to heal your pain, if you have any. Most of all, I wish there's no pain at all.

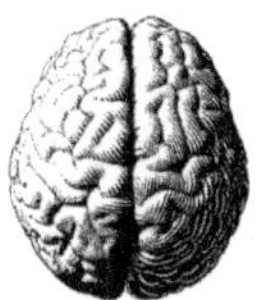

2 0 0 5

[Scribe's note: Darla went into labor on a Saturday evening. I happened to be home, which was lucky for us both. Howard awoke first, hearing Darla's groans. They filled the house, shaking the walls, or so it seemed.

Howard had prepared for this moment. He leaped out of bed, grabbed the go-bag he'd packed for Darla, and shook me. "Come on!" he said.

I rolled out of bed, combed my hair, applied my makeup, and dressed myself appropriately. Darla would be delivering at Massachusetts General (mostly because, considering I was her legal guardian and a staff doctor at the hospital, her care would be heavily discounted), and even though I didn't work with the labor and delivery unit, I couldn't chance someone seeing me as anything but composed.

"Hurry!" Howard yelled, sticking his head into the bathroom.

"Howard," I said calmly. "Start timing her contractions. We don't even need to get to the hospital until they're five minutes apart, at least. There is no need to hurry."

Howard huffed, but he left me to finish my grooming.

When I was ready, I grabbed my own go-bag and helped Howard load Darla into the car. She was sweating and moaning, and I could see her belly tightening under her nightgown. The contractions were irregular, but the shortest interval was barely six minutes.

I won't bore you with the details. We arrived at the hospital—I drove, Howard was too shaky with excitement to be trusted behind the wheel—and the nurses placed Darla in a bed in the waiting room. Her contractions came faster, a nurse hooked her up to an IV and a fetal monitor, she was officially admitted, and we all moved to a private labor and delivery room.

Nobody could have predicted what happened. And I mean nobody—I was there, in the room, and there were no signs. There usually aren't.

When it came time to push, Darla did so. She screamed. She raved. She yelled that her head hurt. She made me even more secure in my choice to never have children of my own.

We could see your head coming out. Howard was green, but he didn't look away. He was overjoyed, and all I could feel was betrayal. I had done everything for Darla, I had kept her out of a nursing home, out of an institution, I had given her a pleasant life, and now, even though I had worked so hard to escape the life our parents had, there I was, in the birthing suite, married, and about to be the mother to a child I did not want.

That I still do not want.

"Stay with us, honey! Stay with us!" the nurse holding Darla's left leg said. "Push! You can do this!"

Darla was flagging, we could all see it.

"Push!" the nurse yelled again. "You'll meet your baby soon! What are you going to name her?"

Darla pushed one final time. She screamed our mother's name, of all things. Her face was bright red, her muscles straining. You slid out in a gush of blood.

The doctors were so busy cleaning you and attending to your needs that they didn't notice Darla go stiff. Her eyes closed, and she kept bleeding, and when the doctors noticed, one of them started yelling for the crash cart, and all of the machines started beeping.

They told us later that she'd ruptured an aneurysm while pushing, and that, although extremely rare, it wasn't unheard of. There was nothing they could have done, and I believed them. Even if an operating room had been prepped and ready for her and I'd been the surgeon on call, I wouldn't have saved her. By the time she had the headache, she was seconds from death.

I didn't say anything, but I did wonder if her lobotomy had something to do with it, if it dictated her death just as it had dictated everything about her life.

Darla was gone by the time the nurse brought you back from the nursery. You were clean and pink and small.

The nurse was crying, as was Howard. My eyes remained dry.

"She cried out a name, there… at the end," the nurse whispered, placing you in Howard's eager arms. "That's what we've been calling her."

I felt numb, but I nodded. The last thing I wanted was a reminder of my mother, but I didn't care enough to change anybody's mind. Howard didn't know how mother had died, only that she was dead.

I had to laugh when I saw the birth certificate for the first time. 'Mother' was listed as Darla Gregory. Under 'Father,' they'd put Howard's name.

As for your name—Darla's scream had distorted it, but that suited me just fine.

Everybody cries out for their mother at the end.

Now that you know everything, who will you cry out for, Keely?]

The Commonwealth of Massachusetts
DEPARTMENT OF PUBLIC HEALTH
REGISTRY OF VITAL RECORDS AND STATISTICS

COPY OF RECORD OF BIRTH

Name   Keely Gregory Rexroth

Date of Birth 06/21/2005   Time of Birth 11:34

Place of Birth Boston

Sex Female   Race Caucasian

Plurality Single

MOTHER

Full Name Darla   Marie   Gregory
       First   Middle   Last   Maiden

Date of Birth 08/12/1960   Birthplace Virginia

Occupation Homemaker   Race Caucasian

Residence 223 Harrowfield Road, Newton, MA 02456

FATHER

Full Name Howard   Arthur   Rexroth
       First   Middle   Last

Date of Birth 12/09/1959   Birthplace Massachusetts

Occupation Salesman   Race Caucasian

Residence 223 Harrowfield Road, Newton, MA 02456

AUTHOR'S NOTE

Many people may finish this book, especially those who have yet to read *Much Too Vulgar*, and think, *Wait. This isn't horror.*

For a long time, I've been urging people to view horror as something other than a bloody monolith. Horror can be gory, sure, but it can also be quiet, profound, uncomfortable, disgusting, taboo, mournful, and thrilling. As a genre, horror pushes you to confront terrifying scenarios and sit with that discomfort until you break through to the other side, changed for the experience.

When I first learned about the history of the transorbital lobotomy, I was stunned. The procedure, as described in the novel, is historically accurate. Based on the leucotomy developed by Dr. Egas Moniz and pioneered by Dr. Walter Freeman, the transorbital lobotomy entailed inserting a sharp instrument, traditionally an icepick, into the eye socket. Once the icepick was inserted, a mallet was used to break the thin bone at the back of the eye. The pick was then used to sever neurological connections in the frontal lobes of the brain.

In theory, the surgery could cure a wide range of mental ailments, from schizophrenia to depression. In practice, the outcome of the surgery was unpredictable, and often left patients incontinent, severely disabled, and unable to care for themselves. Even if patients didn't suffer devastating effects, they frequently experienced significant personality changes, in addition to suffering from the shame and stigma surrounding this surgery of last resort.

Nearly 40,000 Americans were lobotomized before the procedure fell out of favor or became heavily restricted. In 1967, Dr. Walter Freeman performed his final lobotomy on Helen Mortensen, who suffered a cerebral hemorrhage. Following her death, Freeman was banned from operating on patients.

Before you insist that a lobotomy would have been unthinkable for a child like Darla Gregory, let me tell you about Howard Dully. Howard received a transorbital lobotomy from Dr. Freeman in 1960, when he was only twelve years old. Luckily, Howard went on to live a full life, and medical researchers later came to realize, to their astonishment, that Howard's brain had adapted around the damage inflicted by Dr. Freeman's icepick. That's not to say Howard's life was easy—he was profoundly impacted by the surgery he never should have undergone. Dr. Freeman had no compunction about performing lobotomies on children; in fact, his youngest patient was only four years old.

While researching for this book, I had the great privilege to explore the digitized Walter Freeman and James Watts collection housed within George Washington University's Special Collections Research Center. Combing through the files, publications, photographs, and medical reports within that collection was heartbreaking and fascinating in equal measure, and the surreality of the experience brought tears to my eyes.

The more I learned about the lobotomy, the more uncomfortable, agonized, and anxious I felt.

In this novel, the horror is real.

If you would like to learn more about the history of the lobotomy, I would recommend *My Lobotomy* by Howard Dully and Charles Fleming and *The Icepick Surgeon* by Sam Kean.

As always, thank you to my family for their relentless support—my mom, who is an uncompromising and truthful beta reader, my dad, whose attention to detail makes him the world's best copyeditor, and my husband, who always champions my writing.

Thank you to my amazing editor, Alison Hodyna, who helped polish this novel to a shine.

Thank you to my Purgatory Media teammates, who have become

my brain trust, my esteemed colleagues, and most of all, my friends.

Thank you to Leah Richardson, the Director of Archives and Special Collections at the George Washington University, for assisting me in my research.

Thank you to Dawn Kurtagich, Ben Young, Haley Newlin, and Paulette Kennedy for their kind words, support, and encouragement.

Finally, my sincerest thanks to you, my readers, for picking up this book and gifting me your attention.

VIGGY PARR HAMPTON

 is an epidemiologist, host of the podcast "Horror Humor Hunger," and the author of *A Cold Night for Alligators*, *Much Too Vulgar*, and *The Rotting Room*. She is a graduate of Georgetown University and Emory University's Rollins School of Public Health.

Connect with her at her website, www.viggyhampton.com or on Instagram or TikTok @viggyparrhampton